A
WHITE
HOT
PLAN

A WHITE HOT PLAN

Mike and Ayan Rubin

2023

UNIVERSITY OF LOUISIANA AT LAFAYETTE PRESS

http://ulpress.org
University of Louisiana at Lafayette Press
P.O. Box 43558
Lafayette, LA 70504-3558

Printed in the United States

Library of Congress Cataloging-in-Publication Data

Names: Rubin, Michael H., 1950- author. | Rubin, Ayan (Ayan L.), 1950-
    author.
Title: A white hot plan / Mike and Ayan Rubin.
Description: Lafayette, LA : University of Louisiana at Lafayette Press,
    2023.
Identifiers: LCCN 2022058206 | ISBN 9781946160973 (paperback)
Subjects: LCSH: White supremacy movements--Fiction. |
    Murder--Investigation--Fiction. | New Orleans (La.)--Fiction. | LCGFT:
    Detective and mystery fiction. | Novels.
Classification: LCC PS3618.U297 W48 2023 | DDC 813/.6--dc23/
eng/20230113
LC record available at https://lccn.loc.gov/2022058206

PART I

SUNDAY

CHAPTER ONE

At 3:32 a.m. Starner Gautreaux was driving down Vizeau Road in his Ford F-150 Raptor emblazoned with the "Petit Rouge Parish Sheriff's Office" insignia on both doors. Big engine. Huge bumper guards on the front that could push a one-ton vehicle. Blue strobe lights on the roof.

Starner sped up, although it was hard to see through the driving rain despite having the windshield wipers on full blast. If he didn't reach the bridge over the bayou before the water rose, he wouldn't make it home tonight. Again.

Starner hated high water. It always reminded him of the past.

It had been a long day. Eighteen hours straight. Starner spent Friday night sleeping in the office. He had been on duty since Saturday morning, because Judson called in sick for the third day in a row.

Starner resented the fact that Judson, who was twenty years younger, did not have the decency to hold off claiming another sick day. The two of them, both deputies, were supposed to work the whole parish. Not that having to handle everything in Petit Rouge Parish was a hard job. Local elected officials generously called Petit Rouge "rural," but Starner knew it was really just a run-down, pathetic spit of a community wedged between two bayous and a swamp that slunk its way into the Gulf of Mexico.

Starner was resigned to being a lowly Petit Rouge deputy. The job required none of the skills he had acquired as a detective in the Crescent City. A day's work for the New Orleans Police Department might involve investigating two or three murders or fending off gang members trying to gun him down to gain street cred. That kind of experience was not needed in Petit Rouge.

Four hours ago, Starner turned on his siren for the first time in a week and pulled over a carload of drunken teenagers who attended the local all-white, private high school, pretending not to notice them trying to surreptitiously toss their beer cans and liquor bottles into nearby bushes. Rather than issuing them tickets, he escorted the celebrants home to their respective parents, none of whom bothered to thank him.

As Starner rounded the corner and headed toward the bridge, he spotted a flickering, reddish gleam in the woods. Taillights. He hoped it wasn't kids from the senior prom who lost control of their car in the rain.

Starner jammed on the brakes of his truck, backed up, pulled off onto the shoulder of the road, and activated the flashing blue lights to alert other late-night drivers, as if there would be any at this hour, to slow the hell down as they approached the bridge over Bayou Grosse Noir. Turning on the truck's spotlight, he shone it into the woods. It illuminated a tractor trailer that had slid off Vizeau Road, gouged a path through the mud, and lodged itself between two loblolly pines.

Starner kicked off his worn loafers and reached for the waterproof knee boots and rain gear he kept tucked behind the seat. He picked up his flashlight and, as he always did when there was a wreck, grabbed the fire extinguisher from the bed of the truck.

Deep divots trailed from the roadway past scraggly hardwoods and palmettos. Through the curtain of rain, Starner could see the tractor trailer twenty yards ahead. Dark smoke was just starting to spiral out of the rear frame, and a few flames were lapping up from underneath, crawling toward the cab.

He approached cautiously.

A man was slumped across the steering wheel.

Starner ran forward and pulled the door open to help the driver.

The cab was covered with blood.

"Are you all right? Injured?"

The driver didn't respond. He didn't even stir.

Starner directed his flashlight at the man's face. His unblinking eyes were open and glassy.

Smoke coursed around the cab. The acrid smell of burning rubber filled the air.

Starner tried to pull the trucker out of his seat. The man's body was wrapped around the steering wheel. Upon touching the driver's stiff, cold, and immobile hand, Starner realized he had been dead quite a while.

Fire was creeping up from the rear of the trailer, the heat becoming increasingly intense, and there was no easy way for Starner to pry the unyielding corpse free. He squeezed the handle of his fire extinguisher, but the white burst of CO_2 did nothing to thwart the accelerating blaze.

Starner backed away from the rig as the fire crept over the wind deflector and burned through the roof lining above the steering wheel. The rain kept falling and still the flames rose.

A long flare engulfed one of the rig's two fuel tanks.

Starner threw himself behind the downed trunk of a thick cypress tree just before the first explosion occurred, which ignited the second fuel tank in an ear-splitting conflagration, lighting up the sky and causing the long pine needles in the overhead canopy to catch fire and cascade down like a million crimson sparklers, turning the raindrops red in the reflection.

Above the din of the fire Starner heard a massive rushing sound, like a freight engine bearing directly down on him. He flattened himself against the muddy ground.

A third explosion, louder than the first two, shook the earth.

Starner glanced up long enough to see the truck glowing white from the heat, the rain around it turning into steam, before he had to shield his head from the burning limbs that started falling.

The deputy knew there would be no sleep for him now. There was lots to do before sunrise, plus he had to report to Knock.

CHAPTER TWO

The soft buzz of cicadas rose from the alligator weed and button willow that edged the bayou next to the swamp. The Precept carefully worked his way around the faded, yellow school bus that had been backed into the gravel driveway, primed for the next day's run. Through the rain he could discern the dim outlines of two derelict cars resting on cinder blocks, several rusty washing machines, and what appeared to be a disassembled refrigerator.

The ramshackle cottage was just ahead. Looming branches of oak and hickory pressed against its roof.

He adjusted the strap on his shoulder, pulled on latex gloves, and, striding onto the porch, started to expertly pick the lock on the mildewed front door. It was not fastened and squeaked open when he touched it. A mangy dog, hearing the sound, came running around the side of the house, baring its teeth and growling menacingly.

The Precept was prepared. He had scouted the place out thoroughly. He pulled a hunk of raw meat stuffed with tranquilizers and an overdose of powerful sedatives from his backpack and threw it onto the floorboards of the porch. The mutt devoured the offering in two swift gulps, staggered unsteadily backward, panted rapidly, and fell, unconscious.

The intruder entered. An ancient air conditioner wheezed loudly from its perch in the window of the bedroom off the front hall. A television flickered, blaring a canned laugh track that punctuated every other line of an old sitcom. The snoring of the enormous woman on the bed cut through the din. She wouldn't have heard a thing, even had her dog howled.

Sprawled across the flowered coverlet, in a faded nightshirt that bunched up around her layers of fat, Boulette Babineaux looked far older than her sixty years. Her breasts were indistinguishable from the sandwiched mounds of flab that marched from her shoulders to her thighs.

The Precept pulled a small tank from his backpack, turned the valve, and pressed the plastic face-cup tightly over her nose and mouth. As Boulette struggled into wakefulness, he put his other hand behind her tangle of gray hair and pulled her head forward, forcing her to inhale the fumes.

Boulette's eyes opened. They were filled with confusion. Then puzzlement. Then panic. She began to writhe and kick.

The Precept's grasp on her head was firm. The gas flowed into her mouth as she tried to scream.

Boulette struggled, but he easily eluded her flailing arms, keeping the plastic mask affixed to the lower half of her pudgy face.

Thirty seconds passed. She began to take short, frantic gasps. Gulping for air caused her to inhale the chemical mixture even more deeply.

Finally, there was no movement at all.

The Precept remained in position for another minute, just to be sure.

He turned the valve off, checked the veins in her neck for signs of life, and, finding none, carefully stowed his gear. They would find her eventually, of course. An autopsy would indicate that Boulette had suffered a heart attack. The obvious conclusion would be that natural causes finally did in this old, overweight black woman with numerous health problems.

Holding the tank, the Precept headed back through the living room toward the front door when he heard the sound of a vehicle pulling up. A car door squeaked open and then slammed shut. The dusty living room curtains, drooping from their warped wooden dowels, glowed yellow as headlights splashed the front porch.

He stepped back into the shadows and reached for his knife.

Heavy footsteps pounded up the wooden steps. A voice slurred by drink demanded, "What the hell! Who the fuck did this?"

The drunk on the porch had found the dog. The Precept had planned to dump the mutt in the woods on his way out.

The front door burst open. The home's entryway was now blocked by a massive figure, at least six-foot-five and as wide as the doorframe. The big drunk flipped on the light switch and, seeing the stranger in the corner, lunged for him.

The Precept hadn't expected Boulette's son, Debrun, to come home. He was supposed be working offshore in the middle of a fourteen-day-on-seven-day-off roustabout shift.

Easily sidestepping the big man's drunken attack, the Precept raised his arm and gave Boulette's son a vicious blow to the jugular. As he started to turn, however, he was surprised to see that the man had not fallen. A former high school lineman, Debrun fought past the pain as he staggered backward and then, shoulder down, charged at full speed across the small living room.

Ducking low, the intruder was planning to plunge his knife in an upward thrust that would pierce Debrun's heart, but, drunk as he was, Debrun saw the gleam of the blade and, with surprising agility, whirled and knocked the Precept off his feet, causing the weapon to spiral away toward the door.

The Precept reached for his tank, but before he could regain his footing, Debrun had encompassed the stranger in a tight grasp, hoisting him aloft.

Debrun was strong, but the Precept was more supple. Twisting sideways, he smashed the tank into the top of Debrun's head.

"Don't you fuckin' mess with me," Debrun roared as he spun around, his arms now in a vise-like grip around the prowler's chest.

The Precept's torso was pinned, but his arms and legs were free. He kicked Debrun in the balls and again brought the tank down on his assailant's skull.

Debrun staggered but did not relinquish his clench.

Again and again the tank connected, each hammering harder than the last. On the fifth blow, the Precept heard a cracking sound. Debrun's grip loosened.

The tank, now bloody and flecked with pieces of Debrun's hair and scalp, arced up one more time as the Precept drove it directly into the top of Debrun's head. Out of the gap oozed a thick slurry, like reddish-gray oatmeal. A portion of Debrun's parietal lobe had been exposed, and bits of brain dripped onto the floor.

Debrun groaned. His knees buckled. His arms fell uselessly to his sides as he collapsed.

The Precept did not panic. He never panicked.

He calmly picked up his knife and sheathed it. Taking one step back, he then leapt forward, slamming his steel-toed boot into Debrun's neck, breaking it.

Boulette's strapping son was now a lifeless heap.

The Precept was trained to deal with all contingencies. His mental checklist was clear. Turn off the lights of Debrun's car. Can't take any chances, even though the dirt driveway to Boulette's house curved a hundred yards into the deep woods. Locate the keys to Boulette's bus. Put the bodies of Debrun and the dog in Debrun's car. Clean up Boulette's house and lock it up. Drive Debrun's car out back and silently coax it through the woods and off the bank, to be swallowed by the swamp. Return to retrieve the bus and drive it over the parish line from Petit Rouge to St. Bonaventure.

There would be no reason for anyone to be suspicious. Who would miss an itinerant roustabout? Who would call for a crime scene investigation when Boulette's death was so obviously due to a heart attack?

The Precept was smug. All bases were covered.

No problem. Everything will be all right.

But then, the Precept never thought it would be anything else.

CHAPTER THREE

Bea Timms was grumpy when she heard the front doorbell ring. It wasn't even a quarter to seven in the morning. She had been sitting by the old man's bedside all night as he tossed sleeplessly, talked constantly, and complained when it was time to take another pill. Who would bother her patient at this hour?

Bea was dressed in jeans and a flowing blouse. She always refused to wear a uniform or nurses' scrubs when working at a "white home" because she didn't want to be mistaken for someone's maid.

She peeked through the keyhole and, recognizing the visitor, opened the door just a crack and said with an edge in her voice, "Deputy Starner Gautreaux. You again? So early? Well, go on, you know the way. He's out back, as usual, trying my patience more each day, and he's as ornery as ever. Making demands. Do this. Do that. Ordering me around like I worked in his office. And that pipe! Always lit. Morning to night. His hands now shake so much that pipe tobacco is scattered everywhere. That stuff smells to high heaven, stinking up everything in its wake. Don't know why the doctors let him keep smoking it, with his condition and all. But that's not for me to decide. I just do my job, but he's a difficult patient. He's been awake more than asleep all night, wanting me to fetch him this and then fetch him that. You go on while I rest my feet and enjoy a nice cup of coffee in the kitchen. When you're finished, I'll come out and check on him."

The rocking chair that Knock had been sitting in since first light was situated underneath a wide live oak where he could enjoy the colorful flowerbeds flourishing in his spacious backyard. Although it was already warm early on this spring day, he was wearing a woolen sweater. A heavy blanket covered his legs. A confetti of tobacco shards littered the ground around him.

When he was at full throttle, few dared cross Naquin "Knock" Mouton. Despite his advanced years and his withered countenance, Knock was still the sheriff of Petit Rouge Parish and still a political force to be reckoned with. His house, the biggest in the parish other than the antebellum mansion out at the Cottoncrest Plantation, projected power and authority. His wealth and reputation commanded respect.

Knock's formerly broad shoulders were now slumped, bony protrusions. His weathered face was drained of color, like faded leather left too long in the sun. His chest had become a hollow concave. What was left of his muscles were melting away under skin so thin it seemed translucent. His gravelly voice, however, was still strong. "You look like you've been rolling in shit, Starner. Sit down, but don't let the mud and crap covering you get on me."

Even in his weakened condition, Knock's ever-present pipe was blazing, its acrid odor displacing the sweet scent of the roses festooning his garden.

Starner couldn't remember a time when Knock's pipe wasn't lit or in the process of being refilled.

"I came here right away, Knock, soon as I finished with the fire department, the coroner, and Boyo, who brought over his crane and big tow truck. Didn't have time to clean myself up. Wanted you to get all the details as soon as possible. But I did stop on the way to pick up something for you."

Pulling over a wicker armchair, Starner placed a paper bag on the metal table in front of the old man's rocker.

Knock pointed to it with a finger that quivered involuntarily. "Better not be damn medicine! Already got more bottles than a pharmacy. Every few hours that busybody from hospice brings me another pill to force down. Like she's shoving coins in a piggy bank."

Starner reached into the bag, pulled out a stack of paper napkins, and spread them on the table, making room for a plate-size sandwich made on a round, flat loaf of bread, ten inches in diameter.

It was stacked high with ham, two kinds of salami, mozzarella, provolone, pickled olives, diced onions, and chopped garlic, all of which was slathered in creole mustard.

"A muffuletta! Is it fresh, Starner?"

"Wouldn't bring it if it weren't."

Starner took out his pocketknife, wiped it on one of the napkins, and carefully cut the sandwich into quarters. "Brought you some real food for breakfast. The gals on the early shift at the Ganderson's in Lamou made it up special, with authentic muffuletta bread from that New Orleans bakery they use, 'cause those gals are still sweet on you."

Knock leaned forward and whispered, conspiratorially, "What else you got in that bag? Any beer? My tobacco I won't let them take away, but they don't allow me beer anymore. Confiscated it all, dammit. Says it interferes with the drugs. Hell, beer is the best painkiller I know and a shitload better than that watered-down juice they give me with all them damn pills. I'm the law in these parts, but I'm treated like a fucking felon, deprived of all pleasures."

"Got you covered, Knock. Look. Two bottles of Abita Turbodog. Still cold. There're more in this bag and a six-pack out in the truck. I'll sneak it in before I leave." Starner popped the caps off with the bottle opener on his pocketknife and handed one of the cold brews to his boss.

Knock's wizened hands shook as he greedily lifted the longneck to his mouth, not bothering to remove his pipe in the process. Smoke billowed up from his nose and beer dribbled down the corners of his mouth as a blissful expression spread across his unshaven face.

Although Knock tried to keep his hands steady as he ate, the creole mustard and stuffing spilled onto his chin and down into his lap. He attempted to use the blanket to wipe his face, but he was too weak to lift it.

Starner reached over and handed his boss a paper napkin before whipping the blanket to one side, disbursing all the remnants that had fallen, and tucking it back neatly around Knock's legs, which were now just bony sticks. Starner felt like he was wrapping PVC pipe.

The sheriff pointed to a lighter on the table. "Get me a flame for my pipe, Starner, and tell me what the hell happened overnight that has you looking like you've been rolling in a pigsty this early in the morning."

CHAPTER FOUR

"That's it. All done. Start to finish. Less than twenty minutes," the Precept announced, shutting down the camera. "You can unclip that microphone and change your clothes. Hurry up now, we're on a schedule."

Kenny Arvenal pulled off the ammunition belts that crisscrossed his chest and put down the loaded AK-47 he had been holding throughout the taping. When his momma saw the video, how could she not be proud? Not that he and his momma had spoken for a year or more, but once the video aired, she would see he had become world-famous. Maybe then she would love him.

And his stuck-up sister, who had moved up north to Shreveport, gotten married, and had four kids? The sister who wouldn't let her children visit their own grandmother? Who wouldn't talk to her brother and wouldn't have anything to do with the family anymore? She would finally realize that he had amounted to something after all.

And his high school classmates? Well now, a short four years after graduation, they'd finally see he was someone to be reckoned with, wouldn't they? Soon they'd be telling everyone that they went to school with Kenny Arvenal.

Kenny pulled off his camouflage pants and put on his jeans. He removed his camouflage jacket and hung it on a hanger next to the yellow "SBSB" shirt and yellow slacks that all St. Bonaventure School Board bus drivers wore. The outfit was a size too large, but as long as Kenny tucked the shirt in and cinched his belt, he figured he looked fine.

The Precept had thought of everything. He had elevated Kenny from Aspirant to Member. He had arranged for Kenny to become a substitute bus driver and even had filled out the forms for him. Best job Kenny ever had. Learned every route so that he could take over for any driver who had a vacation or called in sick. It was only a matter of time before the name Kenny Arvenal would be on everyone's lips.

Kids made fun of Kenny when he was a schoolboy. "Pencil neck," they'd taunt, or, "Toothpick with a nose," or, "Pimples-on-a stick." They picked on him because of the way he looked and the way he talked. Kenny spoke in such a high-pitched tone that, on the phone, people often mistook him for a girl. And they teased him because he moved awkwardly.

But the Precept had shown Kenny how special he really was. All white people were special, and Kenny more so than others.

Though Kenny didn't understand how, the Precept knew that one of the regular school bus drivers, ol' black Boulette Babineaux, would be unable to handle her route on Monday and that Kenny would be called in to take over for her for the entire week. The Precept had driven Boulette's bus to his farm in St. Bonaventure Parish where he let Kenny stay. Kenny had helped lift his mentor's motorcycle down from the back of the long bus, with its seventy seats and storage compartments underneath for sports equipment and band instruments. He assisted in releasing the thick ratcheting straps snaking in and out of the vehicle's side windows. Afterward, the Precept even let Kenny take the KTM EXC500 Dual-Sport for a spin around the barn, its wide tires gripping the tall grass, still wet from the overnight rain, and its orange frame proclaiming confidence and power.

Kenny was in awe of the Precept. Now he never called him anything but "Precept," even though, while growing up, Kenny had known him as Bubba Mauvais. Bubba was ten years older than Kenny, tough as shit, and quicker than a skittish rabbit. He was always faster than anyone else. He ran faster. He drove faster. Faster on the football field. Faster with his fists. Faster and more accurate with his rifle.

But once Bubba had spent six months in Idaho and returned to Louisiana a year ago as the Precept, he was even better. Knew even more about guns. And explosives. And fighting. And what makes white people special.

Even though his mentor might know a lot, Kenny was the one who would get the glory. That was as it should be, Kenny thought. Recognition properly goes to the one on the front line. To the one who leads the charge across the barricades. To the one who shows no fear in the face of certain death.

Kenny had never been in battle. He had never been in the military, yet he was in the vanguard of the Alabaster Brigade, a battalion of believers who would follow Kenny's example and be inspired by him. The Precept frequently reminded him that they were all part of a proud tradition that traced directly back from the Alt-Right movement to the White Citizens Council to the Knights of the White Camellia to the original Klan.

The Precept told Kenny that, in the future, recruiters would merely whisper the name "Kenny Arvenal," and it would inspire others to join.

Those training to be Aspirants would chant in unison as they did their drills, "KEN-NY, KEN-NY, KEN-NY."

When each recruiting class graduated, the Precept assured him, the newly anointed Aspirants would proudly shout "KEN-NY AR-VE-NAL, KEN-NY AR-VE-NAL" three times, fire their guns in salute, and move on to their assignments, seeking the glory that Kenny had achieved.

Kenny Arvenal. Five syllables. That was important. That was historic. All the important people had five-syllable names.

That great Confederate president, Jefferson Davis.

Fearless heroes like Timothy McVeigh and Lee Harvey Oswald.

Kenny Arvenal would soon take his place among the ranks of such patriots.

CHAPTER FIVE

"Give me another beer. On second thought," Knock said, creaking as he twisted his body, "I can get it for myself."

Starner was shocked by how far Knock had deteriorated in the last few weeks. When the sheriff was in his prime, no one dared cross him. Shortly after he was elected thirty years ago, Naquin Mouton personally took down one of Carmine "the Snake" Micelli's thugs when Micelli's New Orleans crime syndicate tried to muscle its way into Petit Rouge Parish. He beat him senseless and dragged him over the parish line, leaving Micelli's underling propped on the side of a St. Bonaventure Parish highway with a note pinned to his collar warning Micelli that the next lackey the crime boss sent "might accidently be hit by a stray bullet" the minute he entered Petit Rouge Parish. Knock had a stack of signs made that sprouted up during the next election cycle. They read: "Keep Petit Rouge Safe. Everyone Knows, Don't Knock Naq." That's how the old man had gotten his nickname, and it stuck.

Over the years, Knock made the parish an inhospitable place for anyone who, as Knock would say, "didn't respect me." It was just "coincidence," Knock had bragged, that three homes being used as meth labs—by those who had not "respected him"—burned to the ground. Just "coincidence" that an "errant shot" from a "far off hunter who will never be found" happened to kill a drug dealer who was peddling during deer season in the woods next to the park that ran along the bayou. And everyone knew that anyone whom Knock arrested for a felony would be tried by his good friend,

Judge Franklin Fauchère, quickly convicted, and sentenced to serve decades in the infamous Angola Penitentiary.

That was then, when Knock was invincible. But now, Knock couldn't even grasp the bottle in the paper bag.

Knock sunk back in his chair, dejected. "Fuck it all, Starner. It's like someone has been injecting hot pepper sauce directly into my joints. Just pull out your Glock and shoot me now. This ain't living."

"Sure you want to do that and leave the position vacant? Make 'em hold an early election and all?"

"You and I both know," Knock said, "that a special election will have to be called. At the rate I'm slipping, I'm not even gonna make it to this year's primary. Are you having second thoughts about running for my position?"

"Hell, I can't do that, Knock, for all the reasons you—more than anybody—are aware of."

"Yeah. Too bad. The past always comes back, doesn't it, changing the future." Knock shifted in his seat and involuntarily groaned. "Damn! Gonna get that hospice gal to bring me a double dose of painkillers, soon as I finish the beer. Can't let her see that."

Knock tried to give a wry smile, but all that did was reveal his slipping dentures.

"So, we'll turn to present things then. You were telling me about the big rig. Don't that beat all, talking about a wreck to a man who ain't nothing but a wreck. OK. I got it. A tractor trailer on fire. Run off the road. Driver dead. So, what—besides your almost getting yourself killed trying to pull a dead man to 'safety'—is strange about that? Got truckers who don't know any better high-tailing it through the parish late at night, avoiding the weigh stations on the interstate and trying to make up time they wasted lollygagging elsewhere on their route. This guy was probably popping uppers to keep awake and his ticker gave out. Wish I could go like that. Fine one moment, dead the next, instead of having cancer suck the energy out of me faster and faster. He must've broken a fuel line when he barreled off the road and a spark lit it up. Those plaintiff lawyers, the ones from New Orleans with the big billboards on the highway, will be swarming around here any minute. They can smell money four parishes away."

Starner leaned forward in his chair, feigning fascination at what his boss was saying, and pretending to need Knock's advice. As long as the sheriff was alive, Starner knew his place, a place he didn't want to be in but for which he had no choice. His job was to humor the old man, ask for his advice, and act as if that advice was invaluable. "What's strange is that rigor mortis had already set in. The driver had to have been dead at least six to ten hours. Yet, the fire was just starting to really churn when I got there, and all of a sudden everything was fried crisper than oysters in a po'boy."

"Well, fried or not," said Knock, "Acie, our 'fine' coroner, wouldn't have found anything useful anyway, even though he insists on being called to the scene of every death. Thinks he's some kind of super-expert. He's nothing but a damn podiatrist. It's a godawful shame that you don't have to have any real forensic knowledge or experience to put your name on the ballot for parish coroner in this state."

"Yeah," Starner agreed. "And if that's a shame, how he keeps getting reelected is a downright tragedy. Our 'exceptional' coroner/podiatrist couldn't figure out the cause of death of anything unless it was . . . caused by an ingrown toenail."

Knock started wheezing and gasping for breath. His chest rattled.

Starner jumped up to try to assist Knock, but the old man waved the deputy off.

The sheriff's nose crinkled and his mouth spread into a huge grin. He wasn't coughing. He was laughing.

Knock spit out a plug of yellow phlegm, leaned back in his rocker, and gave way to a hearty guffaw.

"Ingrown toenail on a death certificate! That'd be Acie for sure. Hell, Starner, this is the first time since hospice was called in that something has made me smile."

PART II

MONDAY

CHAPTER SIX

Truvi Brady straightened her daughter's collar before sending Abigayle out to the driveway to await the school bus. Truvi couldn't help thinking how fast Abigayle was growing up. It was the second semester of second grade, yet Abigayle had already outgrown the uniforms Truvi bought for her at the beginning of January.

Art had given Truvi money to buy two new outfits for Abigayle. It was yet another example to Truvi of how good Art was to her daughter.

Abigayle looked so cute in the St. Bonaventure Parish school attire that all elementary students wore. White Peter Pan blouse. Navy-and-white plaid jumper. White knee socks. Navy blue Mary Janes.

Even though they lived in Petit Rouge Parish, all public school students attended the regional facilities in St. Bonaventure Parish. The Petit Rouge Parish public schools closed years ago, after white families transferred their children to private schools to avoid going to class with black children, taking their crucial tax dollars with them.

"Time's getting close now," Truvi said, handing Abigayle her blue plaid book sack with the "SBE" patch that Truvi had sewn on the flap. The St. Bonaventure Elementary PTA sold the "SBE" insignia as a fundraiser. It took only a bit of pleading before Art had given Truvi permission to purchase several more of them so Abigayle could have them on her sweatshirt, raincoat, and gym shorts.

Abigayle loved those patches. They had the same white piping and lettering as the crests adorning the big kids' school uniforms, except theirs read "SBH" for St. Bonaventure High, instead of "SBE" for St. Bonaventure Elementary. Even Abigayle's school bus

21

driver, Ms. Boulette, wore a patch on her yellow uniform, though hers read "SBSB," for St. Bonaventure School Bus.

Abigayle started for the door.

Truvi held up her hand for Abigayle to halt. "Didn't you forget something?"

Abigayle ran back to the kitchen table. Truvi bent down, and Abigayle gave her mother a kiss on the cheek.

"You'll never be too old to kiss your momma. Now, go on, you. Scoot out that door. And remember, don't slam it. You know that Mr. Art hates to be disturbed by loud noises. He was working late in his shop and is still out there, but he hears everything."

In the garage that he had converted to his shop, where Truvi and Abigayle were forbidden to go, Art Brady could hear Abigayle bounding out of the house. Ten minutes later he heard the door open and shut softly as Truvi headed out to her job as a cashier at the biggest of the Ganderson's Markets, the one eight miles away in St. Bonaventure Parish.

There was so much to do once they were gone.

Truvi was needy. Art was always looking for the needy. Those who were desperately searching for something, even if they didn't know what it was that they were seeking.

Truvi had dropped out of school at the age of sixteen when she became pregnant with Abigayle. No one in St. Bonaventure Parish wanted a scrawny, black, single mother with a young daughter. No one, that is, until Art Brady came along a year-and-a-half ago.

Truvi was perfect.

Of course, if he hadn't found Truvi, he would have found someone else.

CHAPTER SEVEN

"Y ou come up with anything yet, Ed?"

Edouardine Mitchell didn't turn around. She knew that Starner was looming over her. She could smell the cheap cologne he used and heard him knocking around the office earlier getting a cup of coffee. He must have gone home to take a shower because she hadn't found him asleep on the office couch when she came in.

"You drip some of that stuff on my new blouse," Ed said, "and you're gonna pay for it, understand?"

Edouardine Mitchell had worked for Knock for two decades, and she let it be known, from the time Knock brought Starner in years ago, that she held the deputy's past against him and was not happy that the sheriff had hired—out of some misplaced pity, she was sure—a disgraced, white former detective. Over time, she and Starner reached a truce of sorts. They each did their jobs, but she still didn't like him.

She pulled up her notes on one of the double screens on her desk, deliberately refusing to address Starner face-to-face. "I've checked with FMCSA. Checked with DOTD. Checked with the state police. Ain't no one got a record of that CMV."

Starner didn't say anything, but he realized immediately that what she found didn't add up. CMVs, commercial motor vehicles, had to be licensed. Truckers were required to keep current logs that could be inspected at any time by FMCSA, the Federal Motor Carrier Safety Administration. DOTD, the Louisiana Department of Transportation and Development, was supposed to track the weights and sizes of loads. But the big rig that burned in the woods off Vizeau Road couldn't be traced. The fire had been so hot that both the cab and the engine block melted. No VIN could be discerned. The identification markings on the trailer had been destroyed either before or during the blaze, and what was left of the driver was part of the twisted metal mass.

Starner was unable to stop Dr. Acie LaPierre from instructing one of the volunteer firemen, who was also a full-time welder, to take a blowtorch and cut away a ragged three-by-five section of melted metal that surrounded the body of the driver like some weird, spider-like sculpture bent at ninety degrees. The only recognizable human remains were two soot-blackened limbs grasping a collapsed steering wheel and the toe of a boot fused to a floorboard.

When Starner asked Acie to extract DNA from the foot in the boot or the brittle arms after Acie arranged for the slab to be hauled back to his office, a former grocery store, and stuck in the walk-in freezer next to the big cooler where he kept bodies until he had finished his perfunctory autopsies, Acie had replied indignantly, "What's the use? Don't have the equipment here to do that, even if I had the funds to run such tests, which I don't. If you figure out who he was, let me know. That's the name I'll put on the death certificate. If not, I'll mark it 'unknown,' close my file, and send this whole mess off to the pauper's section of the cemetery."

Since Acie clearly was not going to make an effort to figure out who the driver of the big rig was, and since Ed couldn't provide any answers, Starner headed out of the office and drove his truck to "Ronald Vivochère Sr. and Son: Gently Used Vehicle Parts" to examine the tractor trailer more thoroughly.

Starner braced himself for the visit. He and Ronald Vivochère Jr.—whom everyone called Boyo—had been in high school together. Every time they met since Starner returned to Petit Rouge Parish, Boyo enjoyed constantly needling the former football and baseball star about how far he had fallen, how high the "parts entrepreneur"—as Boyo liked to describe himself—had risen, and bragging about how much wealth he had accumulated while Starner lived in double-wide trailer and remained "just a deputy sheriff" who had to kowtow to Knock, while Boyo not only owned this wrecking yard but also the sole used car lot in the parish as well as a half-interest in a porcelain figurine shop in the New Orleans French Quarter. Boyo loved rubbing that in.

Boyo was more than happy to show Starner through the yard, noting proudly how many acres it covered and boasting about the profits he was raking in. It took them more than fifteen minutes to walk to the rear of the facility through a labyrinth of twenty-foot-high piles of scrap teetering precariously. One of the two huge cranes that Boyo used to move wrecked cars, trucks, and tons of material loomed high above their path. The other one rose in the distance, looking like a mechanical monster about to devour scurrying prey.

"Damn shame," Boyo said, as they approached the blackened mass near the back fence. "No matter how bad things are in a big rig accident, I can usually salvage tie rods, a crankshaft, battery box, an axle or two, or at least a decking saddle to resell. But not on this baby."

Starner walked slowly around the wreckage, using his cell phone to photograph the mangled metal from all angles. He found it hard to believe that this mess was once a tractor trailer rig more than sixty feet long. The fire, plus Boyo's carelessness when moving it to his scrapyard, had reduced the entire contraption to less than a third of its original size.

Trying not to groan from the pain in his knees caused by an old football injury, Starner climbed up on the roof of a nearby wrecked car to view the remains from a higher vantage point. Boyo took a seat in the shade, resting on the bumper of a truck that had neither wheels nor hood.

"You think," Starner called down to Boyo, "you could have at least tried to tow it here intact?"

"Come on! That fire melted everything into a compact mess. Did the best I could. Had to have been some heat."

"Some heat? Boyo, you always were the master of the obvious. Almost got me when the diesel tanks exploded."

"Diesel tanks exploded? That's all?" He looked up at Starner like the deputy had just said the stupidest thing he had ever heard.

Starner could have pummeled Boyo, wiping that smart-aleck expression off his face. But beating up one of the parish's successful businessmen wasn't going to endear him to Knock. Instead, Starner grit his teeth, took out his notebook and pen, and put on his best I'm-just-a-cop-asking-for-the-facts voice. "How much do those diesel tanks hold anyway? A hundred gallons? Hundred-and-twenty? There were two of them ablaze, remember?"

Boyo didn't answer right away. Rather, he signaled for Starner to come down off the roof of the car. His knees aching, Starner carefully clambered down and followed Boyo as they walked around the wreckage one more time.

"Look at this," Boyo said, pointing to what resembled an abstract metallic waterfall, with streaks of brown, black, and silver.

Starner didn't bother bending down to examine it. "Yeah. That stuff covered the driver's body. Those diesel tanks melted everything."

"Mr. Deputy," Boyo said with a big smile that carved deep lines in his sunburned jowls, "you may think you know a bit about police business from the time when you were a fancy cop down in New Orleans, but it's clear you don't know shit about much else. Maybe that's why you're still just a *deputy*. Let me try to fill your thick skull with some useful information. Follow me."

Starner's right hand clenched into a fist. He wanted to punch Boyo in the face, relieving him of a couple of teeth, but refrained. Starner put his hand in his pocket and pinched his thigh forcefully, as if that would relieve his anger. It didn't, but Starner forced himself to swallow his pride. He had been refraining from doing lots of things for a long time, and it was getting more and more difficult to let slights pass.

As they made their way to the front of the yard, winding around piles of wrecked pickup trucks, automobiles, and horse trailers, Boyo took a side aisle. "Watch for that busted windshield on the ground. Guy last week tried to remove it but didn't know what he was doing. Cracked it pulling it out. Stomped on it, he got so mad.

Made him pay for it, of course, as well as the next one that I helped him with. But look, over here, this is what I wanted to show you."

Boyo stopped in front of the burned-out hulk of a Dodge Ram truck. "See this? Wrecked last year in St. Bonaventure Parish. Stupid teenager backed over the gasoline pump on his grandfather's farm. Lucky that he got away with only second-degree burns. So, Starner," Boyo said, with a smirk, "see any melted metal dripping anywhere?"

Starner was once a decorated detective, even if that was years ago. He didn't need Boyo or anyone else toying with him. "Fuck, Boyo. I'm not here to play games."

"Some cop you are! Come to my office."

He strolled briskly back to the prefab metal structure at the front of the yard. It sat on three-foot brick pilings, which kept it dry when Bayou Grosse Noir occasionally overflowed.

As they climbed up the wooden steps and entered through the dented steel door, condensation from the window air conditioner was dripping onto the linoleum floor. An oversized wooden desk, scratched and faded, took up almost the entire end of the narrow building. There was just enough room between it and the wall for Boyo to squeeze by.

Starner pulled the only other chair in the office away from the pond gathering on the linoleum and took a seat as Boyo flipped through piles and piles of paper.

"Knew I had it." Boyo said finally, withdrawing a broken three-ring binder from the bottom of a stack and patting it with satisfaction. "Obvious, isn't it?"

Tired of Boyo's games, Starner remained impassive.

"No, really," Boyo said, "these have all the tables. Look, I'll show you."

Boyo turned the binder around so that Starner could read it. There were pages and pages of rows filled with numbers and columns headed with undecipherable abbreviations.

"It's right here," said Boyo. "Twice a year I sell the stuff with no usable parts to a foundry. The deal is that I load it with my big cranes, they haul, it, and I get a flat price per pound plus extra for each metal they're able to extract. See? Lead melts at six-hundred-plus degrees. Aluminum around twelve-twenty and brass at near eighteen-hundred. Iron north of two thousand. Steel at twenty-six hundred or more and stainless steel at twenty-eight hundred. And then there's tungsten carbide at more than fifty-one-hundred."

"So what?" Starner stood up to leave. "Metal melts. And that stuff melted on the big rig."

"Right," Boyo said, leaning back in his chair. "And the stuff that melted had aluminum, brass, iron, stainless steel, and tungsten carbide. But diesel ignites at less than five hundred degrees. You're the big know-it-all cop. Tell me how that fire got so damn hot!"

CHAPTER EIGHT

"No problem, no problem at all, Precept," Kenny said. He had been filled with self-satisfaction ever since he drove the school bus back to the barn. "Ain't I learnt that route good? Picked up all them kids out in Petit Rouge Parish. 'Course, the ones out there don't fill a third of the bus, and t'aint a white among 'em, but I didn't let on none how them black faces spook me. Was real careful, just like you told me. Stopped at all the railroad crossings. Waved at the teachers at St. Bonaventure Elementary School while dropping off the little pickaninnies. Told them teachers no, I didn't know what happened to Boulette, but I expected she'd be back by next week. Then came the long way back here to the farm with no one the wiser. Done it all just right!"

The Precept nodded encouragement as he opened the cargo latch on the second of the three undercarriage storage compartments on the driver's side of the bus. He pointed to one of the open crates stacked against the wall of the barn. "Go get another bundle—just one at a time, remember."

Kenny pulled the dolly to the rear of barn. He struggled to place another suitcase-sized item delicately onto it. The cargo was heavy, had no handles, and was wrapped in slippery white plastic. Kenny finally positioned the package on the dolly and slowly rolled it to the center of the barn where the bus was parked.

The Precept was not worried. They had two more hours to work before Kenny had to take the bus out again for the afternoon run, and then a few more hours this evening once he returned. At this rate, the bus wouldn't be ready until Thursday night, but that was perfectly acceptable. Tomorrow they would fill up the three storage compartments on the right-hand side of the bus. Wednesday they would pack the smaller boxes behind the mud flaps and under the body panels. That left all of Thursday afternoon and evening to finish up the wiring harness, run it under the bus, snake it above the front axle, and hook it all to the detonators.

Kenny watched with envy as the Precept began to slide the large, white, plastic rectangle into the chamber beneath the bus. Kenny wondered how the Precept remembered which of the existing wires on the items already in the compartment attached to the tangled spaghetti of connectors that he extracted from the top of the latest package. He marveled at how the Precept figured out the way to make it all work—things they were putting in, on, and under the bus—so that just one push of the red button the Precept planned to place adjacent to the steering wheel would ignite the entire load.

It was like magic to Kenny, and he was thrilled to be part of the behind-the-scenes preparation. For him, it was like knowing into which hidden pocket of his coat a magician stuffed a pigeon and in which he placed a bunny, which sleeve contained silk scarves that could be withdrawn in a seemingly endless cavalcade, and which empty box had a false bottom.

But, when the big day came, what everyone saw and heard was the only thing that mattered, not what happened behind the scenes. The magician's assistant didn't get star billing; the magician did. When it was time, the Precept would be invisible. Kenny would be in the spotlight.

Kenny was the one who would be seen. Kenny was the one who would make news. Kenny would no longer be the butt of insults or envy anyone. Instead, Kenny thought, his smile growing even larger, everyone will envy me.

CHAPTER NINE

Starner sat sulking in the back booth at Chez Poêlon, Florene and Armond's roadside café. The name sounded a lot better in French than its English translation: House of the Frying Pan.

Boyo's comment had gotten him thinking. How *had* the fire become so hot? Not from the diesel tanks. That was clear, as his charts indicated. Starner couldn't figure it out. But that was the least of his worries.

Florene emerged from the kitchen with a plate of hot apple pie slathered with sweet mayhaw jelly and a scoop of ice cream. She slid it in front of the deputy.

"Try some of this, Starner. Whatever's bothering you, this'll make you feel better for sure. It's one of Armond's specialties."

"Before lunch, Florene? I've got enough on my mind and don't need more in my stomach."

Florene wiped her hands on her apron and sidled into the seat across from him. "More in your stomach? You haven't eaten anything! Other than to grunt hello when you came in, you've been in a funk here in the corner, downing coffee like you were steeling yourself for a caffeine-fueled battle."

Florene gently patted his hand. "You had that same hangdog look when you came back from your time in New Orleans. Like you were that Greek guy we studied in high school, and your future was a meaningless rock that kept rolling back on you."

Florene's hair, still long and cascading around her shoulders, was beginning to get gray streaks, but to Starner, it didn't make her seem old. To him, it was sexy. Her apron, with the insignia of Chez Poêlon emblazoned over her left breast, was cinched tightly around

31

her still-slender waist. It was a far cry from the skimpy cheerleader outfits she wore in high school, heading the squad while he quarterbacked the team. But her touch was as tender as he remembered.

"Is it Knock? Is that what's eating at you? Everyone says he's in a bad way and doesn't want anyone to see him. Anyone, that is, except you."

Starner wanted to confide in Florene. Wanted to tell her that yes, it was Knock, and it was everything else. It was living alone in the trailer he bought when he moved home from New Orleans. It was turning his back on years of training and not challenging Knock when the sheriff did the "deals" that made him the richest man in the parish. It was learning to ignore the obvious. It was being with Boyo today and wondering how that snot-nosed kid who almost failed out of school had grown up to make loads of money while all Starner had been doing was watching the years fly by, earning only a rural parish deputy's paltry salary. It was surviving the explosion and not knowing why a dead man was still at the wheel of a tractor trailer that caught fire hours after it apparently crashed, a big rig whose melted metal couldn't have resulted from a diesel blast. It was wondering how different his life would have been had he stayed in town with Florene after high school and not gone off to New Orleans and met Cheryl Ann. But if he hadn't met Cheryl Ann and if they hadn't had Bucky . . . Starner's life was full of should-haves and would-haves, of heartache, memories, sorrow, regrets, and grief. He longed for absolution, but there wasn't any.

"It's all about Knock, isn't it? I know that old man is like a father to you," Florene said.

Starner didn't bother to correct her. Everyone assumed the deputy was grateful to the all-powerful sheriff. But Knock wasn't a beneficent father figure to Starner. The deputy knew him for what he was. An ego that had to be fed. A proud politician who disbursed favors as long as one turned a blind eye to things the sheriff wanted to keep hidden.

"When Knock passes . . . if you want to run for sheriff, Armond and I will back you. We'll put signs in our window and, in the evenings after we close up the café, we can help run a phone bank if you want. With our two girls at LSU on scholarships, we've got time to assist and even a bit of money to throw into your campaign."

The ice cream melted on the apple pie and puddled on Starner's plate. "You know that's never going to happen, Florene. Not with the demographics in the parish now. Not with what happened to me in New Orleans. But I appreciate the offer. I really do. Here, let me pay you for the pie."

"Not a chance. This was my gift to you. Come on! You're here almost every day. You can't go without eating anything. At least take one bite before you leave. Tomorrow, when you're hungry, order whatever Armond lists as the special. Maybe then you'll want to talk."

For Starner, there was no point in talking any more. There was almost no point in anything. He knew he simply had been going through the motions for years. Of work. Of existence. And once Knock died, what then?

Florene left the table. Starner stared at the plate glumly before taking his spoon and shoveling up some of the now-soggy pie that had fallen apart, just like his life.

CHAPTER TEN

A rt Brady used four cell phones in the several hours it took him to drive from Petit Rouge Parish into central Mississippi. Intent on avoiding the interstates, Art took two-lane backroads, going through small Louisiana towns like Little Jerusalem, Lebeau, Big Cane, Plaucheville, Lettsworth, and Black Hawk. The route was elevated only slightly above the low-lying alluvial plain, bisecting miles of forlorn fields of sorghum and traversing increasingly decrepit towns with vacant streets and boarded-up storefronts.

He limited his calls to no more than three per phone, and after he reached his limit, Art would stop the car, smash the burner with a hammer, scatter pieces of it out of the window over the few next miles, and then use another. He kept a bunch of such phones in the leather satchel next to him on the front seat. Carefully driving slightly under the speed limit, he eventually crossed the bridge that arched from Vidalia, Louisiana, into Natchez, Mississippi, and from there turned northeast, toward a farm outside of Church Hill.

Three incoming calls today resulted in two potential recruits. That was an excellent ratio. Recruit number one was a Desert Storm vet, now homeless, whom Art met several weeks ago on a trip to Beaumont. He had left the former soldier with a sandwich, two cans of soda, and his card. The other was a tattoo-covered young hitchhiker with a thin beard and silver rings piercing his nose and eyebrows. Art had picked him up outside of New Orleans near a bar, driven him into the city, and given him a card to which was stapled a $20 bill. That card had only one number, and that number was forwarded to whatever cell phone Art was using at the time.

And then there were the additional eleven phone calls Art made while driving. The discussions were short and succinct. Anyone listening in would have thought that the speaker was a farmer hedging the market for his crops. "Buy a put at seven-point-twenty." Or "Your call option creates too much downside risk. We can't change the strike price." Or "Since you can't meet the deadline for the last order, I'll be contacting your Saxon."

It was this last call, the second one to the same person in the past twenty-four hours, that brought Art to a farmhouse in the piney woods near Church Hill, off an unmarked dirt path that intersected with Hog Farm Road. He stood in the kitchen, with its cheap laminate flooring, and spoke to the three people seated in the shabby breakfast nook.

Saxon Fourteen, a man with a scar on his left cheek, was cleaning his Browning Mark III 9mm Luger pistol. Several full magazines were on the table in front of him.

Saxon Thirty-One—barely out of his teens, with spiked hair and a wild look—returned Art's gaze with a twisted smile.

Saxon Twelve, a young, sloe-eyed woman with heavy, black eyeshadow and a low-cut tank top, slouched in her chair.

"The order," Art said grimly, "was to be fulfilled on South Beach in Miami this Friday. Same time, same strike price as the one in New Orleans. But yesterday afternoon I was informed that we're behind schedule in Florida. Two at once. That was always the plan."

"We understand, but sometimes things happen," Saxon Fourteen said, running a pipe cleaner up and down the barrel of the Luger.

Art's eyes narrowed in anger. "Things don't 'happen' unless we make them happen." Art reached over, and, grabbing the pistol from the man's hand, slid it to the far edge of the table. "That was what you promised when you took your oath. That was what you agreed to when you were elevated to Saxon. It is all in service of the greater plan. When the world awakens to the greater truth. When the cobwebs are swept from the eyes of the nonbelievers, the disbelievers, the atheists, agnostics, and Jews. When there are no angels of mercy leading to the path of salvation except us. When the fires of hell are visible, and all Aryan Christians unite to defend the supremacy of the white race."

"But Art," Saxon Fourteen protested, ". . . you see . . ."

"No names!" Art said sharply. "You know the rules. Noms de guerre only." In this group there were to be no names. Names create personal relationships, and Art couldn't risk these three forming any kind of bond with one another or anyone else in the Brigade.

Saxon Fourteen began again, an edge of indignity creeping into his voice, "The load would have been delivered on time if the Aspirant hadn't . . ."

Art held up his hand for silence. "Now you're blaming the Aspirant? Someone I recruited, nurtured, and brought into the fold? Someone I gave to you to train so that you could demonstrate your worth? Someone you vouched for to handle the task? Someone whose training clearly was deficient?"

Saxon Fourteen clenched his jaw in anger, which only accentuated the scar that carved a deep line from his cheek almost to his left ear. It wasn't his fault! Some of Art's recruits were the dregs of society. Saxon Fourteen had done the best he could. Spent eight long months working with that particular misfit.

What, Saxon Fourteen thought, was I supposed to have said a month ago when Art asked if the recruit was ready? How could I ever get to be an Imperial if I even hinted I had doubts about the recruit's ability? If I complained that the recruit was a bum? Shit, Art only recruited bums. And if I had said that the recruit was not ready, Art would have blamed me for not training the recruit properly. Which is exactly what Art was doing now.

Saxon Fourteen looked around the room, trying to figure out how long it would take him to reach over for the Luger, load it, and shoot Art. The others would back him. They were supposed to be autonomous units fighting to reclaim the rights of all Aryans, not part of some damned bureaucracy. Art had gotten too high-and-mighty. Had let his title go to his head! Had let that damn dark-haired, smart-aleck kid who liked to use big words and pretend not to be better than the rest of us Saxons—as if we didn't see him looking down his nose at us—become part of the Alabaster Brigade and work for Bubba. Art had even gone and married a coal-black gal with a pickaninny daughter, claiming it was the "perfect cover." Hell, being covered with shit was more like it. The mere thought of Art getting it on with a black woman disgusted him, and Saxon Fourteen was certain that the other Saxons shared his view.

Art, spotting the man eying the pistol, picked it up, stuck it in the back of his belt, and smiled. "I see it in your face. You worked hard to be a Saxon." He gathered up the magazines and put them on the kitchen counter, out of Saxon Fourteen's reach. "You think I don't appreciate what you've done. That's not it at all. I appreciate what you haven't done all too well."

Art turned to the young woman. "Saxon Twelve, do you want to move from Saxon to Imperial?"

The sloe-eyed woman understood. Imperial was only one rank below Precept. She swiftly drew a hunting knife from the sheathe on her belt and plunged it into the heart of Saxon Fourteen, twisting it to be sure there was no chance of survival.

Spike-haired Saxon Thirty-One laughed and lifted his feet so that his sandals wouldn't get stained by the blood pouring out of Saxon Fourteen's chest as he slumped to the floor.

"Excellent job," Art said to the woman. "You're now promoted. Your title is Imperial Seven. You and Saxon Thirty-One clean this mess up."

CHAPTER ELEVEN

Abigayle bounded off the school bus. With her book sack dragging on the sidewalk and a big smile on her face, she ran toward Truvi, who was waiting for her in front of their frame home, an old Acadian cottage that Art had owned before their marriage. Truvi had barely beaten the bus home after finishing up her shift as a cashier at Ganderson's Market.

"Must've been a good day," Truvi said, kneeling down and giving Abigayle a big hug. The little girl squirmed away, reached into her book sack, and excitedly pulled out of her binder a large piece of paper that she carefully unfolded. It was a crayon drawing. A squiggly line of blue ran down from the left corner, two stick figures were on either side of a felt fleur-de-lis glued in the center of the page, and on the right was a building with a cross.

"Now, that is simply beautiful, Abigayle. Did some professional artist come to school to do this and give it to you?"

"No, Momma, I made it myself!"

"You did? Why, that's the most remarkable drawing I've ever seen. Now this building on the right, that's a church?"

"Of course, Momma. That's the St. Louis Cathedral in Jackson Square in New Orleans, where we're going on Friday on the school trip. You're still going to be one of the chaperones, aren't you?" Abigayle looked like she would cry if the answer wasn't yes.

"Wouldn't miss it for the world, darlin'."

Abigayle did a little dance of joy.

"Now," Truvi said, pointing to the left side of the page, "what's this over here in blue? Rain coming down on these two people?"

"No, Momma. That's the Mississippi River that we're gonna cross on the bridge from Destrehan to Luling to get to New Orleans. Did you know that the river goes in a big half-circle around New Orleans? After we sing on that big stage in Jackson Square, we're going to go up over the levee and get on a riverboat to go to the Audubon Zoo and see elephants and tigers and lions and animals from all over, just like the time we did when Mr. Art took us! It's going to be the bestest day ever. And see right here on my drawing, next to the flower of D. Lee, which is the symbol of New Orleans—although I don't know who D. Lee is—it's you and Mr. Art. Oh, I wish that Mr. Art could come with us, like the last time we all went to New Orleans together."

"I do too, honey. Though I'll get Friday off, he has to work. You know that."

"Still, I wish't he would come," Abigayle said wistfully as Truvi picked up the book sack and the two of them walked up the steps and into the kitchen.

Truvi cut up an apple for the two of them to share while Abigayle bounced up and down in her seat. "Do you know what else happened today?"

"No, I don't think I do," Truvi said, opening a jar of peanut butter into which they would dip their slices of apple. "Why don't you tell me?"

"Well, Gabe threw a spitball at Caleb, and Mrs. Huval made him apologize and moved his desk next to me! Can you believe that? I don't like Gabe. No, I don't. And we have a new bus driver while Ms. Boulette is out sick. His name is Mr. Kenny and he's nice, but he has this squeaky kind of voice, and we all think he sounds like a mouse."

CHAPTER TWELVE

Boyo was getting ready to wrap up for the day when a gray Chevy Silverado double-cab truck sped through the open front gate of Ronald Vivochère Sr. and Son Gently Used Vehicle Parts and came to a screeching halt in front of the office. Boyo studied the pickup through the window. Its grill gleamed, its bed was pristine, and its panels undented. His usual customers drove vehicles that were old and well worn.

The driver got out first. He was a tall man in his early twenties with hair cropped closer than a crewcut. He was dressed in a faded tee shirt, jeans, and scuffed boots. His nose was askew, as if his head had been molded in wax and set down on its side too near a fire. On his left bicep he sported a swastika tattoo.

The man on the passenger side emerged next. He was even younger than the tattooed skinhead and slight, with a mass of jet-black hair and dark-set eyes. His white collared shirt was sharply pressed, as were his khakis.

Boyo opened the front door. "Can I help you gentlemen?" He was trying to flatter them. Gentlemen? They were college-age, if they were even that old. An unlikely pair, at that. The tall one had a bully's swagger, and all the shorter one needed was a necktie to look like a Jehovah's Witness about to hand out a Bible.

The dark-haired kid shielded his eyes, glanced up at the sign, and asked "You're Ronald Vivochère Sr.?"

"No, my father passed several years ago. You guys aren't from around here, are you?"

The kid stuck out his hand. "Glad to meet you. I'm Tommy."

Boyo hid his distrust behind a wide grin and shook Tommy's hand, noting his strong grip. "Folks here call me Boyo. Don't like to be called Ronald Vivochère Jr. And your friend is?"

"Phillip," Tommy said eagerly, before his companion could speak.

Boyo pointed the way to his office on cinder blocks. "Come on in and get out of the heat."

Tommy entered before Phillip, who was so tall he had to duck his head as he walked in.

Boyo squeezed along the wall and settled behind his wide desk, observing the two carefully. "Sorry I have only one seat for customers. It's right over there. Just watch the drip from the air conditioner. As soon as you tell me what you're looking for, we'll go out into the yard. I guarantee that whatever you need, I've got or can get."

Phillip stood by the door, hands in the pockets of his jeans while Tommy sat in the chair and launched right into business. "If you please, Mr. Boyo, we have come to your establishment in search of amalgamations of metallurgical accumulations."

Phillip tried to stifle a sneer. That kid loved to use big words but had no idea how to talk to people. He resented the fact that the Precept made him Tommy's bodyguard and ordered him to let Tommy take the lead in everything. Phillip was certain the kid couldn't lead the way out of a forest if the path were lined with neon lights.

Boyo's suspicions, already raised, were heightened. No legit customer spoke like Tommy. "You want scrap? Hell, I got tons of that, no question. Literally, tons. You want ferrous or nonferrous? Or are you looking for something specific, like copper? Got bare bright, copper roofing, and more. Sheet iron? There's shitloads of that in the back, and I can give you a flat rate for 300 series stainless steel. You bring a flatbed in here and I'll use one of my cranes to load up whatever you want. Ain't nothin' too large or too small for me to sell, buy, or handle." Boyo watched them carefully. He did not see a flicker of recognition on their faces as he mentioned the types of detail that interested true buyers.

Phillip jumped in before Tommy could respond. "We're just looking for plain, old scrap metal, like from a wrecked 18-wheeler.

Doesn't matter what its condition is, even if it's all burned up. You have anything like that?"

Boyo forced a smile, the one he used when he was about to scam someone. Who the hell were these guys? "You got your permits with you? Always got to log in those permits, you know, for bulk buyers. Let me get my book. It's down here somewhere."

Boyo bent under the desk and, hidden from their view, loudly shuffled papers with his left hand while, with his right, he took his Browning 9mm pistol from the lower drawer and slipped it into his pants pocket. He sat upright, placing the big logbook on top of a stack of papers. "Your permits?"

Tommy's eyes grew wide. He hadn't expected such a question. "You need bureaucratic documents?"

Philip put his hand on Tommy's shoulder to silence him. The kid couldn't handle anything. "No problem. You got scrap. We got permits. They're out in our truck, in the glove compartment. Right, Tommy?"

Tommy nodded.

As they walked outside to the Silverado, Boyo kept his hand in his pocket, grasping the Browning, as he continued bantering. "You guys must really know what you're doing. Scrap metal permits aren't easy to come by. You working for somebody else or are you doing this on your own? If you got permits, you must know Stan in the permitting department. He's the one who's got to add the approval stamp each year. Or are you working for Pepperneck Charlie over in Winona, Mississippi, and using one of his chits? Pepperneck is always hiring college boys to try to scrape up a good deal. And, of course, if you want a good deal, there's no better deal than the one you can get right here."

Boyo figured if they answered any of those questions in the affirmative, he was going to run them out of the yard at the point of his gun. Everybody in the scrap metal business knew that permits were issued as a matter of course, there was no Stan in the permitting department, and no Pepperneck Charlie.

But neither of the boys responded to his inquiries. Instead, when they got to the Chevy, Tommy opened the passenger-side door and reached into the glove compartment, "The permits are right here."

When he turned around, he was pointing a small handgun at Boyo.

Boyo's eyes twinkled with delight as he pulled out his Browning. "You boys think you can scare me? You guys are as transparent as a whore's thong. Get off my property. I don't know why you're looking for a wrecked 18-wheeler, but if I see you around here again, I'm going to shoot first. Understand? Put that shitty, little pistol away before you plug yourself in the foot."

Boyo was so delighted by the fear he saw in Tommy's eyes and the way Tommy's hand trembled that he didn't notice Phillip leaning on the truck bed and slipping his arm down to retrieve a crowbar. "Fuck all this talk!" The skinhead with the swastika tattoo swung the crowbar and caught Boyo square in the face, breaking his nose and knocking out one of his front teeth.

Trying to ignore the pain and the blood filling his mouth, Boyo got off two wild shots, but Phillip attacked him again, breaking Boyo's forearm and causing him to fall to the ground in agony.

Retrieving Boyo's Browning, Phillip pulled the scrap dealer to his feet. "No more games, old man. Where's the fucking 18-wheeler? We know it's here."

Caressing his injured right arm with his left hand and spitting out blood, Boyo managed to say, "In the back."

Tommy's hand was still shaking as he thrust his pistol against Boyo's forehead. "Show us!"

Boyo slumped back down on the ground. He spoke slowly. It hurt to even move his lips. "It's a long walk. I can't make it in this condition. You drive. Lots of twists to get there. I'll tell you which turns as we go. Take the damn big rig and leave me the hell alone!"

Phillip picked up Boyo was if he were a bride being carried over the threshold and tossed him into the bed of the Silverado. Boyo groaned as he hit the metal.

Phillip sat on the truck bed rail, relaying directions to Tommy as Boyo, who was growing weaker and weaker, instructed them on how to maneuver the Chevy through the scrapyard to the back gate where the remains of the big rig sat in the shadow of a large crane. The long, flatbed wrecker that Boyo had use to haul the burned-out 18-wheeler was parked beside it.

Boyo's voice was filled with agony. "There it is. Your fucking 'metallurgical accumulation.' Can't be driven. Has to be picked up and placed on the flatbed. Know how to work a crane?"

"Of course," said Phillip. He opened the tailgate, kicked Boyo out, and using the Browning, shot him in the head.

PART III

TUESDAY

CHAPTER THIRTEEN

Starner had been at his desk for several hours before the sheriff's office officially opened at eight. He hadn't slept much, but that was typical. He could never seem to make it through the night without waking up four or five times. He'd get up, drink a beer, and try to fall back asleep. That never worked. He'd watch TV, turn it off, walk around the outside of his double-wide in the dark listening to the crickets and owls, go back inside, attempt to read a book, and close his eyes in the hope that exhaustion would overtake him. But the bad memories keep flooding back.

Ed's desk had a view out the front window so that, when she sat down, her back was to Starner. She could see the big magnolia tree that shaded the parking lot and everyone who drove in or out. Ed didn't look up when Judson Jorée finally strolled in, not even apologizing for being more than an hour late. The first words out of his mouth as he wiped his nose with the cuff of his uniform while pouring a cup of coffee, were, "Just when the weather gets nice in the spring, I get sick. Got to be allergies."

Ed warned him, without turning around, "Don't you be gettin' any of your germs in my area."

"As you wish, Miss Edouardine," Judson said in a tone of voice that meant he wasn't going to do anything he didn't want to do.

Starner looked up and covered the top of his coffee cup with a paper napkin. "Go sniffle out in the parking lot, Judson, not in here. Besides, you're supposed to be on patrol already. You've missed three days this month and you're behind in your ticket quota. If Knock was here, he'd be chewing your ass out by now."

"I'm entitled to every one of my sick days, and I'll take 'em as I need 'em. Don't worry, I'll exceed my quota by the end of the month, old man. . . . Remember, we both report to Knock. You're not my boss."

Ed shook her head in disbelief as Judson exited, slamming the door. "If my son—and he's about the same age as Judson—had shown that attitude to me at home, my husband would have given him the what-for."

Starner didn't respond to Ed. She was rubbing salt into the wound he carried, criticizing him for not dressing down Judson while reminding him, not so subtly, that Bucky, were he alive today, would have been a year or two younger than Judson.

Starner drained the rest of the coffee from the cardboard cup and, crumpling it, tossed it into the trash can. He couldn't sleep because of the past, and he found no respite here in the office. He forced himself to focus on the present—which, under the circumstances, was bleak enough—and gave a sigh. "Ed, just note the time he came in—seventy minutes late—and dock his pay. Play it by the book with him. Knock wouldn't have it any other way. But in any case, what were you saying, before Judson sauntered in, about the state troopers coming here?"

Ed reached into her bottom drawer, pulled out a package of antibacterial tissues, and started wiping down her desk, keyboard, and all the surfaces nearby. "I ain't gettin' no cold from Judson. Now, you listen up good, because I ain't your or anybody else's secretary, and I'm not wasting my breath saying anything twice. As I was telling you, they said that they were coming around ten thirty and wanted to look at the remains of the big rig that you found. They saw the report about the wreck on the InterForce website into which I have to input all our accident dispatches. Apparently, they want to follow up on a tractor trailer side-swiping a car and running it off the road in St. Bonaventure Parish. They have a surveillance tape from early Saturday evening—from some bank branch on Chastaine Boulevard—showin' a semi barrelin' toward the Petit Rouge Parish line a few minutes after the car got pushed off the road. I told 'em that rig was all burned up and it wouldn't be no use, but they insisted."

Starner steeled himself for another wasted day. Knock was insistent that no other law enforcement entity take action in "his parish" without "his troopers" being involved to make sure that outsiders didn't interfere with any of Knock's "side deals." What would the state police find to examine? A charred wreck.

CHAPTER FOURTEEN

An hour later, Starner was waiting in the scrapyard outside of Boyo's office when a state police van pulled up and a man and a woman exited. Starner instantly recognized the senior officer, Earl Elkins. Years ago, they had served together in the New Orleans Police Department.

Earl gave Starner a not-so-friendly punch in the arm as a greeting and said to the young woman in her flawlessly creased uniform, "This is my old buddy, Starner Gautreaux, the former pride of the N.O.P.D. Starner, this is Trooper Debbie Lesiker."

Lesiker, her hair tied back in a ponytail under her regulation blue flat-brimmed hat, nodded in acknowledgment.

"Why the hell aren't you already inside, Starner? Waiting for some crappy warrant from some shit-ass country judge? You know that we don't need a warrant to examine a wrecking yard's books and records. They got to turn them over whenever we ask, or they'll lose their license."

Starner saw that Earl's attitude hadn't changed one bit. Still believing that whatever he wanted to do was justified because he had a badge, and still blustering through life with his supercilious swagger and ramrod posture. Earl was that way back in New Orleans, thought Starner, shaking down drug dealers and bullying local businesses into "voluntarily" comping him lunches and dinners to avoid his threats to enforce obscure and ignored ordinances. It was just like Earl to parlay his many arrests—arrests made, more often than not, when drug dealer X rolled over on drug dealer Y in exchange for Earl's letting the former continue operating—into a series of promotions, leading eventually to his heading up a state police unit. On the other hand, that wasn't much different from how Knock's deals operated.

"The door's open, Earl. I've already been in there. Help yourself."

Earl stalked up the steps to the scrapyard's office. He wasn't inside more than a minute when he stuck his head out the door and yelled, "Lesiker, bring your camera and shit and get in here."

Waiting until Lesiker gathered her gear, Starner followed her into the metal building.

"Hell, Starner," Earl complained, "look at the crap all over this place."

Debbie Lesiker was working her way around the tiny office, snapping pictures as she went. "Like a tornado hit. How would anyone know if there's anything missing?"

Starner had arrived at the scrapyard twenty minutes earlier and had been shocked at the condition of the office. It had been ransacked, the air conditioner pulled off the wall, and the desk turned upside down. Boyo's file drawers were emptied, their contents scattered everywhere. Moreover, when Starner arrived, the entrance to the scrapyard was unbolted, and Boyo's office door unlocked. Starner knew that Boyo was way too possessive of his "gently used parts" to leave his facility and his files accessible to just anyone. Either Boyo knew the intruders, or he was trying to hide something and make it look like a robbery.

Earl impatiently opened every cabinet and flipped through the papers on the floor. "Know where Boyo keeps his logbook, Starner?"

"You two can excavate this office on your own. I'm going to sit in my truck with the air conditioning on. Come get me when you're through."

Earl kicked a pile of papers. "Fuck it all, Starner. Just show us where he towed the semi. We'll take it from there."

"When you're ready to kiss ass, I'll consider it. Your authority extends to books and records, not anything else."

Officer Lesiker tried to hide her astonishment. No one ever talked back to her boss that way.

Earl made a show of pulling out his cell phone. "I'll fucking call the state superintendent."

"Go ahead. You and I both know that's a hollow threat out here."

Earl knew Starner was right. Sheriff Naquin Mouton never let any state law enforcement official take one step beyond what the law precisely allowed. Why, there was even that time, a decade ago, when Knock went to court and got Judge Franklin Fauchère to issue an injunction preventing the state police from investigating a shooting in Petit Rouge Parish.

"I'll be back to wipe that shit-eating grin off your face, Starner. Just watch me." Earl spun on his heels and exited Boyo's office. Debbie Lesiker stopped taking photos and rushed out after him.

Starner stood on the office steps and locked the door while the state police van spun out on the crushed oyster shells that lined the yard around the office and headed toward the front gate.

Starner climbed in his truck and steered through the labyrinth of rusting and smashed vehicles until he got to the area where he and Boyo had walked just the day before. But the burned tractor trailer wasn't there. The flatbed wrecker was missing as well, and the door to the cab of the crane had been left open.

Parking his truck, Starner walked around the area in amazement. Heavy treads had churned up muck from the former location of the semi to the back fence, which now sported a gaping hole. Why, Starner wondered, would someone load what remained of the 18-wheeler back onto the flatbed and then drive through the fence and out onto Vizeau Road?

There were a lot of muddy tire tracks on the ground, and Starner's truck arriving on the scene added even more. Off to one side, however, the ground looked like someone had been trying to make a snow angel in the mud amidst a confusion of footprints and ruts. He bent to look more closely and spotted a halo of dark splotches around the mud angel's head, a scattering of circles and ovals, none bigger than a nickel. Each was reddish-purple in the center encircled by a cracked, gray edge. From his days on the New Orleans Police Force, Starner instantly recognized that this was drying blood, blood that had been there at least a day. A few more hours in the sunlight and it would all be completely gray.

Petit Rouge Parish did not have a crime lab. Knock said there was no need to spend money on "fancy equipment and stuck-up graduates in lab coats." Nevertheless, Starner gathered up a number of blood samples and placed them in an empty Skittles bag he found under his front seat. Knock might not care about preserving evidence, but Starner did, because now, in addition to what made the big rig explode and then melt, there were three more unanswered questions. Whose blood was this? Where was the tractor trailer? And where was Boyo?

Starner figured he'd start with the last one first, which is why he drove over to Boyo's rambling house, one of the biggest in the parish (although not as big as Knock's) to have a chat with Lydellia Vivochère.

CHAPTER FIFTEEN

"No, Starner, I haven't seen Boyo since the middle of last week." Lydellia sat in a gold-colored rocking chair in the living room, a cigarette dangling from her lips as she stroked the calico cat that crawled into her lap. "I haven't spoken with that little shit since then either, and I don't care to without my lawyer. So, if he's not at the yard, he's probably over in St. Bonaventure."

Starner, who was perched on the sofa, took a sip from a china teacup and placed it gingerly on the delicate saucer resting on the coffee table that was built atop a model of a red 1966 Cadillac El Dorado convertible. He was careful not to disturb the half dozen eight-inch porcelain clowns that crowded the table's glass surface.

This was the first time Starner had been inside Boyo and Lydellia's house, and she proudly pointed out their "fabulous collection of handcrafted art." In addition to the clowns on the table, gaudily painted porcelain Mardi Gras masks adorned with purple and gold silk ribbons hung from the walls. Dozens of porcelain circus figurines crowded not only every shelf of the bookcases that lined two walls of the room but also the mantle above the fireplace. Clowns, lions and their tamer, elephants marching with trunks raised, tightrope walkers, and even a garishly decorated horse-drawn circus truck with a calliope.

"So, I take it," Starner asked, trying to choose the right words, "that means you and Boyo have been having . . . a problem?"

"A problem? That's a polite word for the crap he's been slinging. That man is going to be the death of me, Starner. All that money we were generating started going to his head. Didn't matter to me that he kept his wrecking yard in such a mess. I let him pretend he understood what's really going on with the debits and credits of that scrap shit. Each month I have to straighten out the books he keeps messing up, make sure the insurance is paid and the bank is kept happy. As for the figurine shop in New Orleans, which is the real moneymaker, I run that entirely by myself, remotely you understand. Hire and fire the sales staff. Supervise inventory acquisition. Boyo assumes he is a success, and he is, but it's all because of me. And it's a good thing, too, because, as you can see," she said, pointing to the gold-flocked wallpaper, the heavy blue damask curtains that shrouded the windows with silver braids hanging from the bottom of each fold of the fabric, the tall lamp by the wall with its base made of seashells topped by a shade encircled with painted goldfish, the chandelier that was too big for the room and which caused Starner to stoop as he entered, and the purple rug on which her rocker rested, "I'm the one with the good taste."

Starner tried to appear impressed by the décor and uttered what he hoped she would take as appreciative, "Mmm," in response. It was no surprise that Lydellia was the reason behind Boyo's financial success. He had gotten her pregnant when she was a high school junior, married her before she miscarried and found out that they could not have more children, and out of guilt, gave into her every whim.

"Even allowed him to start making some of the yard's bank deposits without passing them by me first," Lydellia continued, "but Boyo not only let our money go to his head, he also let it go to his crotch as well, if you know what I mean."

Starner maintained a professional, stoic expression. He had long ago discovered, working the streets of New Orleans, that the best way to keep people talking was to say nothing. Folks are uncomfortable with silence. They want a conversation to continue. He learned that if he'd leave a gap, others would fill it in, and Lydellia loved to hear herself talk. Of course, she had always been a talker. Even in high school, her constant patter was something Boyo couldn't resist. Her hair, now dyed wine red, was as bouffant as ever, and her voice had not diminished in volume as she entered her late thirties.

"Now, I don't mind him cattin' around a bit. I understand a man's got to have some of that from time to time, especially if he is proud of his . . . well, an appendage as big as Boyo's is something to be proud of, I guess. His 'casual dates' never bothered me as long as it was one night here and one night there, as long as it was only one night and as long as the money kept flowing in a straight line from the businesses into the bank accounts that I watch over like a hawk."

She stroked the cat in her lap. "I took it for granted she was just a one-night stand. But no! I found out he had been meeting up with one gal on a regular basis. Would leave the wrecking yard to be with her for some 'afternoon delight' and then come back, work the rest of the day, and eventually return home."

Starner gave her a quizzical look, as if he were going to ask another question at this point, not that he intended to do so. He was just creating another opening for her to continue, and he was not disappointed.

"Did I suspect anything, you were going to ask? Hell no!" As she said this, she apparently dug her fingers into the cat's back, because it let out a startled yelp, leaped off her lap, and scurried under one of the long damask curtains, its tail protruding onto the purple carpet. "Well, not at first. He comes home from that stinking yard smelling like sweat and oil and who knows what all and I make him take a shower before supper and throw his stuff in the washing machine. It's so dirty I don't want to touch it. So, I never got a whiff of that gal on him. Nonetheless, he tripped up when he started doling out money to her. Boyo thought he was so clever, giving her cash, but I noticed the discrepancy between his ledger and the deposits when I was doing the month-end reconciliation. Over three thousand dollars! When I confronted him last week, he admitted it. And that's when I kicked him out. He snuck the damn ledger out with him. You want more tea? I'm going to get me another cigarette."

Lydellia rocked forward, reached over to the claw-footed side table, opened up a mother-of-pearl box, withdrew a cigarette, and grabbed a six-inch silver lighter in the shape of a dragon. She snapped its tail, and a flame came shooting out of its snout. She inhaled deeply and then let the smoke escape from the corners of her pursed lips. "Boyo should have known better than to cross me when it came to the businesses. Since I ran last month's numbers and he took the ledger back, I've been checking with the bank every day. He was making deposits all regular-like, until early last week, that is. 'Course, I don't know if they match up with the ledger, but I've fixed his wagon. Moved all the money into a second set of accounts that only I control. Already hired a big-time divorce lawyer from New Orleans. Planning to go to the wrecking yard with her tomorrow. I don't give a rat's ass if Boyo is there or not. I'm going to retrieve the logbooks and ledger and then sue that little shit 'til he screams."

Lydellia leaned back in her chair, happily contemplating having complete control of what little remained of Boyo's money and independence.

Starner reached into his breast pocket and pulled out a pad and pencil. "What was her name again?"

"The lawyer?"

"No, the woman Boyo has been seeing."

"Oh, that bitch? Angel-something is her stage name. Think her real name is Susie Faye, Shayna Faye, something like that. She's a stripper over in St. Bonaventure Parish at Good Cheeks."

CHAPTER SIXTEEN

When Starner got back to the station after visiting Lydellia, he found Ed crying. He had never seen her in such a state. For the first time since Starner came to work for Knock, Ed abandoned her I-only-speak-to-you-about-business attitude and was talking to him as if he were someone whose help she really needed.

Between sobs, Ed told him that her brother—Cooper, the St. Bonaventure Parish school superintendent—had called from Boulette's house and wanted someone from the Petit Rouge Sheriff's Office to come right over. Ed said she was fearing the worst. She and Boulette were cousins, more like sisters almost, and she knew that Cooper wouldn't be calling her unless something serious had happened. All Cooper said was to get someone over there pronto, and Judson was nowhere to be found.

Starner told her he would head over to Boulette's immediately, even though it meant that, because he hadn't eaten anything at Florene's café, he'd have to wait until supper to get some food. It wouldn't hurt him to miss a meal every now and then, he ruefully thought. He kept one of his uniforms from his time in the New Orleans Police Department, more out of inertia than anything else. Occasionally when he was searching for something in the shed behind his trailer, he'd find the cardboard box where the blue jacket and slacks were wrapped in plastic, pull them out, and marvel that he had ever fit into them. When he was younger. When he was robust and trim. When Cheryl Ann, Bucky, and he were a family.

When Starner finally got to Boulette's place, Cooper rushed off the porch to greet him and quickly ushered him the bedroom where Boulette's corpse lay decomposing on the bed. The odor in the room was stifling.

Cooper said he had already called the coroner, and they agreed not to contact Ed until Acie LaPierre had done a preliminary examination. Cooper wanted to tell Ed himself, which was fine with Starner.

The two of them sat on the porch in rusted metal chairs waiting for Acie. "Boulette was the best driver I had," Cooper said. "The kids loved her. Gonna be tough to break it to them. Not as hard as telling Ed, of course. Boulette loved those kids, and they adored her. She was an institution to a generation or more of school children whom she bused from Petit Rouge Parish into St. Bonaventure. Her funeral will be a parish-wide event."

Cooper and Starner chatted until a red Toyota Highlander drove up. It had big "Dr. Acie LaPierre: Petit Rouge Coroner's Office" signs plastered on both front doors. While he went inside to examine the body, Starner started writing down the bullet points he would include in his report, the one he knew Ed was going to read in detail over and over before filing.

"Let me make sure I have all the timing down, Cooper. You couldn't raise Boulette on the phone, so you decided to come out here to check on her around eleven fifteen, right?"

"Right. We have a substitute driver—remember skinny Kenny Arvenal? His momma used to have the fabric shop in town before she lost it to the bank. I figured Boulette was sick and had called Kenny to substitute, but I was worried about her. Boulette was Ed's second cousin on her Auntie Bibs's side of the family, you know."

Of course Starner knew that. Everyone in Petit Rouge Parish was related, grew up together, or knew each other. If a local married someone from outside of the parish—or occasionally, even from outside of the state—and returned with a spouse, the couple was woven back into the tight web of linked affiliations. Starner had lived in Petit Rouge long enough for people to think of him as a parish fixture. Strangers were those who barreled down the rural highway, got caught in the town's speed trap, and had to fork out their hard-earned money to cover the exorbitant fines imposed by Judge Fauchère. Strangers were the ones who drove leisurely, stopping for gas while touring the scenic Louisiana backroads on their way south to New Orleans or those who paused to eat at Armond and Florene's Chez Poêlon, pleasantly delighted by how good the food was. Strangers were gawkers who filled the tour buses headed for the historic Cottoncrest Plantation on the edge of town, coming solely to see the antebellum mansion with its elegant gardens, costumed docents, and murderous past, eat in its renowned restaurant, and shop in its overpriced gift emporium.

Knock made certain that outsiders did not remain unknown in these parts for long. Well, none except those who kept to themselves in the part of the parish that Knock had redlined. Those in the redlined area minded their own business and never came into town anyway, not even to buy gas or supplies.

"So," Starner asked, "you drove out here, rapped on the door, and when no one answered, you let yourself in? Was it locked?"

"Locked? Well, yes, it was, and Boulette almost never clicked the double-bolts 'cause you have to know where you're going to even find this place way the heck out in the backwoods. Can't see it from either the bayou or the swamp beyond. 'Course, I had the key Boulette gave me. The last time she was in the hospital with her heart problems, she worried about Gertie, her dog, getting fed. Come to think of it, where is Gertie? Haven't seen that mutt since I've been here."

Cooper turned toward the woods and whistled. No response. He called out, clapping his hands, "Gertie! Gertie! Come here, girl." He waited a minute, looked around, but saw and heard nothing. "She'll show up sooner or later, whenever she gets hungry. I'll leave a bowl of food out for her before we go and come back for her this evening. You know, I thought it curious that Boulette would lock herself in when she was sick. The minute I opened the door and smelled that awful stench, I knew something was wrong. Found her in the bedroom. Her ticker finally stopped working. Damn shame."

At that moment, Acie came out of the house pulling off his examination gloves. "You got it on the nose, Cooper. Heart attack. That's the way to go. Peaceful. In your own bed. No need to do an autopsy. I've called the funeral home. The hearse will be here shortly. Starner and I will wait for it. You may as well go back into town and start making arrangements."

Acie spoke in the tone of someone immensely self-satisfied with his efficiency. Starner knew, however, that Acie confused speed with both efficiency and competency, and thoroughness wasn't even in his vocabulary.

There were actually two funeral homes in Petit Rouge Parish, but Acie didn't need to tell Starner and Cooper that it was the folks from Graunier's Funeral Parlor who were coming. The parish funeral homes remained segregated by custom. Black residents would only use Graunier's. The white funeral parlor didn't have any trained mortuary cosmetologists who could make a dark-skinned person in an open casket look right, and no "self-respecting white family" would dare be caught seeking Graunier's services. The invisible color line operated throughout the parish, even in death.

The rusty porch chair squeaked as Cooper rose out of it. "Thanks, Acie. Nothing more I can do here. I'll call Ed from the car and then head over there to comfort her. Also got to phone my wife. We'll need to get Ed and her husband over to our house for dinner tonight to talk about things and figure out how to contact Boulette's son, Debrun, and break the news to him. He's been working fourteen-sevens offshore, and I don't know whether he's in the middle of a fourteen-day shift on a rig or has the week off."

Cooper drove away. Acie went back to his red SUV and started making calls.

Starner couldn't sit on the porch any longer. He decided to walk around the house and scout out the scene. An old habit from his days in New Orleans, where he never assumed anything about a death until he closely examined the entire location.

Nothing missed Starner's observation. The wooden siding was mildewed. The raised cottage, resting on four-foot-high brick pilings, was surrounded by weeds. A spindly tallow tree had pushed up through the floorboards of the rear stoop and was now almost as tall as the cracked aluminum awning. Starner did not find any of this unusual. Boulette's home was like many others in the parish. Her son spent most of his time offshore, so either he wasn't helping her very much or she simply had gotten used to things the way they were.

As Starner rounded the back and approached the front porch again from the side of the house nearest to the bayou, two things caught his attention. First, there were tire tracks leading off the muddy driveway and heading toward the woods. Second, on this side of the porch, under the corner of the house, was a hunk of meat covered in dead ants and surrounded by two dead mice and four dead squirrels.

CHAPTER SEVENTEEN

Tommy and Phillip knew better than to speak to the Precept when he was in this kind of mood.

The Precept led them into the barn. They had expected him to scream at them in anger, but when he finally broke the silence, he enunciated each word slowly in an ominous, measured tone. "There . . . is . . . nothing . . . that . . . either . . . of . . . you . . . has . . . done . . . right."

Tommy and Phillip waited, shoulders slouched, arms at their sides, for whatever was about to come next.

The Precept stalked across the barn's dirt floor, settled on one of the many suitcase-sized bundles wrapped in white plastic, and pointed his pistol at them.

Tommy and Phillip tensed up, but neither moved. Whatever the Precept was going to do, he would do swiftly. There was no action either of them could take that would prevent it.

But the Precept surprised them. He put the revolver on the plastic sheeting and dropped his handkerchief over it. "This is how things are supposed to be. Only a white handkerchief left resting on a bit of white. Pure white. The perfect color. Nothing usual. Nothing suspicious. Nothing out of place."

As Tommy and Phillip started to relax, the Precept swiftly grabbed the handgun and dashed forward, arm outstretched, until the barrel touched Tommy's cheek. Tommy tried not to blink as the cold steel pressed against his face.

Phillip simply stared straight ahead. He was not about to interfere or even watch. It was fine with him if the Precept wanted to kill Tommy.

"If anything raises concerns, however," the Precept said, tapping the pistol against Tommy's face, "that's a problem. And we have a problem because you haven't done your job." He glanced over at Phillip. "You're as much to blame as Tommy. You're both Imperials, and even a newly minted Saxon wouldn't have made the kind of stupid mistakes you two did."

The Precept backed away and signaled them to take a seat on the white plastic-wrapped containers. "The Supreme Kommander knows all. He is aware that folks are talking about state police coming into the parish to review a situation at the wrecking yard. Your assignment Saturday night was simple. Meet Saxon Fourteen. Get the tractor trailer from him after he had 'taken care' of the Aspirant who was driving it. You assured me your tasks had been accomplished, didn't you?"

"Yes," Tommy responded, gaining confidence as he spoke. "We gave you a confirmatory affirmative that was not inappropriate, given the scope of the undertaking and the inopportune position in which Saxon Fourteen left us."

The Precept did not raise his voice, but his anger was palpable. "Words of more than three syllables ain't gonna cover up the crap you caused. The big rig didn't go to Florida, as the Supreme Kommander's plan called for. It was burned in the fucking woods."

"You may be a Precept, but I know you're aware of who I am. You want to shoot me? Go ahead. There'll be hell to pay, and you know it. Given the circumstances, we—or I should say, I—acted with creative alacrity. As I told you before, when we got there, Saxon Fourteen was arguing with the Aspirant—about what, we have no idea—and before we knew what was happening, Saxon Fourteen shot him. There were bullet holes in the windshield and instrument panel. Blood was everywhere. Even though we're Imperials, Saxon Fourteen did not obey us. He left, and I did the best I could to remedy the problem. There is no way the big rig could be driven across state lines. It wouldn't pass inspection at the first weigh station. Any cop driving down the highway would undoubtedly pull it over for having a broken windshield. My resolution was ingenious, if I have to say so myself. Ran the thing off the road so that it looked like an accident, and, better yet, arranged for all the evidence to burn up. Body. Blood. Bullet holes. Spent cartridges. Everything. A few packages of R-37 explosives did the trick. Three in the undercarriage. One in the engine block. I got Phillip here to set the detonators on a timer so that, long after we left, first the diesel tanks would blow and then the R-37 would ignite. I think I deserve approbation rather than censure. I solved the problem."

The Precept, still standing, leaned against a stall door in the barn and directed his pistol away from Tommy's head and toward Phillip's. "Damn it, Phillip! You didn't call me before things got out of hand! I don't care what Saxon Fourteen did to the Aspirant. Using the R-37 destroyed the cab all right, but it also destroyed the trailer that was to haul the rest of the R-37 the Supreme Kommander wanted transported to Florida. The last thing we need is for anyone to figure out what the Alabaster Brigade possesses before we get to deploy the goods this Friday."

The Precept's anger was no longer in check. His voice grew harsh. "How dare either of you think you have the talent, much less the authority, to fix anything on your own? After you told me what happened, after I reminded you that explosives always leave traces behind, you still took matters into your own hands, making things even worse. Trying to 'clean up' by grabbing what was left of the rig at the wrecking yard. Killing the owner to boot. What the shit were you thinking?"

Phillip said nothing, even though the guy from the wrecking yard deserved to die. After all, he had pulled a pistol on them.

"There's not a thimbleful of smarts between the two of you! I lost precious hours last night disposing of what's left of the big rig, plus the flatbed from the wrecking yard and its owner. Had to put all three where neither Kenny nor anyone else will find them. And now, we don't have all the explosives we needed to get to Florida or a tractor trailer to take them there."

The Precept swung the barrel of his pistol back and forth between the two fools.

Each waited stoically.

But the Precept didn't shoot. "You have committed your lives to the Alabaster Brigade. If you want to survive, you'll do precisely as I say. Nothing more, and not one thing less. Maybe the Supreme Kommander will order me to spare you. If so, maybe—and this applies even to you, Tommy, with your big words and high-and-mighty attitude—maybe both of you won't be demoted to Member or be busted all the way back to Aspirant. Maybe, you understand. No promises. Any screwups from this point on, however, and you know what the consequences will be. Wait for my instructions. I'll contact you. Now, get out of here before Kenny returns from his afternoon bus route. Kenny doesn't know about you, and that's the way it needs to stay."

CHAPTER EIGHTEEN

It was twilight when Starner arrived back at Knock's house. Bea Timms tried to dissuade him from coming in, saying the old man was tired, but Starner insisted.

Knock lay on a hospital bed that had been placed in the center of his long living room with its two chandeliers. The antique furniture had been pushed against the walls. The top of an expensive sideboard whose drawers were made of intricately inlaid wood was covered with a plastic tablecloth on which rested prescription containers filled with pills, medicine bottles, a box of nitrile gloves, sterile gauze, and surgical tape.

The old man tried to smile, but the only thing showing under his upper lip were gums because he had removed his dentures. "Back again, Starner? Bring me something else good?"

Bea huffed. "If'n you want to kill yourself quicker, you go right ahead and take whatever the deputy is trying to sneak in. But I'm not having any part of it. My job is to keep you comfortable, not to watch you down something that'll only make you throw up, like you did after the last time the deputy was here."

Starner held out his hands to show that they were empty. "Got nothing with me. Right now, it's just business."

"As if!" she said, as she walked out of the room and closed the door behind her.

Knock reached under the covers, retrieved his dentures, and snapped them in place. "Find the damn control and crank up the head of this bed, Starner, so I can see you better. Are you really here on business?"

Starner adjusted the bed and pulled up a chair. "A whole lot of business, Knock. First, don't know if you've heard, but Boulette's dead. Died of a heart attack. I'm sure Ed's going to need a few days off to deal with it. Second, Earl Elkins came out to Boyo's yard, wanting to investigate the 18-wheeler crash. I got rid of him. I know you don't want the state police messing around in Petit Rouge. After he left, I checked out the yard. That smashed big rig is gone. Who would want that melted mess? It's been stolen, along with Boyo's flatbed. Why? Plus, someone got hurt. I found what I'm certain are bloodstains near where the flatbed had been parked. I looked for Boyo's pistol before Earl arrived. It wasn't in his office drawer where he kept it. I'm thinking Boyo got into an argument. You know what a hothead he can be. Maybe he shot the guy, loaded the flatbed with what was left of the big rig, and took off, although for the life of me I can't figure out why. But I've checked the hospital here and in St. Bonaventure Parish. No reports of anyone coming in with a gunshot wound. So, no big rig and no way right now to know the identity of driver of the tractor trailer. If only Acie had the balls to run a DNA test on the remains stuffed in his freezer, I bet we'd find something. No gun. No Boyo. I went to his house and Lydellia told me she kicked him out last week. I have a lead, though. Boyo apparently was shacking up with a stripper over in St. Bonaventure. The reason I'm here is to get your permission to go question her over there. Boyo might have stashed the flatbed wrecker at her place. The sooner we find Boyo, the sooner we will get some answers. So, let me head over to St. Bonaventure to interrogate the stripper and find Boyo."

"Goddamn it, Starner! I get sick and the whole parish is going to hell! Now you want to go gallivanting over to St. Bonaventure?" He slumped back on his pillow and closed his eyes.

"Are you awake?"

"Of course I'm fucking awake. Can't sleep worth a damn. I'm listening. Go on. I know you got more to say."

"We don't have a lot of time, Knock. Lydellia could come in to register a missing person's report tomorrow. She wants a divorce and needs to serve Boyo with papers. Judson can't handle this. You and I both know that boy has no tact. He can barely write a traffic ticket without insulting the driver."

Knock raised his eyes to half-staff and blinked, as if trying to bring Starner's face into focus. "I am fully aware," he said wearily, "of what Judson can and can't do, and his can'ts outnumber his cans by a lot, but that's not your concern. This ain't New Orleans, Starner. It's not the big leagues. Suddenly, you're a forensic scientist identifying blood? Are you sure it's blood? And if it is, do you know if it's human blood? For all you know, Boyo could have been shooting at the rats that crawl all over his yard. Come on! And speaking of rats, I don't give a rat's ass about Boyo's whereabouts. He's been playing the field for years. Can't keep his zipper up. If Lydellia kicked him out, he might have thought he'd make his place look like it had been robbed. Or maybe he took off and his place really was robbed. If it wasn't Boyo but one of the scavengers, bottom crawlers, and scum who frequent his yard looking for bargains and decided to rob him, that guy is surely long gone from Petit Rouge by now. Report it to Earl Elkins and let him worry about it. That'll keep him away from here. Number one No one investigates anything in my parish but me and my team. Number two, no one in my employ crosses parish lines to investigate anything anywhere else. So, let Lydellia file her missing person's report. You'll dutifully note it and that'll be that. If he turns up, good for her. If he doesn't, good for him. But nothing in this is good for you. Just drop it."

Starner had hoped that the confluence of events might have piqued Knock's interest in trying to find Boyo, but the sheriff's response merely confirmed what Starner already knew. Knock wasn't interested in solving crimes. He wasn't interested in figuring out why a fire had gotten so hot that it melted a big rig. He was interested only in protecting "his parish" from outsiders, and since the big rig and Boyo were gone, "his parish" was back to its pristine obscurity, safe from prying eyes that might stumble upon what Knock had really been up to all these years.

As the old man's breathing became heavier and he finally began to snore, Starner tiptoed out of the room. He stuck his head in the kitchen to let Bea know he was leaving and softly closed the front door behind him.

Walking down the wide steps of Knock's multi-columned, three-story home, its walkway and the two moss-covered oak trees in the manicured front lawn illuminated by hidden lights, Starner continued to rue his fate. He knew a murder scene when he saw one. The splotches weren't "rat's blood." Someone had been shot. Either Boyo had done it, or someone had shot Boyo. A crime had been committed and needed to be solved, but Knock wasn't interested, and Starner was tied to Knock as long as the old man was alive.

CHAPTER NINETEEN

"Come on, Momma," Abigayle said, holding out her hand, "just one more chapter. Pinky promise."

Truvi smiled. It was past Abigayle's bedtime, but she had finished her homework, laid out her uniform for the next day, moved the dirty dishes from the table to the kitchen sink after dinner, taken her bath in record time, and gotten into her pajamas.

"Ok," said Truvi, extending the little finger of her right hand and wrapping it around Abigayle's little finger. "Pinky promise. But only half a chapter, you understand, It's a school night."

Abigayle gleefully fluffed her pillow, pulled her dolls around her, arranging her bed just so, and said, "Too bad Mr. Art has to work late again."

"Yes, dear," Truvi agreed. "It was a long weekend, with his having to spend most of the time in his workshop, and the last two days he's had to travel all over the state for his consulting business. He's due home tonight, but he'll get here after you're asleep. So, don't make any noise in the morning, hear? He needs his rest."

"Will you tell him I helped make him a surprise for his supper?"

"Of course, darlin'. When he tastes those cookies you and I baked this afternoon after school, he's gonna be so happy."

"Can I have another cookie now? Please."

Truvi laughed. "You're gonna be a lawyer or a politician, for sure, when you grow up, trying to negotiate like that. No, you can't have a cookie now, and if you don't pull those covers up and get ready for me to read you the next chapter, then pinky promise or no pinky promise, I'm gonna turn out the lights."

Abigayle snuggled under the covers. "Ready!"

CHAPTER TWENTY

I
t was almost midnight. Art Brady made sure that the garage doors were locked, the white noise generator was turned on, and the blocking software was activated before he used an encrypted phone, one that he would destroy immediately after this call was over.

"Damn it, Bubba. I didn't make you a Precept—the only Precept in this region—for nothing. We've known each other far too long for you to flake out on me now. Remember when I brought you up to Idaho for training? Absolute adherence to superiors is required in all circumstances. So, yeah, I know Phillip and Tommy messed up the deal with the truck driver, but given the greater mission that's at stake, there's a reason I told you to 'forgive' them, especially Tommy. I know you're angry at him, and you have every right to be. Hell, I'm furious that, because of them, I can't stage an 'event' in Miami simultaneously with one in New Orleans, but that's the way it's got to be. Tommy must be protected. Without him, we couldn't have gotten the explosives. Without him, we wouldn't have received the operating funds. Tommy's the key, and given all that's passed between the two of you, there's a chance he's going to set you off or vice versa, and I can't have that. I'm ordering you to take yourself out of the Phillip/Tommy loop, at least until Friday."

Bubba started protesting, but Art abruptly cut him off. "That was a command, not a request. Tommy needs to believe he's part of the operational team or he'll tell his uncle. If that happens, a shitstorm could break loose that would undermine all my plans. Friday is the day. New Orleans is a go. I've worked too long and too hard for things to fail now. We have to keep Phillip involved and watching out for Tommy, and the two of them need to be side-lined, away from the real action. You found Phillip at NightHawk and trained him. You know that he's a dyed-in-the-wool true be-liever. Come time to act, he'll do what's needed and follow the chain of command. Have Imperial Seven, Maggie Mae, take over as their contact. Get her to read Tommy and Phillip the riot act and give them a task they can't possibly mess up."

Bubba responded in the appropriate manner. Art might call him by his first name, but Bubba knew his place and that was to refer to Art by his official title. "Yes, Supreme Kommander, I un-derstand. Eighty-Eight."

That's more like it, thought Art. He formed the Alabaster Brigade and ran it like a military operation. Insubordination would not be tolerated. Acquiescence to superiors was mandatory. A Kommander directed the Precepts who ruled over the Imperials, who were superior to the Saxons, who outranked the disposable Members, like Kenny, who were one step above the removable Aspirants. As Supreme Kommander, Art ruled over them all. Bubba was now not only showing the proper respect, he appropri-ately ended the conversation with "Eighty-Eight," the coded salute of the Alabaster Brigade. H is the eighth letter of the alphabet. "Eighty-eight" stood for "H.H."—Heil Hitler.

Art knew that he and his Alabaster Brigade would purify the world by intense fire and immense faith. They would rid the world of blacks, Jews, Islamists, Catholics, atheists, and agnostics. Everyone who stood in the way of the truth. The way of the Lord requires an army whose spirit is pure and whose courage is resolute. Nonbelievers must repent or be destroyed. Doubters must believe or cease to exist. It's right there in the Gospel. The Prophet Nahum said: "Who can stand before his indignation? Who can abide in the fierceness of his anger? His fury is poured out like fire and the rocks are broken asunder before him."

Fire would pour out on Friday. The war on nonbelievers was about to begin.

"Now," said Art, "here's what I want you to tell Maggie Mae to do."

PART IV

WEDNESDAY

CHAPTER TWENTY-ONE

Ed was still upset when Starner got to the office Wednesday morning. She and Cooper hadn't been able to get in contact with Debrun. The contractor he worked for said his shift on the rig ended five days ago, and the company helicopter had dropped him off in Morgan City as usual. Boulette's son hadn't posted on his Facebook page or Instagram account. The few friends of his they knew about hadn't heard from Debrun since last week.

"Maybe," Ed implored Starner, "you could run by Boulette's house again. Here's the key that Cooper had. Please check for anything there that might help us find Debrun. Another phone number maybe. Or perhaps he's with some girl Boulette knew about. Anything so that we can let him know about his mother's passing."

Starner reluctantly agreed.

After turning off the rural road that dead-ended a mile past Boulette's place, he drove his truck down the long dirt drive toward her weathered house. As he rounded the last sharp curve before reaching the front yard, he had to pull far to the right to avoid deep ruts caused by Boulette driving her school bus in and out every day. Slowing down, he observed a tire track leading off into the woods. If it was there yesterday, he hadn't noticed, because he had been rushing to meet Cooper and had not been concentrating on much else.

Starner stopped, exited the truck, and followed the track cut into the alluvial soil. The dirt was now dry and hardened, so it could have been made during the weekend's rainstorm.

He followed the churned-up tire trail into the woods. It was just a single line that abruptly stopped twenty feet away from the driveway next to a tree, so it must have been a motorcycle. But if someone rode one in here, Starner wondered, how did it get out? There should be an exit track, but he didn't see one. The forest floor was covered with a thick carpet of leaves that left no trace of what had happened. Had the driver walked his cycle out of the woods? Why do that? And why would anyone have been in this area on a motorcycle in the first place?

Starner got back into his truck and slowly drove into Boulette's front yard, honking the horn in the hope that Gertie, Boulette's mutt, would come bounding out from under the porch or from around back, but no dog appeared and there was no barking. The only response was the low murmur of crickets chirping.

Starner used Cooper's key to enter Boulette's house. It almost felt like his old days as a detective back in the New Orleans Police Department, investigating a case. But this wasn't a crime scene, he had to remind himself. He was only here for Ed's sake, to see if he could find a way to contact Debrun, as if some scrap of paper would magically appear and provide vital information. Fat chance of that, he thought.

He started in the bedroom where Boulette's body was found. It still carried the stench of death. On the top of her dresser, next to a pile of dirty clothes, he located her cell phone. Debrun's number, the same one Ed had been calling continuously, was in her contacts folder, but her phone reflected no calls to or from him during the last week.

The drawers in Boulette's dresser were a mess, jammed with underwear, tattered scarves, faded sweatshirts, rumpled slacks, two open bags of potato chips crawling with ants, and a box of half-eaten chocolates.

The kitchen was equally disorganized. Dirty dishes were strewn across the sink. A pan on the stove was encrusted with what looked like stale oatmeal. The bathroom was no better. Roaches swiftly scuttled away as Starner opened the door. The mirror on the medicine cabinet was cracked, and the tub hadn't been cleaned in weeks.

Yet, Boulette's living room was immaculate. Every chair was in place. The embroidered pillows on the sofa were fluffed and arranged just so. The ragged rug, mottled with signs of wear, was stretched taut. The thin curtains were pulled shut. The mantle over the fireplace bore no evidence of the thin layer of dust that coated the kitchen windowsills, and the small plastic busts of Martin Luther King, Abraham Lincoln, and John F. Kennedy were placed precisely as if aligned with a ruler.

It didn't make any sense to Starner. Why would Boulette keep her front room so neat and leave all the others in such disarray? Was she expecting a visitor? Had she been cleaning up when she had her heart attack? If so, why go back to her bedroom, which was down the hall, rather than stay near the front door and call for an ambulance?

Starner turned to leave, and as he did, his foot caught on the edge of the area rug. He righted himself before he fell, but the woven fabric shifted under his shoe and was now badly rumpled. The deputy picked up one edge to straighten the rug when he noticed something strange and pulled the entire thing up, tossing it on the couch. The floor underneath was splotchy, as if someone had wiped a portion of it down with bleach and, in that effort, lifted off part of the cheap stain coating the wooden boards.

As he examined the rug, he noticed that what at first glance appeared to be signs of wear may actually have been something else. Flipping it around 180 degrees and repositioning it, Starner saw that the "wear" stains aligned perfectly with the marks he discovered on the floor.

He wished he still had a crime kit like the one he used when he was with the N.O.P.D., but Knock wouldn't spring for one, calling it "fancy equipment" for which Petit Rouge Parish had no need.

Starner pulled out his pocketknife and probed the spaces between the pine flooring. He was able to pry up dust, lint, rug fibers, and some tiny cracked, gray flecks that might have been dried blood. He found a dusty glass in the kitchen cupboard, wiped it clean, and deposited his findings in it. Starner regretted not having a bottle of Luminol or Fluorescein to spray on the rug and floor. These would luminesce bleach, if that's what the discolored areas of the rug and wooden floor had been treated with. But why would Boulette be bleaching anything in this room? Luminol and Fluorescein also luminesced blood. Boulette's body didn't have any marks on it. Could there have been blood in the living room that an intruder was trying to eradicate? It didn't make any sense. Nothing seemed to be missing from the house. Boulette died in her bed, and there was no sign in her room of a struggle.

Back in New Orleans, the necessary investigative tools, like Luminol and Fluorescein, were readily available in a locked cabinet in Starner's police van. He also kept his gun locked up when at home, because Bucky was almost four years old at the time and got into everything. He would make believe he was a policeman and try to walk around the house in Starner's shoes. They fell off his little feet with each step. He would arrest his teddy bear, using the toy pistol that Grandpa Fogel had given him. One minute Bucky would say he wanted to be a detective, just like his dad, and the next he'd say he wanted to be a quarterback on the Saints football team.

For years, thinking of Bucky was too painful for Starner, but occasionally, like now, the memory of the good times would come roaring back, mixed with an aching sadness.

The memory of how Bucky loved going to the Superdome for football games, the two of them sitting side-by-side in the high rows near the top, the little boy munching on chicken tenders while they watched the players far below them on the field and relished the replay on the big screens.

The memory of planning Bucky's fourth birthday party, when his little boy pleaded to have a Saints football theme.

The memory of purchasing kid-sized Saints hats and T-shirts for all of Bucky's preschool classmates who would be invited. Of tacking up Saints posters in the living room and promising Bucky that although they had to be taken down after the party, he could put them up in his bedroom.

The delight Bucky showed when unfurling the bright six-by-eight-foot Saints flag Starner had bought and how Bucky insisted that they hoist the flag so that "everyone in the neighborhood could see it, Daddy!"

There was nothing Starner wouldn't do for Bucky. He had gotten his ladder, climbed onto the roof of the second story of their home, up the steeply pitched asphalt shingles, secured a pole to the chimney, and raised that flag.

He remembered how Cheryl Ann playfully accused him of being a damn fool who could have broken his neck up there.

How he laughed, saying, "Bucky will only turn four once."

How she gave him a peck on the cheek when she said, "I don't know who's the silliest youngster around here, Bucky or you!"

Those memories reminded Starner that all the joy had gone out of his life years ago.

He locked Boulette's door behind him, and, lint-and-dust -filled glass in hand, slumped in one of the rusty porch chairs. He hadn't found anything that would help Ed and Cooper locate Debrun. He hadn't found Boulette's dog. What was he to do? Drive back to the highway, park behind a tree, and wait for motorists to drift into the Petit Rouge speed trap? He regretted that, with all his carefully honed detective skills, he had been reduced to being a lowly traffic cop spending his hours watching cars—and life—pass him by.

But why, thought Starner, should he continue to coast through life, blinders on, letting Knock dictate what he could and couldn't do? When he was part of the N.O.P.D., his advice to those seeking to make detective was to look for discrepancies. Crime scenes, he'd say, tell a story. Look for any object that is not where it should be. Think about what should be there but isn't. Be suspicious of things that don't match up.

A lot of things recently were not matching up, such as the contrasts between Boulette's bedroom and living room, and the marks on and under the rug.

What else out here might not match up?

But who would care? Not Knock. Not Acie the coroner, who had decided Boulette died of a heart attack. Starner thought he should care, but he owed his livelihood to Knock. The old man had given him a job when no one else would. Yet, given how loyal Starner had tried to be to Knock, he didn't think it right that the old man would spend his final weeks treating him like this. And when Knock died, then what? A new election would be held. A new sheriff would take over. Given the demographics of the parish and his checkered past, Starner knew he would be out of a job. Yet, even with all that, Starner just didn't have the energy to cross Knock, not while the old man was dying.

Starner walked over to the side of the house where he had found the scrap of meat with the dead squirrels and mice. They were still there, their tiny carcasses half eaten away. He brushed aside the ants that were feasting on the rotting flesh and tossed what was left of the critters and the meat into the bed of his truck. He didn't want Gertie to eat any of this when she returned from wherever she was wandering.

He sat in the cab, removing his loafers and retrieving his boots. The least he could do while he was out here was to look for Boulette's dog in the tall grass behind the house that ran to the swamp. Ed would like that, he thought, if he could find Gertie, figuring she was probably back there somewhere scavenging and covered in fleas and ticks.

Speed-trap enforcer and dog catcher, thought Starner. Some life!

CHAPTER TWENTY-TWO

Kenny Arvenal couldn't stop grinning with delight. He accelerated once he left the rural backroad, racing down the dirt driveway. The rear end of the school bus swerved as he hit the brakes, raising a cloud of dust in front of the barn, and he managed to slide to a screeching stop just like a stunt driver in the movies. He was really getting the hang of it. He could make this bus do anything he wanted. And in just two more days everyone in the world would know how this school bus, with him behind the wheel, upended history.

Kenny's expression changed, however, as soon as he jumped off the bus and saw Bubba coming out of the barn.

Bubba was not happy. "What was that all about? You know my instructions."

Kenny took a step back. The last thing he wanted was to anger the Precept. "I try to do everything you tell me to." Kenny had always tried to follow Bubba Mauvais's instructions, even before Bubba became the Precept.

"I'm to drive like an old woman when I'm in public," Kenny continued, apologetically, "picking up them pickaninnies from Petit Rouge and dropping them off at the school in St. Bonaventure, but," Kenny's face brightened, ". . . but in this part of St. Bonaventure, out here on the farm, there ain't never nobody around 'cept you and me. Can't hurt to show you I have some real control over this thing, can it?"

"Real control," Bubba upbraided, "is never doing anything that might raise even a hint of suspicion. Doing something now 'for fun' might mean that you'll forget and do something 'for fun' in public later. Can't risk that."

Kenny responded earnestly "I promise, Precept. There is nothing I want more than to make sure the plan is a success. I learnt everything you taught me. I remember exactly what you wrote for me to say when we made the video last Sunday—'Whoever refuses to stride on the straight path of belief in the supremacy of the white race is an infidel who deserves to dangle'—man, I love that, 'deserves to dangle' is a really cool way of saying things—anyway, 'who deserves to dangle over the fires of hell. Achieving the true God's justice and order requires nothing less, and if it takes chaos to open people's eyes, we must obey His word.'"

Kenny solemnly bowed his head. "Amen." Then he looked up like an eager puppy and puffed out his chest. "See, I got it all solid-like in my mind. I believe, Precept, I really believe. You have made me the messenger of the true God. I won't let you down."

CHAPTER TWENTY-THREE

"Following a school bus is for prosaic proletarians," Tommy complained. "It's crap work, Maggie Mae."

"That's Imperial Seven to you, shithead," she shot back.

"Fuck your numbered title," Phillip said angrily. "If we're with the Precept or the Supreme Kommander, that's one thing, Maggie Mae. But not here. After all, we were Imperials long before you were elevated. So, don't stand on ceremony with us!"

Maggie Mae's response was sharp and immediate. "It has nothing to do with 'standing on ceremony,' you cretin. It's about respect for rank. The Supreme Kommander made me Imperial Seven, and Seven outranks the two of you, as Imperials Nine and Ten."

"No fucking fair," Phillip said under his breath.

"I heard that! You dare question the Supreme Kommander's decisions?"

"It's not," Tommy interjected, "that we question the Supreme Kommander. It's just that an assignment such as this . . . from you . . . is ill-befitting our capacities."

Phillip saw the fury on Maggie Mae's face and backed away from Tommy. After all, Phillip thought, he had done more to help the white race than Tommy or Maggie Mae. Did they have a Nazi tattoo, like the one he got when he was first promoted to Saxon, a year before he became an Imperial? It proved to the world that he was Anglo-Saxon to the core. Had either of them firebombed a black church over in Napoleon Parish, like he had done? Not a chance. It was the bombing that first brought Phillip to Bubba's attention. Phillip worked harder than anyone. Didn't think he would have to continue to prove himself. He even let Bubba, who wanted to be called "Precept" all the time, convince him to team with weird Tommy and keep the kid out of trouble. And then Bubba went and made Tommy the boss! Anyway, what had Maggie Mae done that allowed her to jump rank over them both? Fuck it all. Fuck Tommy. Fuck Maggie Mae. Well, he wouldn't mind fucking her. Throwing her down on the ground. Ramrodding her until she screamed and then doing it again. And again.

Maggie Mae pulled out her knife and sliced the air in front of Tommy's nose. "Look, you little shit. You'll do as I say, because I outrank you. You'll do it without question. Understand?"

Tommy didn't budge. "I thought violence was for our enemies. The Jews. The blacks. The nonbelievers. Internal violence is counterproductive."

"I'll counterproduct your nuts off if you don't shut up!"

Maggie Mae almost thrust her knife into Tommy's gut, just as she had done to Saxon Fourteen, but she caught herself. She knew that the Supreme Kommander had made it clear Tommy was to be accommodated in every way. She didn't understand why, but, unlike Tommy, she had risen in the ranks by never questioning her superiors. She performed diligently as an Aspirant. She slept with those she had to sleep with to get her level of Member and again to be promoted to Saxon. She killed Saxon Fourteen on the Supreme Kommander's instructions and been elevated to Imperial for her efforts. She was not about to imperil her position now. She put the knife back in its leather sheath, took a deep breath, and spoke as calmly as she could, as if addressing a child. "The Precept made it clear. You are to follow my instructions, and these directions come straight from the Precept. I don't want to hear another word about how you think you can 'fix' a plan you already broke. The Supreme Kommander is not about to let you steal another tractor trailer to make the Florida run before Friday. The Supreme Kommander has given an order to the Precept, who has given it to me. Don't deviate from your assignment one bit. You have a simple, easy task. We've been over it time and time again. You are to follow that school bus this afternoon and tomorrow. Then on Friday, when it heads down to New Orleans, you are to trail it. You are to make sure nothing goes wrong. Simple enough. You'd have to be even bigger idiots than I think you already are to mess that up."

CHAPTER TWENTY-FOUR

Starner strode through chest-deep grass and lanky pussy willows along an old logging road toward the rear of Boulette's acreage. Every few yards, he called out, "Gertie, come here, Gertie." He was sure the mutt was around here somewhere.

The path terminated half a mile down at a rotting boat landing at the edge of the swamp. Though its planks were long gone, the few termite-infested wooden pilings still visible were listing in all directions.

Starner yelled a few more times for Gertie, and, getting no response, turned back toward Boulette's house when he noticed something that gave him pause. Where the road stopped, ten feet from the water's edge, the dirt was barren and smooth. No paw prints of foxes, raccoons, or deer coming for a drink. No tracks left by egrets or cormorants coming to groom themselves by the shore. No ribbon-like marks left by cottonmouths slithering into and out of the swamp. It was as if someone had run a brush or pine limb over the area in an effort to comb away any signs of disturbance.

Look for the discrepancies, Starner had preached when he was a detective. Like Boulette's house, with its messiness everywhere except in the living room. Like this patch of ground without a trace of weed or wildlife incursion.

In the meantime, however, he decided to make one last attempt to find Gertie. Sure that his waterproof boots were laced up tightly before entering the murky water, Starner stepped out carefully. He progressed about five yards from the shore and halted because he knew that, below the dark surface of the swamp, the bottom could drop off abruptly from a few inches to more than ten feet.

Starner peered out, thinking he might spot a small patch of high ground to which Gertie could have swum. He called out her name again and again. No barking response came from the wood. No splashing sound of a mutt leaping into the swamp and heading back to shore. Nothing except the water shimmering in spots. It didn't appear to be from the play of light, and it wasn't from Gertie. It came from something below the surface. An alligator? Gators can move faster than a man can run, at least for a short distance. Starner was far enough from the shore that a gator could come at him with a vengeance. He unholstered his pistol, knowing full well that his Glock was not powerful enough to stop an angry gator, though it might scare the critter away.

Starner slowly backed toward dry land, keeping an eye on the shimmering spot the whole time. He withdrew a quarter from his pocket and tossed it at the area immediately behind the murky roiling water, thinking it would distract the gator.

The spinning coin skimmed the surface twice, but no creature rose out of the swamp. Rather, on the third skip, instead of bouncing ahead, it ricocheted with a clang off something metallic. He broke a limb off a nearby tree and probed the water. It was the top of a car. Someone had run a vehicle into the swamp.

Starner hated to call Lydellia for help, but he knew that Knock would not tolerate an outside wrecker coming into the parish. Boyo's was the only game in town. Since he was missing, the deputy had no choice to but to reach out to Boyo's wife.

Forty minutes later, Rod showed up in one of the scrapyard's big tow trucks. Rod had worked for Boyo for years, running equipment, sorting scrap metal, and acting as his general handyman. Everyone knew Rod. His father had been the preacher at the tiny black church on a bayou in Napoleon Parish before it was burned down by an arsonist a few years back. The culprit was never caught.

Starner met Rod in front of Boulette's cottage and directed him down the logging road, where the truck's wide wheels flattened the vegetation that had overtaken the path. As they neared the old dock, Starner asked Rod if he knew of Boyo's whereabouts.

"I don't mess with none of that. I just get going with whatever Mr. Boyo tells me to do, and when he's not around, like now, I occupy myself doing what I think he would want and doing what Ms. Lydellia directs."

Rod backed the truck down to the water's edge, waded into the swamp, and diving below the surface, hooked a chain to the rear axle of the car. He then climbed, dripping wet, onto the wrecking truck's deck. Sunlight streamed through the tall cypress trees and leafy mangroves, the afternoon heat intensified, and Rod's ebony face glistened with sweat as he watched the winch straining and smoking.

Slowly, the roof and back windshield of a submerged vehicle broke through the swamp's dark water, causing ever-widening ripples to swirl outward as it rose.

Starner leaned against the rough bark of a pin oak and watched, lost in thought, brooding over how water seemed to bracket his existence. Unlike the expanding ripples now before him, however, his life had contracted inward.

With Hurricane Katrina threatening New Orleans the last week in August 2005, the police chief and mayor declared a state of emergency, requiring all first responders to remain on duty until otherwise instructed. Starner knew he would not get back home for quite a while. His house would remain high and dry, he thought. No worries. No need to panic. No need to evacuate. He told Cheryl Ann to grab Bucky and enough food and water to last a couple of days and not to worry about Fogel, Cheryl Ann's father, because the nursing home where he lived knew what to do in a storm. He promised Cheryl Ann he'd come back for her and Bucky as soon as the hurricane passed.

But it turned out that they weren't safe. Cheryl Ann's childhood home, the one they bought from Fogel after Cheryl Ann's mother died and remodeled themselves, the one that stood for a hundred years and in all that time never even had water encroach on the yard, no matter how bad a storm, was quickly inundated.

Water initially sloshed across the front lawn. It rapidly rushed up to the front door, shattered both side glass panels, gushed through the opening, shorted out the electricity, overturned the refrigerator, and dislodged the stove from the kitchen, depositing it in the living room. The dining room table Cheryl Ann inherited from her grandmother was reduced to rubble. The unrelenting torrent pounded the staircase, eventually sweeping it away. The water rose as high as the ceiling of the first floor, but it didn't stop there. It invaded the second story of the house, saturated the wallpaper and demolished the family photos on the wall above the king-sized mattress in the master bedroom. It tossed furniture around in a swirling mass. Bucky's toy trucks and stuffed animals floated out through the smashed second story windows. The snapped gas lines caused the house to reek with the odor of rotten eggs mixed with sulfur. And the water kept rising higher and higher.

Starner wasn't able to return home until a day-and-a-half after the levees broke, finally getting there courtesy of a Coast Guard skiff. The only way he was able to recognize his house, which was now just one of many rooftops barely piercing what appeared to be an endless lake stretching to the horizon, was by the battered Saints team flag attached to the top of the chimney, the flag Bucky had asked him to display for his fourth birthday party, which was due to take place the first week in September.

Slimy, silt-filled water covered everything but the peak of the roof. Starner balanced there, chopping through the shingles and tar paper with a Coast Guard ax, calling out for Cheryl Ann and Bucky but never getting a response.

He finally found their bodies floating in the attic. Cheryl Ann was still clutching Bucky in her arms. They both had looks of unbridled panic frozen on their faces.

Starner thought he had buried the horror long ago, but now it all rushed back at him.

He returned to the tow truck and welcomed the sun beating oppressively on his head, hoping it would drive away the dark thoughts. Fixate on what's happening now. The past only brings pain, Starner reproached himself.

Suddenly, the high mechanical whine from the winch went silent.

"What's up, Rod? You still got a ways to go to get that vehicle out of the swamp."

"Gotta shut it down for now. Gonna burn this thing out if I'm not careful, and Mr. Boyo will have my ass for sure if I do. Have to let the engine cool down for at least twenty minutes. That car is stuck real good. The mud down there is like a big suction pump pulling the car back in."

"Anything else you could try right now," Starner asked, looking at his watch, "short of us simply twiddling our thumbs while we wait?"

Rod took off his well-worn John Deere cap, wiped his brow, scrunched up his face in thought and said, after some contemplation, "Maybe . . . maybe, I could try to drive the tow truck, real slow like, further up onto the logging road. That might pull it out. Got to be careful, however, not to snap the cable."

"Tell you what," Starner said, walking over to the water's edge, "I'll watch the cable and signal you if I see a problem."

Rod nodded in agreement, got into the cab, and put the powerful vehicle in gear. The big wheels spun as the tow truck inched forward. The cable was taut, but it held, and a Jeep Grand Cherokee emerged slowly from the swamp until it was completely clear of the water. Its windows, which had been rolled up, were thickly coated with the clay muck that covered the bottom of the swamp. Brown water poured out of every crevice.

When the stream rushing from the Jeep became a mere trickle, Starner tried the driver's side door. It was locked and wouldn't budge. He walked around to the passenger door. Its handle was inoperable.

Taking a crowbar from the back of the tow truck, the deputy smashed the passenger-side window, reached inside, and unlatched the door.

Sprawled on the front seat was the swollen body of a huge man covered in sludge.

Debrun!

On the floor of the back seat, resting under a bunched-up, mud-coated blanket, appeared to be another, smaller body.

Starner bent down to pull the covering away. It was not a blanket. It was the matted coat of a curled-up dog.

CHAPTER TWENTY-FIVE

The hearse from Graunier's Funeral Parlor pulled up and parked next to Acie LaPierre's red Toyota Highlander just as Acie was completing his perfunctory examination. Starner helped Acie arrange Debrun's body on the plastic sheet he had laid on the ground.

Gervais Graunier was dressed, as always, in a black suit, white shirt, and black tie.

Starner had known Gervais for years. He was a sixth-generation member of the family that owned all the Graunier Funeral Parlors throughout the region. Siblings, cousins, and in-laws ran the lot of them, honoring a tradition started by their ancestor, a free man of color who began the business in New Orleans right after the Civil War, catering to the aspirations of the newly freed slaves in those heady days of Reconstruction before the northern troops withdrew and the anvil of Jim Crow fell upon the south.

Gervais ran the Graunier Funeral Parlor branch whose service area extended from Petit Rouge Parish into St. Bonaventure and beyond. He looked dispassionately at the corpse lying on the ground. "Yep, that's Debrun, all right. No question about it."

Acie cavalierly pulled off his gloves. "You'll have your work cut out for you, Gervais. Debrun ran his car off the road. Wasn't wearing a seatbelt. What the hell he was doing back here off the logging road beats me. Must have been drunk as a skunk. No need to do any toxicology tests. It's clear what happened. He drove wildly back here, mistook the old landing for the road, and ended up going into the swamp at full speed. Probably ran into a big ol' cypress stump that's down there in the muck somewhere, broke his neck, and drowned. His momma ain't alive, so you don't have to prettify him up for her. It can be a closed coffin funeral. Of course, if that happens, you won't be able to charge extra for your mortuary beautician, will you?"

Gervais didn't respond, nor did the deputy expect him to. As coroner, Acie signed off on the death certificates the mortician needed to proceed. Gervais had to tolerate Acie in order to maintain his funeral parlor.

When Gervais returned to the hearse to withdraw the collapsible stretcher, Acie glanced over at Starner and gave him a conspiratorial 'we're-two-white-guys-forced-to-deal-with-a-black-dude' smirk. The deputy pretended he didn't see it.

Acie started for his SUV. "I've made enough trips out here, Starner. Twice in one week, for God's sake! Once for Boulette. Now for Debrun, who drowned with Boulette's mutt. Do yourselves a favor. Bury that damn ol' stinky dog somewhere in the woods. It smells worse than the corpse, and that one ain't no bed of perfumed roses."

Gervais overheard everything, though his face betrayed no emotion. He had his professional expression on, one of silent respect for the dead combined with unending patience, but both Rod and the deputy knew what Gervais was thinking: Acie didn't even have the decency to help load Debrun's body onto the stretcher.

Gervais withdrew a pair of gloves from his coat pocket and started to move the corpse, but he was having a bit of difficulty. Debrun was a big guy.

"Here. I'll help," Starner offered. Gervais handed him a second pair gloves. By the time the two of them swung Debrun's body onto the collapsible stretcher, Acie was gone, the taillights of his Highlander disappearing as he rounded the curve of the logging road leading back toward Boulette's cottage and from there to the highway.

"Did Acie," Gervais asked quietly, "do his usual 'expert' job?"

"Speediest 'forensic' examination ever."

Before Gervais covered the corpse with a sheet, he used two fingers to open each of Debrun's eyelids and looked carefully. "Want to see this, Mr. Deputy? You too, Rod?"

Making room for Rod as they both peered over Gervais's shoulder.

"Didn't drown," Gervais said, "no matter what's on the death certificate Acie signs."

"How can you tell?" asked Rod, as Gervais draped the sheet over Debrun's body. "Don't you have to cut into his lungs or something?"

"No need," said Gervais, "although I gotta do that to prepare the body for burial."

Rod had a puzzled look on his face.

"The whites of Debrun's eyes weren't bloodshot," Gervais said, as he loaded the body into the rear of the hearse, the wheels and supports of the stretcher folding in on themselves as he pushed. "When you drown, your lungs fill with water. There are little pockets in the lungs—alveoli—where red blood cells pick up air and transfer carbon dioxide. These tiny areas are covered with a chemical—surfactant—so the pockets can open and close when you breathe. But water destroys the surfactant. The alveoli collapse. When you drown, your eyes become bloodshot from lack of oxygen. Well, technically, it's called petechiae—red or brownish-red spots caused by ruptured blood vessels within the eye. But Debrun's eyes are clear. No matter what Acie writes down in his report, this man didn't drown."

Starner already knew this, having performed a quick examination of the body before extracting it from the Jeep. He did not mention it to the coroner. Acie did not respond well to anyone challenging his authority, and it would have done no good. The coroner was happy in his ignorance. So Starner did not point out to Acie that Debrun's broken neck and battered skull couldn't possibly have resulted from running his Jeep into the swamp. Its windshield wasn't even scratched, nor was there any hard object in the vehicle that could have smashed the back of Debrun's head, pierced his skull, and exposed part of his brain.

Debrun was dead long before his Jeep hit the water, a fact that led to one, and only one, conclusion. Murder. Acie, damn podiatrist and politician that he was, didn't know or care enough to realize that.

Starner seethed knowing that Knock would let Debrun's death go and rely on Acie's report that it was the result of an accidental drowning. Knock's pockets were well-lined from deals that maintained the public image of Petit Rouge as a sleepy, backwoods place where nothing untoward ever occurred, where the strongest "violent" acts were high school kids using speed limit signs for rifle practice, where serious crimes were never committed, and where no death was ever classified as a homicide. Knock wouldn't allow anything to dispel that illusion.

The clarity of Debrun's eyes—along with the uncharacteristic neatness of Boulette's living room and the charred truck driver whose body had hardened into rigor mortis well before the explosion—confirmed the suspicion that had been nagging at Starner. Debrun's death was likely not the only homicide in Petit Rouge Parish this week.

CHAPTER TWENTY-SIX

Starner called Cooper once Gervais drove away and asked him to break the awful news to Ed. He regretted deceiving both of them about the cause of death, but Acie's report was going to be the final word. The deputy told Cooper he had no idea why Debrun drove down the logging road but that Acie determined he and Gertie had drowned in the swamp.

By the time Starner got back to the office, Ed was gone. Distraught and unable to stop crying, she called in Judson's girlfriend, Irénée, to cover for her. Starner surmised that Irénée would probably be there the rest of the week, answering the phones though not doing much else, her mouth always full of chewing gum and her head as vacant as a spent shotgun shell.

As he entered, Starner was accosted by Lydellia, whose mood was anything but pleasant.

"Thank God! You certainly took your sweet time getting here. I sure hope you have the authority to do something! Judson's out writing traffic tickets, and while Irénée here has been polite and all, either you take charge and issue a warrant or search party or posse or whatever you have to in order to locate Boyo or I'm going to the state police, and I don't care what Knock thinks about that."

"I tried explaining to Ms. Vivochère," Irénée said, "that if she'll just fill out a missing person's report, you would take it from there. But I don't know where Ms. Ed keeps those forms."

"They're over here," Starner said, heading toward the file cabinet.

Lydellia angrily stomped the three-inch heels of her moss-green shoes on the wooden floor. "I don't need to fill anything out. My lawyer and I went over to the wrecking yard. We saw where the fence was breached. My lawyer's assembling an inventory of equipment. The stuff that is there and the stuff that's missing, like the extra-long flatbed. We both looked for Boyo's logbooks and metal transaction ledgers but couldn't find them. Dammit. Rod was either too stupid or too lazy to have gone to the back to see where the fence was broken. Gonna fire that good-for-nothing as soon as I get my hands on Boyo's neck. My lawyer's assured me that once I give her the go-ahead and she goes to the state police Commercial Vehicle Enforcement Division, she and the CVE will be able to get a judge up in Baton Rouge to issue whatever orders are necessary. So, don't talk to me about paperwork!"

Starner sighed and pointed to an empty chair. "Lydellia, just take a seat and we'll work through this. You won't have to fill out anything. I'll simply take a statement from you, you'll sign it, and I'll take it from there, all right?"

"No! It is not 'all right'! My lawyer—she's top-notch and from New Orleans—told me not to sign anything, so I won't. This is the second time you and I have talked, once informally at my house and once here, all formal-like. I've given you all the information you need. You've been warned. The state police are coming in. If you don't find Boyo first and bring him back, I'll have them swarming all over this parish. It'll be up to you to explain to Knock why you let it happen!"

"Have it your way, Lydellia. I'll simply note in my report that you designated Boyo as a 'missing person' and confirmed it orally. That'll be sufficient."

"What will be sufficient," Lydellia said with exasperation, "is for you to do your goddamn job, Starner. Don't try to calm me down. I've known you too long for that. Everyone in the parish is aware that Knock's on his deathbed, Judson's an idiot, and you've been cowering behind your deputy's badge for years. Well, make yourself useful for a change. Find Boyo so that I can serve him with divorce papers and take him for everything I haven't already taken him for."

She paused as she turned to leave. "And if you need the tow truck again, or anything else, you call me like you did this morning. I've taken practical control of everything as of today, and by tomorrow I'll have legal control over it all!"

CHAPTER TWENTY-SEVEN

When Starner arrived late in the afternoon, Knock was in his garden, languishing in his rocking chair and wrapped in a blanket despite the fact that the temperature was almost ninety degrees. His pipe was blazing, and he was surrounded by two hulking men in slacks and polo shirts. Starner didn't recognize them, although he had a good memory for faces. Both had athletic builds and appeared to be in their midfifties. One was a slab of muscle with a keg of a chest and a pylon of a neck below a broad, broken nose. The other was even taller—six-foot-five or more—with a linebacker's build and a thick mane of salt and pepper hair pulled back into a short ponytail that hung over his collar.

Spotting Starner, Knock raised his head in acknowledgment. "You called me from the office about Lydellia, and I've thought it over." His voice was weak and reedy, and he spoke as if he was afraid he was going to run out of breath before he finished up whatever he had in mind to say. "Meet my guests. Frankie . . ."

The towering man with the ponytail nodded.

". . . and Ribeye."

The other glared grimly.

Starner addressed the old man directly, ignoring the other two. "And good afternoon to you, Knock. Feeling any better than you did yesterday?"

"I feel about as shitty as I look." Knock shifted painfully in his seat. "Enough of the pleasantries. You know my rules, Starner. Lydellia's on the warpath. You asked to question the stripper in St. Bonaventure Parish, but I'm not going to let you do that. No cross-parish investigations will be conducted by my deputies." He gestured in the direction of his two threatening-looking guests, his bony hand shaking with tremors. "Just tell them what you want to find out."

"Come on, Knock. You really want to use these . . . ? What are they? Out-of-parish P.I.s?"

Frankie, the one with the ponytail, snorted with disdain.

"Starner," Knock said, "Frankie and Ribeye are very experienced."

"As private investigators?"

Frankie spoke up. His voice was deep and gravelly. "Let's just say we're good at extracting information."

"I've got this under control, Starner," Knock said. "They'll report to you. They'll do as you instruct."

"So, they're employees? Consultants? You say you don't want anything run out of your office, so is this official? Unofficial? What's their capacity?"

"They're friends, Starner. And they work for someone who's a special friend of mine. They're doing this at his request . . . as a favor to me."

CHAPTER TWENTY-EIGHT

"Why Paolo told us to do this is fucking beyond me," Ribeye complained, as he drove the polished black Cadillac Escalade toward St. Bonaventure Parish.

Frankie moved the passenger seat all the way back, but it still didn't go far enough to enable him to stretch out his long legs. "What the hell do you care why Paolo does anything? This is a no-brainer. Paolo said do whatever Knock wants, and all the old man asked is that we follow his shitty deputy's 'instructions.' So, why do you care if we have to go talk to some stripper at Good Cheeks? The deputy didn't tell you what you had to do with her afterward. You can stick your dick up her ass, for all I care. I'm going to get mine sucked by the one with the biggest bodacious tits I can find."

Ribeye smirked. "You think Knock knows that Paolo owns Good Cheeks?"

"How do you think the old man got so rich? He and Paolo have had a deal going for years."

"I still don't get it, though, Frankie. Knock got his reputation by kicking Carmine 'the Snake' Micelli—Paolo's uncle—out of Petit Rouge Parish, and then turns around and partners up with Paolo?"

"Get your head out of the crapper, Ribeye. It's because Paolo is smart. Smarter than the Snake ever was. The Snake ruled only through guns and intimidation. Smarter than dick-face Tony, the Snake's son, who is nothing more than a fancy-assed loan shark. Smarter than you or I will ever be. That's why, when the Snake died, Paolo—and not his fat slob-of-a-son Tony—took over. Because he fucking knows how to do business the right way. Why do you think that you, me, and the others in the Red Zone can't stop at a gas station in Petit Rouge, can't buy anything in a store there, and can't eat at that diner with the fancy French name, as if we would want to in the first place? Why does Paolo insist that we always drive five miles below the speed limit in Petit Rouge? Because he bought safe passage, security, and complete privacy for everything he does in that parish."

Ribeye steered the SUV into the curve that cut between seemingly endless fields of sugarcane, their green stalks sandwiched in tight rows. He agreed that Paolo had found a sweet spot in Petit Rouge. In the Red Zone, where Knock forbid his two deputies to go, there were safe houses, three meth factories, and a fully equipped lab for making designer drugs. Locals knew better than to stray into the redlined area. The "no trespassing" signs were kept freshly painted and clearly posted. All it took was a call to Knock to report an unwanted entrant. As quick as you like, Knock himself would show up and rush the fool off to the judge, who would lock him up for a week. Once anyone got a taste of Knock's Petit Rouge jail, they were so grateful to finally get out after posting an inflated bail bond, that they weren't about to return to the redlined portion of Petit Rouge Parish ever again.

Of course, Ribeye thought, that was before Knock got sick. There hadn't been any such incidents recently, anyway. People in the parish knew better than to fuck with Knock. Besides, you had to know where you were going to even make your way to the redlined area.

Ribeye brightened as they crossed the St. Bonaventure Parish line. They'd be at the Good Cheeks Gentlemen's Club in a few minutes. The roadway, recently repaved, was an improvement over the rough asphalt of Petit Rouge's streets. Signs along the highway boasted that St. Bonaventure had a Rotary Club, a Kiwanis Club, a Lion's Club, and a Junior Chamber of Commerce. They passed a Dollar Store, a Walmart, a McDonald's, a Dairy Queen, and a Burger King. To their right was a four-screen movie theater where teenagers gathered on the weekends. To their left were grain silos, feed stores, and bars.

"Do you think," Ribeye said, pausing at a stop sign as a cane truck coming from the cross street made a turn, "that the deputy really wants us to find that Boyo Vivochère guy—and what kind of stupid name is 'Boyo' anyway?"

"I don't think," Frankie responded, "I just do what I'm told to do. That's enough for me. Thinking will only give you a damn migraine. Hell, given how little you have up there, it could give you a fucking stroke."

CHAPTER TWENTY-NINE

The music emanating from the big speakers surrounding the bar of the Good Cheeks Gentlemen's Club pounded away relentlessly. A half dozen farm hands from the local sugarcane fields were sitting at tables near the stage, gawking at a girl listlessly going through her pole-dancing routine. Beneath the pancake makeup on her face and body, she was sizing them up while tossing her ponytail, brunette with neon green highlights.

The bartender, seeing Frankie and Ribeye enter, recognized them immediately and pointed to a door to the left of where the girl with the ponytail was wrapping one leg around the shiny pole, leaning backward, and raising her other leg high over her head.

Paolo's two men walked purposely down the dingy hallway, past curtains made of strings of pastel plastic beads separating the performance area from backstage. The glitter that once covered the three wooden stars on the dressing room door had long since fallen off, exposing cheap plywood.

Not pausing to knock, they found Sora Faye alone, putting on heavy eye shadow.

They questioned her for fifteen minutes. When they didn't get the answers they wanted, they asked her the same questions again, only louder.

Sora Faye retreated to the corner of the tiny dressing room, clad only in a thong. "I told you. You can ask me again and again, but it's the truth. I ain't seen Boyo since Sunday night."

Frankie stood between Sora Faye and the door. "Sunday night? That doesn't sound right to me. Way I understand it, you had him twisted around your little finger. Can't believe you'd go all this time without at least talking to him."

The pony-tailed brunette-with-green-streaks strutted off the stage, lit up a cigarette, grabbed the tumbler of whiskey she had left on a table behind the curtains, and pulled on a tattered robe. Her picture was on the sign outside Good Cheeks. It showed her sucking her finger seductively. She was billed as "Chastity." Below that was a photo Sora Faye, labeled "Angel Bird."

Hearing a man's voice coming from the dressing room, Chastity called out from the hallway, "You got company in there, girl? I gotta be back on in ten minutes."

Ribeye emerged and blocked the doorway to where Frankie and Sora Faye were talking. He snarled, "Get the fuck out of here. This is a private conversation."

Chastity didn't budge. She gave the muscular man a saucy look and opened her thin robe, revealing that she was completely naked. "Want some private time with me, big fella? I promise I give better head than Sora Faye. You'll be real pleased with what I can do."

Ribeye eyed her appreciatively. "Maybe later." He went back into the dressing room, slamming the door shut behind him.

Frankie, who towered over Sora Faye, lowered his bulk into a chair, confining her to the corner to which she had retreated. His eyes were now level with her chest. He pulled out a switchblade and flipped it open. "Those are nice big tits. All natural? Bet you're real proud of them. You won't get many tips if you have a big scar across one of them, will you?"

Sora Faye crossed her arms in front of her breasts. Her lower lip began to quiver. "I ain't lyin'."

"Didn't say you were, gal." Frankie signaled for her to put her arms down. She did as instructed. He tapped the side of his knife's blade against her left nipple, causing Sora Faye to shiver at its touch.

"Sunday night? Was that really the last time you spoke with him?"

Sora Faye realized that whatever this big man was planning to do to her, there was nothing she could do to prevent it. Just like she couldn't prevent any of the things other men had done to her since she was twelve, starting with her stepfather. "OK. Hadn't seen him since Sunday, but he did call me Monday morning, as soon as he got to the scrapyard. Told me that if it was a slow day, he'd be comin' back to our place late afternoon. And I said don't bother, I gotta work a double shift today. Wouldn't get off until after ten at night, but he could bring dinner. He got us, like, a nice place. Furnished apartment overlooking Bayou Grosse Noir with cable TV, internet, and wall-to-wall carpeting that's almost new."

"You haven't spoken to him or seen him since then?"

This was the fifth time he had asked the same question. She could read men. He was just playing with her now. No longer believing he was really going to cause her harm, her fear subsided. "Shit no! And he better show up. Rent is due next week and I sure as hell don't have it."

Sora Faye deliberately gave Frankie's crotch a long look, making sure he was aware of her provocative glance. "Got a big load down there?"

He let her push the knife away. Sora Faye's face softened, as did her tone of voice. "Look, I know you guys must work for Paolo, I ain't ever done nothin' to cross Paolo. Never! Love that apartment. Best place I ever lived. Gotta have that rent payment if Boyo don't show back up." She slipped out of her thong. "You guys want to do a double? One in front, one in back? Give me enough for next month's rent and I'll definitely make it worth your while."

Ribeye, still standing in front of the closed door, grimaced. "The last thing I want is to have Frankie's balls anywhere near mine."

"That's because," Frankie said to Sora Faye, with a smutty smile, "mine are twice the size of his." He gestured for Ribeye to leave the room and turned back to her, admiring her slim figure and smooth skin. She couldn't be more than eighteen, if she was that old. "Let's you and me discuss this privately. I'll give you money for your rent, and you can give me whatever I need."

CHAPTER THIRTY

Judson Jorée lounged against his police cruiser, an insulated cup of coffee in his left hand and a radar gun in his right. He had parked in his favorite spot, behind one of the two giant, moss-covered oak trees that grew on either side of the sharp curve in rural Vizeau Road, a quarter mile away from the St. Bonaventure Parish line. Once cars crossed into Petit Rouge Parish, the speed limit dropped abruptly from 55 to 40. The traffic sign indicating this was green with mildew and half-hidden by palmettos, just the way both Knock and Judge Franklin Fauchère liked it. Whizzing down the macadam-patched concrete, vehicles coming from St. Bonaventure either failed to see the sign or ignored it, thinking that there was no earthly reason to slow down out here amidst what appeared to be overhanging hardwoods, high weeds, and not much else.

Judson sported a self-satisfied grin as he clocked the blue Chrysler 200 LX Sedan. He'd show Starner! Criticize him for not meeting his ticket quota? Why, since yesterday, when Starner upbraided him while they were both at the sheriff's office, Judson had written over twenty tickets. All to outsiders, of course. Wouldn't be smart to ticket someone who could vote for Knock or Judge Fauchère.

Not meet his quota? Hell, he'd double it! Triple it, maybe. Thanks to him, cash would flow into the parish coffers. That would make both Knock and the judge happy. After all, most of the money received from tickets was split between the judicial budget and the sheriff's office.

And what next? Well, Knock would be dead soon. And Starner—the grim-faced deputy whose life seemed to be mired in the past—had no future to speak of.

Nothing is going to stand in my path, Judson thought. Going to maintain a sterling record while Knock is alive. And when he's gone, I'm going to leverage my way into a cushy spot with the state police. Higher pay. Better benefits. Leave this damn parish. Perhaps be assigned to Troop B, which handles New Orleans. Lots of over-time pay there, plus triple time during Mardi Gras. Beaucoup fine women to pick from. Not like the skanks here in Petit Rouge or the sluts over in St. Bonaventure. Of course, Irénée is no skank, but she and I have just been hooking up. Nothing serious on my part. Why, with my good looks plus some new threads, once I move to the Big Easy I'll attract them long-haired, big-titted, short-skirted New Orleans gals and have the salary to entertain them proper.

Smiling at the thought of the evenings he'd spend in New Orleans with classy women at his beck and call, Judson checked the locked-in reading on the radar gun that memorialized the speed of the Chrysler as it had rounded the curve and passed by the oak trees. The driver hadn't spotted him yet.

Climbing into his cruiser, Judson turned on his siren and flash-ing lights and pulled out onto Vizeau Road in pursuit of the of-fending sedan.

Seeing the lights in her rearview mirror, the driver of the Chrysler steered to the shoulder of the road next to the steep ditch still half-filled with water from the weekend's rain. Judson pulled in behind, turning off the siren but leaving the blue strobes on the roof of his car blazing.

Adjusting the brim of his hat and grabbing his ticket book, Judson walked over as the black woman in the driver's seat rolled down her window. She was in her forties, nicely dressed. A silver cross hung from her necklace. Perfect, thought Judson. A church-goer. This was going to be easy. And quick.

"Do you know," he said politely, "how fast you were going?"

"Of course!" the woman responded in exasperation.

Judson didn't like back talk or criticism. Not from Starner, and certainly not from a black woman foolish enough to argue with a white officer of the law. Judson jutted out his chin and said curtly, "Then you know you were speeding."

"Was not!"

"Lady," Judson said in a tone that clearly meant he thought she was nothing of the kind, "I have you on the radar gun."

"You can 'have' anything you damn well please, but I wasn't speeding. I know all about this area. Soon as I hit the parish line, I put the speed control on forty. And that's what I was doing. Forty!"

Judson was determined that this uppity black woman would regret her remarks. "Your speed control ain't worth spit. Got you recorded at forty-two. That's two miles over the limit. And that's a misdemeanor. Eighty-dollar fine, plus court costs. I'm going to write you up a ticket. You can either pay it by mail or contest it in court. Up to you. Give me your driver's license and registration."

Judson was surprised when the woman didn't reach into her purse and do exactly what he had commanded. Rather she started to open her door.

Judson backed up and pulled his gun from his holster. "Don't you dare! Get back in there, you black bitch!"

The woman slowly put both hands on her dashboard, palms down. "Now, officer," she said through angrily gritted teeth, "look what I'm doing. I'm not going to give you any trouble. Put your pistol away. That's a Beretta 92FS, 9mm semi-automatic with a three-dot sighting system, right?"

Judson was amazed at her knowledge, but it only made him grasp his pistol more firmly. He assumed a firing position, aiming at her head.

The woman took a deep, cleansing breath and spoke to him slowly, trying to calm him down. "Are you aware of who I am? I'm the sister of Sheriff Isaiah Brown of St. Bonaventure. Surely you know my brother!"

Oh crap, thought Judson. But he didn't change his stance or his expression.

"Now officer," the woman continued, "I'm certain that this is just a misunderstanding. I happen to know there's a high level of courtesy between those in the law enforcement arena and their immediate family members. Two miles over the speed limit? Seriously, you really aren't going to ticket me for that, are you? Just give me a 'firm warning' and I'll be on my way."

All them blacks to stick together, thought Judson. A black sheriff in St. Bonaventure! Thank God for the white D.A. in that parish. Extend 'courtesy' to someone like Sheriff Brown? Not a chance. The law in Petit Rouge Parish began at the parish line, and it was a bright line not to be crossed by anyone. Knock would back him up on that.

"First," said Judson, "throw your keys out the window."

"What?"

"YOU HEARD ME!" Judson was screaming now. "KEYS! TOSS 'EM!"

The woman did as instructed, lobbing the keys at Judson's feet.

Judson's temper was at full blast. "Get out your license and registration, bitch! Real slow! Put them both in your left hand and hold them outside the window."

The woman followed his commands.

Judson snatched the papers from the woman and backed away from the car, never lowering his gun. "Jarnayce Brown Mitchell," he read out loud from her license. "Age 48. This address is in New Orleans—you still live there?"

"Yes, sir," she said, pointedly showing the "proper degree" of deference this sallow-faced officer obviously expected and wondering if she had stepped into a 1950s time-warp, when any sign of "disrespecting" a white cop led to a pistol-whipping or worse. When Isaiah hears about this, she thought, he'll be incensed. He'll know what to do to fix things.

"Well, Jarnayce," Judson said contemptuously, "I'm going to ticket you for driving over the speed limit. I'm also writing you up for resisting arrest and attempted assault on an officer. That last one's a felony. The fine is going to be over $900. You want courtesy? I'll give you courtesy. Rather than hauling your black ass into the Petit Rouge Parish prison, I'm going to let you keep your license, but you better pay that fine promptly or Judge Fauchère will toss you behind bars. Put both hands back on the dashboard and sit still while I finish writing all this up."

CHAPTER THIRTY-ONE

R ibeye kept a watchful eye on the speedometer as he drove into Petit Rouge Parish. He didn't exceed 35 miles per hour although the speed limit was 40. It wasn't the cops he was worried about. It was Paolo. Paolo ordered his men to never cause a problem in Petit Rouge, and he brooked no opposition. Fail to obey him explicitly and you didn't get a second chance. In fact, that was what Ribeye and Frankie were good at—eliminating those who crossed Paolo.

Ribeye enjoyed the work. Unlike when he and Frankie were collectors for Tony, the loan shark who simply wanted his debtors roughed up so that they would eventually pay up, Paolo had no compunctions about rubbing out anyone who crossed him. Ribeye and Frankie were Paolo's enforcers.

So, Ribeye wondered, why did Paolo want them to help Knock by merely questioning the stripper? Want them to "assist" some washed-up deputy?

Ribeye didn't ponder it further. He didn't need to worry about such things. Frankie did the thinking for both of them.

Frankie was in the Cadillac Escalade's passenger seat, trying to get comfortable. With his size and height, he needed all the leg room possible in this vehicle, but it was never enough. He peeled a stick of gum and stuck it in his mouth. "That Chastity gal was a good lay, huh?"

Ribeye nodded, smiling at the memory. "I like 'em that way. Hard body. Tight ass. Shaved muff. Dirty mouth."

Frankie gazed out the window as the Escalade crossed over the bridge at Bayou Grosse Noir. "When we get to Knock's tomorrow morning, you let me do the talking, hear?"

"Don't I always?"

"Most of the time. But this is important. Those girls will rat out anyone if they think it'll help them, and we got to assume that everything they told or did for us will get back to Paolo."

"You think I don't know that, Frankie? Paolo won't mind that we'd mixed a little pleasure with business at Good Cheeks."

Frankie gave the back of Ribeye's head a not-so-friendly whack. "You don't get it, do you? The point of this assignment was to help Paolo further grease the wheels with Knock. No one from St. Bonaventure messes with Petit Rouge. No one from anywhere does. Paolo pays Knock good money to have free run of the Red Zone. When I tell Knock what I found out from Sora Faye—that this Boyo guy really has up and disappeared, on his wife, on his slut girlfriend, on his business—what's going to happen next? No one just vanishes like that, leastwise no one in high cotton like that fella. Means, don't you know, that something is wrong, big time. Knock, sick as a dog or not, ain't gonna like it. Boyo's business is regulated by the state and the Feds. Now, they're both likely to start swarming down here. That's not good for Knock's setup. And what's bad for Knock is even worse for Paolo."

CHAPTER THIRTY-TWO

"We're closing the kitchen now, Starner," Florene said, wiping down the tables. "Want anything else?"

Starner slumped in his usual seat in the side booth at Chez Poêlon. "One more hit of coffee, Florene. Then I'll get out of here."

It was his fourth cup this evening, but it wasn't as if it would keep him from a sound night's sleep. Starner hadn't slept well in years. He had tried giving up caffeine after Cheryl Ann and Bucky died, but that hadn't prevented him from tossing and turning in the dark or drifting off into nightmares from which he'd awake with a start. So, he went back on caffeine. Back on whiskey. Back on wine that came in gallon-size plastic cartons.

Starner longed to close his eyes, shut his subconscious off, and sleep peacefully. Just once he wanted to drift awake well after daylight streamed through the curtains in the bedroom of the double-wide trailer he called home since moving to Petit Rouge Parish. But blissful slumber eluded him year after year.

Florene brought over a large thermos bottle and a 12-ounce Styrofoam cup with a lid and took a seat in the booth. "The bigger one is iced coffee. The smaller one's café au lait. You can bring the thermos back tomorrow. Guess Armond and I overestimated how many folks would be in tonight."

That was too true. The deputy had been the only customer in the place for the last hour and a half, working his way slowly through Armond's sensation salad, with its sharp, vinegary dressing and its snowfall of grated Parmesan cheese. Through a thick slice of Armond's meatloaf laced with tender ground lamb and chicken livers, giving it a smooth texture and silky taste. And through Armond's latest creation, a four-inch-high blueberry-banana double cheesecake.

He paused between mouthfuls. "How much longer are you and Armond going to keep this place open? Got to be tough. Less and less traffic passing through each month, especially in the evenings."

"Oh, we'll get by," Florene said, unconvincingly. "If we have to, we can always close Chez Poêlon and go work at that fancy restaurant at Cottoncrest Plantation. They keep dangling an offer before us, but neither Armond nor I want to do that. Don't want to be preparing dinners for busloads of tourists who prefer something served fast and seemingly 'authentic,' as if using extra cayenne pepper and Tabasco sauce makes anything Cajun. Have you seen what they're passing off as 'Cajun' elsewhere? I've had people from up north tell me they've had Cajun Cod, as if you could catch cod down here, and blackened pasta, whatever the heck that is. Even had a visitor last year from London who swore that they served 'Cajun burritos' in some pubs there. He wanted to come here to taste the real thing. A 'Cajun burrito'? Can you believe? That's about as 'authentic' Louisiana cooking as trying to come here and ask for a slice of kangaroo 'prepared the Cajun way.' Ridiculous!"

Spotting a fingerprint on the edge of the next table, Florene took out her dishtowel and wiped it away until the chrome glistened. "No, as I told you before, we've lived carefully, saved our money, and with our two girls on scholarship at the university, we're okay. Besides, what would I do with Armond if we shut this place down? He could never go back to working for someone else. Besides, he's happy in his own kitchen, reinventing old dishes and creating new ones."

Florene put down her dishtowel. "But what about you, Starner? What would make you happy? You haven't been happy in years. First it was Cheryl Ann and Bucky. Then it was the trial and the verdict. And now, Knock's dying. It's a lot to deal with."

That was an understatement. Cheryl Ann and Bucky were never far from Starner's thoughts. And the trial? He had known it would be a travesty from start to finish. The year after Katrina, the year after Cheryl Ann and Bucky died, the last year he remained a detective on the New Orleans police force, Starner sold his water-logged casket of a dwelling at a loss without even bothering to fix it up. Hadn't bought flood insurance. FEMA money wasn't enough to do the needed repairs, and he didn't have the heart to venture down his old street anymore. He wanted to be free of those awful memories, the sooner the better.

Starner was living in a dumpy apartment not far from the shabby Achilles Housing Projects, trying to save every penny he earned to pay off the mortgage balance that remained on his ghost house, when the second disaster of his life began.

He had been driving back to his apartment late one night in his N.O.P.D. cruiser when he spotted two men exiting the back of a closed bodega, each holding bags. He turned the corner slowly. They spotted the police car and started running.

Starner called for backup. Thought he had them cold for burglary.

He gave chase on foot down the side alley through which they ran, unholstering his gun in case he needed it.

A cruiser screeched around the corner cutting the burglars off where the alley intersected the next street. Two officers jumped out brandishing weapons. A second marked vehicle arrived, siren blaring, and the officer in it ran forward, Taser in one hand, pistol in the other.

Seeing the cops in front of them, the thieves panicked and started trying to open every door in the alley. Starner yelled "Stop. Police!"

One of duo reached for a ladder dangling from a fire escape and started to swing himself up it. The other bent low behind a dumpster.

A warning shot rang out from the officer with the Taser.

The man on the fire escape didn't stop. He scampered up higher and higher.

The Taser-toting cop yelled, "Fucking come down right now or I'll shoot!"

When the robber didn't halt, the cop made good on his threat. The man, shot in the back while he continued climbing, tumbled off the fire escape and fell into the alley with a thud.

The other burglar panicked and started firing.

He was silenced by a barrage of bullets from the three cops who had arrived on the scene after Starner called for backup.

Starner approached cautiously from his end of the alley while the other three, from their end, crouched low as they approached.

Behind the dumpster a body lay sprawled on the ground, blood pouring out of four holes in his torso. The hoodlum who fell from the fire escape had a bullet hole in his back.

Starner shone a flashlight on their faces.

They were teenagers. Maybe not even fifteen yet.

While waiting for the ambulance and other law enforcement personnel to arrive on the scene, the three cops, Dolan O'Callaghan, Benoit Medoux, and Chuck Cifaldi, cornered Starner "to get their story straight."

Chuck, the shortest but beefiest of the three, was the ringleader. "No problem," he explained. "The kids fired first, right?"

Dolan and Benoit nodded affirmatively.

"We had no choice. Couldn't be helped, given the situation. We all acted in self-defense, right?"

Dolan and Benoit agreed, but Starner did not. "That's bullshit, Chuck. The kid on the fire escape was climbing up and not even facing us. If he had a gun, where is it?"

"You're a fool, Starner! We're sticking to our account. You're either part of our team or you're the opposition. What do you want to be? It's three against one, plus all the shots from the pistol that's still in the hand of the one next to the dumpster."

"But that's not the full story and you know it."

"It's the story that will sell. It's the one everyone will believe—and will want to believe."

Starner refused to engage in a cover-up although Chuck tried hard to persuade him to join in their ruse right up until the ambulance arrived. Chuck led the attendants to the bodies, regaling them with how the "perps almost got the drop on us when they started firing first."

When the investigation got under way, Starner told the D.A. exactly what had happened, which is why Starner became the state's star witness and avoided prosecution, while O'Callaghan, Medoux, and Cifaldi were arraigned on second-degree murder charges.

Although still employed as a detective during the investigation and trial, Starner was ostracized by his colleagues on the force for ratting out the others. Officers he had known for years refused to speak with him. Someone welded his locker shut, so he was given a new one in the hallway, outside the changing room. His union reps were too busy with the defense of Dolan, Benoit, and Chuck to help him. The union held a press conference accusing the kid behind the dumpster of firing numerous times, threatening seasoned officers with families who risked their lives in the line of duty and who had to make split-second decisions when faced with a murderous gunman.

There were no body cams in those days. It was Starner's word against three decorated policemen, two of whom outranked him.

Their trial was a farce. "White Cops Shoot Unarmed Black Teenager in the Back" blared the headlines. Marches were organized. Demonstrators occupied the mayor's office. There was a public outcry for the resignation of the three cops as well as for the resignation of the chief of police, who had publicly supported their actions as being appropriate under the circumstances.

Starner, who willingly testified against O'Callaghan, Medoux, and Cifaldi, was genuinely shocked by the criticism he received when he honestly admitted unholstering his gun, even though he never fired it.

The New Orleans district attorney tried the case himself. The police union, sparing no expense, brought in a top-notch lawyer from D.C. to defend the cops who became known as the "Achilles Three" because of the housing project in which the shootings occurred. The union was justifiably afraid that, in such a racially charged situation in such a racially divided city, a guilty verdict would result in a federal investigation of both the New Orleans Police Department and the local police union, something the Crescent City's African American community had been trying to get for years without success.

A jury was finally seated, though the out-of-town defense attorney used plenty of slick tactics to keep the number of black
jurors on it to a minimum. He'd ask potential black jurors, but not
white ones, "Do you have a relative or friend who has ever been
arrested?" An affirmative answer enabled the lawyer to convince the
judge to grant a "for cause" dismissal, given the significant amount
of publicity the case had received and the criticism of the police
department being lobbed daily by the media and local activists.

"Have you ever personally had a run-in with any law enforcement officer that you felt was unjustified?"

"Have you ever gotten a traffic ticket you believe you didn't
deserve?"

"Don't you, in your heart of hearts, think black people in this
city are unfairly targeted by the police?"

On and on the defense lawyer probed until he got the judge to
reluctantly eliminate juror after potential juror "for cause." Finally,
nine white jurors and three black jurors were empaneled.

The trial lasted four and a half weeks. Demonstrators filled
both the courtroom and the streets surrounding the Orleans Parish
courthouse every single day, regardless of the weather.

When Starner was called to the stand, the D.C. defense attorney
cross-examined him with a vengeance. How could Starner be sure the
boy behind the dumpster didn't fire first? Why would a fellow officer
shoot someone unless he felt his life was in danger? How could the
detective dispute the forensic expert who linked the bullets lodged in
the two police cruisers to the gun fired by the boy behind the dumpster? And, most damning of all, two questions back-to-back.

The first: "Didn't you unholster your gun?" Starner answered
simply, "Yes."

The second: "You wouldn't have done that if you hadn't feared
for your life, isn't that correct?" Starner fumbled for an answer.
It was like being asked, "When did you stop beating your wife?"
Whatever he said would be taken the wrong way.

Finally, he said, "Whenever there is an active pursuit, there is
always the potential for danger."

When it came time for closing arguments, the defense attorney harped on Starner's delay in answering the second question and his "hesitant and evasive response." Striding forcefully
before the jury, the D.C. lawyer pounded the point home. "Of
course Officer Starner Gautreaux unholstered his gun. The only
reason for him to do so was because he feared for his life and
thought he might have to use his pistol. It is only by grace of
God that the shooter didn't fire at him, and it is only by the
grace of God that Officers O'Callaghan, Medoux, and Cifaldi
had the presence of mind to fire back when viciously attacked
by someone intent on killing them!"

The jury did not deliberate long and quickly returned a verdict
of not guilty.

The next morning, Starner was unceremoniously fired from the
police force.

The press had a field day, proclaiming "Achilles Three Acquitted."

Mention of Starner was relegated to a short paragraph that he
had been summarily terminated for "insubordination."

No one in the white community trusted an officer who would
testify against "upright public servants who put their lives in danger every day." And no one in the black community wanted anything to do with a detective who ran around chasing teenagers with
his gun unholstered.

In the weeks following the verdict, there were riots in New
Orleans. Some stores in white neighborhoods were looted. The
cops came down against the violence with force. The state police
and the National Guard were called in. "Peace" was eventually re-
stored, and when the publicity and clamor finally abated, Starner
was nothing more than a thirty-two-year-old, unemployed has-
been, a former police officer with no wife, no child, and no pros-
pects. He was a pariah in the city he had so faithfully served.

Just when Starner was sure he had no future, Knock took pity
on him and offered him a position as a deputy. Why? Because
Knock had known Starner's family for years. Because no one in
Petit Rouge Parish, black or white, would ever publicly question

Knock's actions or decisions. And because Starner had no bargaining power whatsoever and could be hired dirt-cheap.

Theirs was a marriage of convenience. Of necessity. Or maybe, not a marriage at all. More like a macabre dance where the invitee can't leave the one who brought him to the soiree, no matter how distasteful the coupling became.

That was many years ago. Knock still paid Starner next-to-nothing, and Starner still didn't have the ability to complain or another place to go if Knock laid him off.

So, Florene was exactly right. It was all about Cheryl Ann and Bucky. About the trial and the verdict. And about Knock dying.

CHAPTER THIRTY-THREE

S tarner was just leaving the café when Bea Timms called and said Knock wanted to see him immediately, even though it was after 9 p.m. The lights on the wide veranda were illuminated when he got to the sheriff's big house and rang the bell, but no one answered the front door.

The deputy walked around the corner of the house down a brick pathway flanked by LED lanterns in the shape of 1890s gas lamps. Bea was propping Knock up in his favorite rocker in the garden. Starner hung back, knowing that Knock wouldn't want him to see what it took to get the sheriff prepared for a visitor.

Bea had trouble positioning Knock in his chair. She packed three pillows around his sides in an effort to keep him erect, but even with these in place he was too weak to sit upright on his own. "Truss me like a pig about to be roasted for a *cochon de lait*," Knock insisted, and she dutifully lashed him to the rocker, using rope from one of the many shelves in his four-car garage. Then, she covered him with a blanket, as he had instructed, tucking the loose ends of the rope under his legs so that no one would see them.

After Bea adjusted the Japanese lanterns strung from the trees so that Knock was in the shadows, she took a seat in a nearby garden chair. It was only then that Starner emerged, as if he just arrived.

Knock raised an arm to weakly wave a greeting but didn't say anything.

Bea took that as a cue. "You wanted your deputy here, Mr. Knock, and the other two as well. I made those calls, although I don't know why this couldn't wait until morning. I imagine you want to discuss business. Well, that's fine. Far be it from me to watch over you, even though it's my job. Remember that as you sit out here in the dark and run the risk of getting pneumonia on top of everything else that ails you."

As she got up to leave, Bea turned to Starner. "I'll be inside. If he needs anything, just call out."

Once she was beyond earshot, Starner pulled his chair close to Knock and patted the old man's hand. It was clammy and had prominent veins surrounding bony knuckles under paper-thin skin. "As you can imagine, Ed's all broken up about Debrun. His death, plus Boulette's, has put her in a state. Irénée is filling in, but don't expect anything to be done right—if done at all—other than answering the phone. The office, however, is under control for the time being. So what was so important that you needed me to come over right away?"

The sheriff's voice was weak, barely above a whisper. "My friends have talked to the stripper. They'll be here any minute."

With that, Knock's head drooped to his chest and he fell asleep.

Moths flittered around the Japanese lanterns overhead, fireflies darted in and out of the lush plantings in the expansive garden, and the low thrum of crickets provided a constant wash of sound. Starner sat there listening to the old man's slow, shallow breathing, noting that his diaphragm hardly moved under the blanket. The sheriff seemed more frail with each passing hour.

After ten minutes, Starner sensed movement behind him and turned around. Bea was escorting Frankie and Ribeye into the garden. She bent down to check on her patient and gently wake him. "Mr. Knock, the other folks you asked me to call are here."

The sheriff raised his head and blinked, as if trying to focus. Clearing his throat, he croaked, "Tell Starner what you found out."

Frankie opened his hand palms up and addressed Knock directly. "Empty handed, Sheriff. Don't know where Boyo is, but he sure ain't in St. Bonaventure with the stripper. He set her up nice and then left her holding the bag for rent. Great guy, huh?"

The look on Knock's face indicated he was having trouble following the conversation.

"Thought you two were experts in extracting information," Starner said. "We already knew he was missing. All you've done is confirm that?"

Frankie, accustomed to intimidating people, glared at the deputy with a don't-fuck-with-me expression.

It didn't faze Starner, who merely smiled.

Frankie, irritated, ignored him and directed his comments to the old man. "Believe me, Sheriff, if Boyo had been around, we would have found him. But he ain't there. He could be in Mississippi or Texas or south of the border, but he's not in this area. We talked to that stripper but good. She didn't lie to us. If she had, I would have cut her."

"Yeah," Ribeye added. "We told Paolo, and he put the word out. If this Boyo guy shows up anywhere Paolo does business, he'll know about it right away."

Frankie pulled Ribeye to one side and whispered angrily, "I told you to let me do the talking. Go back to the Escalade."

Ribeye shrugged his shoulders as he sulked out of the garden.

Starner observed this little drama between Frankie and Ribeye with amusement, wondering why Paolo Micelli would be interested enough in Boyo to 'put the word' out? Starner was not chagrined with their inability to obtain any useful information, knowing that if he had been allowed to go to St. Bonaventure, he would have gone beyond just questioning the stripper. He would have insisted that she take him to the place where she and Boyo were living to see if any clues could be gleaned there. He would have checked the property records to find out if Boyo's name appeared anywhere as an owner, landlord, or tenant. He would have quizzed the bartenders at the club, as well as the others who worked there, and the regular patrons. He wouldn't have just chatted up the stripper and come straight back.

Starner started to speak to Knock but the old man had dozed off again, his chin against his chest, drool dripping from one corner of his mouth.

Frankie gestured to Starner to follow him to the side of the garden. "Look, errand boy, you tell your boss, when he awakes—if he awakes—that we've done what he asked and we kept your nose clean by eliminating the need for you to venture into St. Bonaventure. I'm leaving my card on the table. If he needs us any more, tell him to dial that number rather than calling Paolo. We're here for Knock—per Paolo's instructions—until Knock dismisses us. Ribeye and I will be over in the Red Zone, but we can be back this way in twenty minutes if needed."

After Frankie left, Starner, still fuming at the way Frankie talked to him, settled into one of the garden chairs next to the slumbering invalid, ruefully musing that Lydellia was a pain, but maybe she was right. Maybe it was time for him to do his "goddamn job," as she had so pointedly put it. Not the job that Knock expected of him, which was to dutifully overlook anything that caused wrinkles in the fabric of the parish that Knock had carefully woven to shroud all things Knock wanted left unseen. Perhaps it was time to do the job he worked so hard to earn and which he lost so quickly years ago.

Starner resolved to start acting like the first-rate detective he once was.

CHAPTER THIRTY-FOUR

"You like that, baby?"

"Don't stop, Maggie Mae. Don't stop. One more time. Keep on like there's no tomorrow."

Sloe-eyed Maggie Mae threw back the thin covers. Bubba Mauvais was spread-eagle, his head on the pillow and his back on the mattress.

"It ain't all about you," she said, positioning herself on top of him and starting to rock up and down. "Besides, after Friday, the Supreme Kommander is sending both of us off in different directions." She rocked harder. "Stay still, dammit. Let me do this at my own pace."

Bubba groaned with delight. Finally, she rolled off him, grabbed one of the four remaining marijuana joints on the nightstand, lit it, and, inhaling deeply, nestled against his chest. "What about Florida?"

"Art hasn't told me shit about that, and I don't expect he will. I'm sure he's planning something there in the future, but no matter what, New Orleans is about to have one helluva shock, along with the rest of the country. Here, give me a drag on that."

He took it from her hand, and said, after exhaling, "This is definitely good shit."

She twirled the hairs on his chest. "Can Kenny be trusted to carry through?"

"I got Kenny so wrapped up in the Supreme Kommander's theology that he'll do anything and everything he's told. Got him spouting the mantra on his own. He even scribbled down one of Art's favorite sayings, the one Art gives to all new Aspirants, and nailed it to the wall above his bed. 'Chaos must again reign supreme. Only then will the nonbelievers believe.' Oh, Kenny is a true believer all right."

"Well, fuck, I am too!"

"Of course you are baby," Bubba said, stroking her left breast. "We are all true believers. Wouldn't be doing all this if we weren't, right?"

Maggie Mae brushed his hand away and sat cross-legged on the bed. "True belief is all well and good, but given what the Supreme Kommander wants, it has to be coupled with competency."

"Well then, come couple with me, right now." Bubba turned on his side and reached over toward her.

Maggie Mae playfully swatted his cheek and scooted further away from him. "Keep your hands off my snatch for a minute, will you? This is serious. Phillip's got a hair-trigger temper, a chip-on-his-shoulder, and the sense of a horsefly buzzing around a pile of shit. And Tommy? He's trying too hard to prove himself but just can't. With his fancy three-syllable words and his I'm-smarter-than-you attitude, he's a catastrophe waiting to happen. Anyone can see he don't fit in down here in south Louisiana. Together, that pair is as combustible as a package of R-37. And you've gone and made me their goddamn babysitter. They screwed up the Florida shipment. Caused you no end of trouble. Once we're all out of here, how long do you think it's gonna be before someone finds that burned-out wreck in the woods behind your place? Or the body of the guy from the wrecker yard they killed? Those two have created problem after problem for the Supreme Kommander, as well as for you and me. Why does he keep them around anyway? Why not dispose of them, the same way I got rid of Saxon Fourteen and got promoted to Imperial Seven? He made that decision in a split second!"

Savoring the joint and mellowing out, Bubba leaned back on the pillow. "Why ol' Art, the Supreme Kommander, does some things and not others ain't my worry, and it better not be yours, babe. He has a reason for everything. No need to fret. Don't tell anyone, but I took the backhoe and buried both the wreck and

Boyo but good. Covered them up. Planted a row of pine seedlings over them, along with a raft of poison ivy. No one's gonna find nothing. The poison ivy will spread all over and those pine trees will sprout up before you know it. Nobody's ever gonna be the wiser."

"You might bury that stuff, but that won't be the end of things. Come Friday, you're supposed to head back to Idaho and I'll be driving to San Antonio, where the Supreme Kommander has planned the next event to occur on the downtown Riverwalk that those Texans are so proud of there. If something causes a problem this Friday in New Orleans, who's the Supreme Kommander going to blame? You? Me? Both of us? Do you think he's going to show any compassion before he offs us, even if the two of you go back years together? Not a chance. If Phillip or Tommy mess up anything at this point, it could be your neck and mine that are at risk."

Bubba gave a toothy grin. "You're right, babe."

"Don't patronize me, you big fart! Of course I'm right."

"No, I mean it. You've got a point. We can't let Phillip and Tommy fuck up one more time, especially since they're toting more than a thousand bucks in cash authorized by the Supreme Kommander in case they have to cover any unexpected expenses. I understand his not wanting to leave a credit card trail, but why so much? As I said, I ain't about to question anything the Supreme Kommander does, although I agree with you that he seems to bend over backward when it comes to Tommy. Tell you what. Tomorrow, you follow those two but don't let them see you. Watch them watch Kenny drive his route. If anything goes awry, step in right away and fix it. Can you do that?"

"Why the shit should I do that? I already told them to call me if problems arise! You want me to follow them into the bathroom and wipe their asses too?"

"No, babe. I want you to be an insurance policy for both of us."

Maggie Mae flashed Bubba a smile, the one she gave when she wanted men to believe she thought they were terrific. Bubba was full of crap, but she was not about to let him know what she thought. Watching Phillip and Tommy was a job for a Saxon, not an Imperial like herself. She would do whatever it took to get ahead, however, whether it was lying to men or laying them. "Good idea, Prefect. Eighty-eight!"

Bubba sat up and gave her a kiss. "Great, Imperial Seven. Eighty-eight!" he said, while putting his head down at the foot of the bed. "Now, you put your face up there next to the pillow. Good. Let me adjust my legs. Right. You adjust yours. Yes, that's it! Let's do the numbers. Sixty-nine and 88! Eighty-eight and 69!"

PART V

THURSDAY

CHAPTER THIRTY-FIVE

Ashrimp trawler bearing the name *Creole Lady* hugged the marshy coastline, working its way in the dark toward the narrow opening that led into the Istrouma River. The sliver of moon left in the sky provided scant illumination. It was 2:30 a.m., and even if someone had been watching the water from the shore at this hour, there was not a chance they would spot the trawler. Its navigation lights were shut down. The red and green sidelights had been turned off since midnight. The blinking LEDs atop the highest point on the masthead of the sturdy steel framework from which hung the wide otter trawls—cone-shaped nets to catch brown shrimp—were in the "off" position. Even the stern transom lights, which alerted a vessel coming up from behind, were dark.

Captain Clebert Lessoile was not worried. His wide face, thick beard, and perpetual good-humored smile projected utter confidence, a look which allowed him to charm his way out of countless difficult situations. Besides, he had made this run many times before. The members of his regular crew were fast asleep in their homes. By the time they got to the dock at Cocodrie at 5:30 a.m. for today's shrimping expedition out into the Gulf of Mexico, he'd be there to meet them.

The only ones on the *Creole Lady* besides the captain were two of Paolo Micelli's men, Smokey and Duffle Bag—Clebert didn't know their real names and didn't want to know them. He had picked the pair up a half hour ago on a spit of land in Timbalier Bay where they had anchored their aluminum bateau.

Steering to the designated spot miles out in the Gulf of Mexico, the three of them launched butterfly nets, held open by metal frames, and retrieved what the low-flying aircraft had dropped into the water—more than two dozen bobbing black barrels, each with its own radio beacon. Now the only thing left to do was to make the delivery.

The trawler proceeded despite the lack of illumination. Paolo Micelli had advanced big bucks so that Captain Clebert could outfit the *Creole Lady* with cutting-edge sonar, infrared sensors, black lights, night vision googles and binoculars, and a host of other items that made navigation in the dark easy.

The vessel's first turn was where the slow-moving Istrouma River dribbled out from the marsh. It moved laggardly up the twisting Istrouma until reaching a Y-shaped cut surrounding a low-lying island dotted with what was left of once-mighty cypress stands, their crowns dead from the increasingly brackish water that was poisoning the trees as the saltwater intruded. This was the entrance to Boueux Bayou.

If it had been after sunrise, no commercial fisherman, much less any weekend angler, would have taken a boat into this area, for they would have seen not only the numerous signs warning of "Shallow Bottom" and "Cypress Stumps," but also the decaying hulls of two vessels that had ignored the posted warnings and were tilted on their rotting sides in the watery pass.

The signs were invisible now, the black of the night sky meshing with the dark bayou's surface. The trees on the nearby banks blotted out the stars on the horizon. Clebert did not turn around, however. He simply cut the engines on the *Creole Lady* to just above idle and pushed a button on its navigation panel. He was careful not to touch the one that triggered the EPIRB, the Emergency Position-Indicating Radio Beacon that signaled distress and would bring the Coast Guard speeding to the rescue. Rather, he pushed the button on the equipment that Paolo Micelli had supplied him without charge. It sent a signal to Micelli's engineers stationed at the camp a mile upstream where Boueux Bayou had been closed off, beyond the Y-cut.

As soon as Micelli's men verified that it was the *Creole Lady*'s electronic beacon, they threw a switch. A series of telescoping poles topped with red lights rose up from the muddy water, marking a curving path through which the trawler could safely travel.

Once Clebert cleared the area, he pushed the button again. The red lights flickered off and disappeared below the water's surface. No vessel could safely navigate this area without guidance, for not only were there hidden cypress stumps that could tear the bottom out of even a shallow bateau, but there were also sharpened metal projectiles that Micelli's men had inserted just below the water's surface. These would impale and overturn any airboat that attempted to skim this part of the marsh unless they were retracted by the same electronic impulse that made the telescoping lights rise.

Clebert was in awe not only of the amount of money Micelli had spent on security to protect the camp and his other "investments," but also of Micelli's cleverness in buying up thousands of acres of swamp and marsh and designating it a "wildlife protection area." That made hunting without a permit in the area impossible. Micelli's arrangement with "friendly" officials allowed only those he trusted to get permits. The defined protection area also kept helicopters transporting roustabouts to offshore rigs and aircraft running reconnaissance on the receding Louisiana coastline from flying over the area, because the special designation he was granted also established a bird sanctuary to be left undisturbed by anything that might disrupt the flight patterns and nests of the eagles, geese, ducks, and hundreds of other species that made their homes in these parts.

Clebert expertly navigated through Boueux Bayou's increasingly narrow confines in the heart of Petit Rouge Parish until he came to a dock surrounded by buildings elevated thirty feet above water level and mounted on a forest of concrete stanchions designed to protect it from hurricane tidal surges.

As the trawler approached, klieg lights atop the buildings' roofs flared on. Micelli's camp was the only one on the bayou. He had bought out all the other owners and torn their cabins down. Captain Clebert shut down his engines, clipped the end of the thick cigar he withdrew from his breast pocket, and lit it while standing at the top of the ladder leading from the deck to the bridge. Everything was going according to plan. The packages would be unloaded, and the captain knew he'd be on his way again in less than twenty minutes. He did some quick mental calculations and, satisfied with the conclusion he reached, took a deep drag on his cigar, and exhaled.

At this rate, Clebert thought contentedly, he might even make it back to Cocodrie by 4 a.m. Heck, given what he was making on each run for Micelli, before year end he'd be able to pay off the bank that held the loan on the *Creole Lady*.

CHAPTER THIRTY-SIX

Kenny gunned the engine of the four-wheeler as he barreled down the path that led into the back woods of the Precept's 1,100-acre spread. The sun had not yet risen, but the stars were no longer visible as the sky turned a luminous orange, heralding, for Kenny, the last day before he achieved worldwide fame. And to think it was the result of his training here! Bubba Mauvais's family had owned this property in St. Bonaventure Parish for years, and when Bubba's parents died and Bubba came back from Idaho as the Precept, this was where he brought Kenny for his months of instruction.

But Kenny's training was over now. Tomorrow he would ascend to the heavens in glory.

Kenny knew the Precept would not object to his riding the squat vehicle. In fact, the Precept gave Kenny the keys weeks ago and told him he could use it whenever he wanted. Now was a great time for a final trek through the property. After all, last night the Precept said he had something very important to do and might not be back before Kenny's first bus run today. There was plenty of time to take a final spin before the Precept returned this afternoon and they finalized everything prior to tomorrow's historic mission.

As Kenny drove into the woods, he continued to marvel at how the Precept had the best of everything. The best plans. The best knowledge. The best equipment.

After all, didn't the Precept drive the KTM EXC500 Dual-Sport motorcycle that Kenny had helped him unstrap from the back of Boulette's bus on Sunday? Hadn't the Precept said it was the best dual-sport bike in the world? Lightweight orange frame. Maxxis Enduro tires for the toughest terrain. Engine tweaked personally by the Precept, who told Kenny it could hit 115 miles per hour flat out. One thing was for sure. The Precept never lied.

Hadn't he given Kenny permission to muck about in the four-wheeler in which he was now joy riding, a Polaris XP Sportsman with cool camo trim? Three throttle control. Gun scabbard. 2,500-pound winch, and heavy-duty brush guards front and rear.

Those brush guards were helpful as Kenny headed off the trail into the woods. The profusion of growth leaping up from the forest floor was so dense he could barely coax the Sportsman along faster than a creep. Kenny reluctantly returned to the main path, which was like a narrow riverbed twisting through a cavern of branches, bushes, trees, and climbing vines in multiple shades of green, brown, and gray.

Just as the Precept taught Kenny about the true word of the Lord and how salvation for the world will spring from disaster, the Precept also taught him how to identify much of the vegetation that sprang from the rich soil. Kenny was proud he knew that the spindly trees with their muscled bark marching along what used to be a fence line were ironwood. He spotted several multi-trunked yaupons whose leaves could be used to make tea. He noticed Chinese privet in dense patches, forming almost impenetrable hedges, sweet gum with their star-shaped leaves and furrowed bark, and fifteen-foot-high patches of thin water oak. Plus, leaves upon leaves upon leaves resembling animal paws, broken hearts, card-deck spades, and five-pointed stars ranging in size from magnolias as broad as Kenny's hand to creeping fig as tiny as his thumbnail.

Kenny was exuberant as he foolishly leaned back, accelerated, and made the front two wheels of the Sportsman rise into the air like a trick horse. But he reared up too far. Before Kenny could regain his balance, the four-wheeler overturned and fell to the ground, throwing him to one side. The vehicle narrowly missed crushing both of his legs.

Kenny was shaken up but not frightened. He knew it was God's will that he not be injured today. He was protected by the Lord because he was doing the Almighty's work. The Heavenly Father would not allow anything to keep him from tomorrow's mission.

Kenny dusted himself off and managed to get the four-wheeler upright again. He paused a minute, staring at the forest. The plants, as different as could be, were all a part of God's plan, just as the Precept said. Some plants were better than others. The massive live oak and the tall loblolly pines were the chieftans and all the rest were their servants just as, the Precept explained, Aryan Christian men are kings and everyone else must serve them. Either those who are inferior—blacks, Catholics, Jews, Hindus, Muslims, and anyone else who didn't worship a white Jesus—acknowledged the superiority of the Aryan race and converted to the only true religion, or they deserved to die.

And yet, Kenny thought, until he started driving Boulette's bus, he never really dealt with black people for extended periods. His momma's pastor got him a scholarship to a tiny, private, church school. Twenty kids per grade. All white. He never worked with blacks, and his interactions with them were blissfully few.

Still, Kenny thought, the kids he had been driving to and from school this week, pickaninnies all, weren't that bad. They respected him and said, "Good morning, Mr. Kenny," as he picked them up at their bus stops. He hadn't heard them make fun of his high voice, like the kids he grew up with did. And when he dropped them off at their homes in the afternoons, they often high-fived him as they skipped off the bus.

No! Kenny pushed these thoughts aside. Blacks were not the same as whites and never would be. They were not created in God's image. They were meant to be made an example of, for the sake of bringing about God's kingdom. The Precept said—and the Precept was always right—that black folks were "spiders dangling over the fires of hell who needed to be dropped into the licking flames." They were "specks of insignificance to be blown away in a wind of jellied fire." They were creatures with damaged souls, beyond redemption, not good for anything at any time, and could never be equal to Kenny. Or the Precept. Or the Supreme Kommander. Or any Aryan true believer.

Kenny re-mounted the four-wheeler and motored down a side trail, one he had not taken before. He checked his watch. There was still time to explore the area briefly before getting back to the barn and starting Boulette's bus on the morning run.

As he drove along, Kenny noticed a new path etched by the treads of a tractor or some other big vehicle. He followed it through the woods to a freshly cleared area, its brush and trees pushed to one side. Its center, the size of a baseball infield, consisted of packed dirt into which had been planted with small pine trees. They must have been there a while, thought Kenny, because poison ivy was already creeping around them.

How like the Precept, Kenny thought, to be planting trees, just as he was planting the seeds of change in the world, a world where only the true believers deserved to live. A world that would begin to take shape tomorrow. A world that would revere Kenny Arvenal who, like Christ, had to die so that the kingdom of heaven could come.

CHAPTER THIRTY-SEVEN

Starner helped Gervais Graunier move Debrun's body to the metal table in the mortuary section of the funeral home. They were both clothed in white PPE, personal protective equipment, and looked like spacemen in suits, with impermeable screens atop full bibbed hoods that completely encircled their heads and extended to their chests. The suits had a particulate respirator through which they breathed. Examining gloves covered their hands and forearms and were firmly attached to a head-to-toe, single-use gown comprised of three-layered waterproof fabric. Thigh-length plastic boots adorned their legs and feet.

"Can't be too careful, Starner. Make sure everything is sealed tight. Minute I cut him open, pathogens will be able to get to you. Airborne bacteria and infectious spores can penetrate your skin. They can access your body through your mucus glands and head straight into your bloodstream."

Gervais got out his tools. "Acie said he didn't need to do an autopsy because the cause of death was 'obvious.' That means I can go straight to the embalming. Contrary to what Acie assumed, Ed and Cooper want an open casket. The only thing I got to be careful about is preserving the face so I can restore it. Are you sure you're up to watching this?"

"I've seen worse," Starner assured him, "Don't worry about me. Cut away."

Starner was used to dealing with corpses from his time as a New Orleans police detective. He was the first officer on the scene after a gang victim had been hacked to death with a machete, his arms and legs severed from his body. He led the team that found a wife and her lover murdered by a vengeful husband, each with a shotgun blast to the face that obliterated their features. He was called to the edge of a drainage canal where a body lay decomposing, covered with ants and pecked at by buzzards. All this and more. He was inured to the sight of death . . . except that of Cheryl and Bucky.

Gervais drained the blood from Debrun's body using the sharp blades of a trocar to puncture the dead man's lungs and abdomen. The hose to which the device was connected vacuumed out the cadaver's gas and fluids. Gervais cut out the internal organs and stuffed them into a viscera bag.

The two of them flipped the body over, face down, exposing the back of Debrun's head. Using a scalpel, Gervais made a curving slice that ran from one ear to the other, across the top of the dead man's scalp, then down almost a foot along the back of his neck, and up again until the point of beginning. Next, Gervais grabbed the hair behind Debrun's ear and pulled the section he had separated off in one piece, a process that made a sound like a Velcro strap being undone. This exposed the top of Debrun's skull, his muscular neck and shoulders, and the top of his spine.

"Just as you thought, Starner," Gervais said, pointing to the three-inch ragged hole in Debrun's skull. "He didn't die because his car ran off the road. Not even a head-on auto accident could have produced these injuries. Someone must have hit him with a hammer or a piece of lead or something damn hard to cause damage like this. Note the cracks here and how they are spaced. This wasn't a single blow. Someone whacked at Debrun a number of times. But that didn't necessarily kill him. You know, the human body's a wondrous thing, and the skull is even more amazing. You can have all kinds of damage to your head and still survive. Why, in them olden times, back in the days of the pyramids, the Egyptians used to do brain surgery. Yep, can you believe it? I read about how they drilled holes in the head, removed portions of the skull, and the patient still survived. Don't know how they did that without anesthesia, but I read all about it in *Deep South Funeral Director* magazine. I once embalmed a guy who had a nail lodged in his head. He hadn't died of that. Fact is, he lived for six more hours, wide awake—in pain but wide awake—talking to the guys who found him. Cause of death? Internal bleeding from his fall off the scaffold, not the pop from the nail gun as it bounced off the roof and discharged as he fell. So, bad as this injury was for Debrun, it's not what killed him."

Gervais then pointed to a section of Debrun's exposed spine. "See up here. These are the C4 to C7 vertebrae. This is what did him in."

Gervais repositioned the surgical light to illuminate the area. The delicate bones in his neck were crushed, completely separated from the rest of his spine.

Starner started to walk out of the room.

"Getting a little nauseous? That's to be expected. You can go wait out there until I'm done."

"I could eat a po'boy while you did this, Gervais. No, I'm going to get my cell phone from the next room so that I can photograph this."

"Not a chance. Not if you ever want to use that phone again. No way to sterilize it afterward without ruining it. The dead not only have tales to tell, as you can see, but they also have diseases to spread."

"I'm taking photos and that's the end of it. Understand? Got to have proof that Debrun was murdered. Plain and simple."

Gervais put his tools down and walked in front of the door, blocking it. "Don't you go and endanger my business! Acic's death certificate says auto accident, and that's what I'll agree happened. He's the coroner. I can't handle a body without his certificate. No way I'm putting my livelihood in peril by undermining anything Acic does."

"But you see what I see. You cover this up and you could be an accessory to murder. Your funeral home license could be yanked."

"Don't pull rank on me, Starner. I like you, sure. But you're not a trained medical examiner. You aren't qualified to make a medical determination. You don't have any power over me. I was willing to let you in here early this morning before anyone else showed up. Glad to help you satisfy your curiosity about what happened. But that's as far as I go. I'm not going to get crosswise with either Acie—I got to stay on his good side to handle the bodies and conduct funerals—or with Knock, who controls both this parish and you. If you want to watch as I wire up Debrun's jaw so his mouth won't be open and sew his eyes and lips shut, that's okay with me. If you want to see how I pump him up with formaldehyde, glutaraldehyde, methanol, ethanol, phenol, and water, you're welcome to do so. Heck, if you want to observe me putting makeup on his face, lips, and ears so that he'll look as 'normal' as possible when I place him all peaceful-like in his coffin, artfully hiding the top of his head and what I've cut away, you can do that too. What you can't do, however, is take a photograph. Not without Acie's permission, which I'll make sure you won't get. So, once you walk out the door, you may as well go ahead and leave. My staff will be here shortly. Not only do we have to finish up Debrun, but we also have to start on Boulette. The family wants an open casket for her as well, and I've had to rush order an extra-large one."

CHAPTER THIRTY-EIGHT

"You gonna sleep the day away?" Maggie Mae asked, as she slipped into her tank top.

Bubba Mauvais turned on his side and pulled a pillow over his head.

Maggie Mae went to the refrigerator, got a tray of ice cubes, and dumped them over Bubba's bare crotch.

"Damn, girl!" Bubba yelped as he leaped out of bed.

"Get your ass in gear. You left Kenny alone all night? When I woke up, I was surprised to find you snoring away. Thought you would have been long gone. You were supposed to be out of here three hours ago. If Kenny screws up and anything goes wrong tomorrow because you weren't at the farm this morning . . . well, then childhood friend of his or not, the Supreme Kommander will off you in a minute."

Bubba smiled bemusedly, sidled up, pressed his naked body against hers, and started to pull down her panties.

Maggie Mae affectionately but firmly pushed him away. "Got no time for that now. Those two idiots, Phillip and Tommy, are supposed to be out on the highway waiting for Kenny to start his run. If I'm going to follow them without their knowing it, I've got to be there before they arrive. That was your idea, remember?"

Bubba flashed his I'm-such-a-charmer-you-can't-resist-me grin and started to draw her back onto the bed.

Maggie Mae pivoted on her left foot and swung her right leg out, forming a perfect ninety-degree arc from her torso, and swatted Bubba in the gut with her bare heel, knocking him down. "I'm serious, you fucker! You might be able to mess with the Supreme

Kommander all you want because of how far the two of you go back together, but I'm gonna be a Precept and then Kommander one day. Gonna show all those liberal, lesbian feminists, all those commie Jews—aren't all Jews commies in one way or another—all those humanists and Papists, all those blacks, browns, yellows, and shitty mulattos of every hue, that there is but one true way. I'm going to bring the wrath of the one perfect God of all Aryans down on the unrighteous, and no roll in the hay, as good as it might be, will stop me. So crawl back into bed if you want, but you gave me a command as Precept, and I intend to follow it to the letter."

CHAPTER THIRTY-NINE

Tommy tried to hide his contempt for Phillip as they sat in the Chevy Silverado. "There's enough coffee if you want some. My thermos keeps it hot for hours."

"I've tasted that shit you make. Like flavored water. You don't know crap about how to make good coffee." Phillip took a last swig of beer and tossed the can out the window, where it landed near the empty one he had thrown earlier.

"You're going to drive drunk? We have a job to do!"

"Shut your trap and mind your own business! Just sip away at what's in your fancy-ass flask. You, with your expensive shoes, expensive shirts, and your high-and-mighty attitude. You ain't no better than me, crap face! I'm doing my job by keeping you out of the shithouse. I don't know what you're good for, but it ain't for doing anything worthwhile. The Precept told me to drive you, so that's what I'm doing. Maggie Mae told us to follow the goddamn bus, so that's what I'm going to do. I don't need any advice from you! I've run the backroads in this parish since I was a kid on a moped. Then, here you come from out of state, like you're a big swinging dick. Bet your little pecker's 'bout the size of a two-inch nail."

Phillip reached under the seat and retrieved a third can of beer. "Keep your eye out for the bus when it rounds the corner on the way to its first pickup and call out if you see it. I'm going to take a leak."

As Phillip opened the driver's door, climbed down, and unzipped his pants, Tommy carefully sealed the top of his thermos. Phillip's insults didn't rile him because Phillip was nothing but a tool. A piece of clay that couldn't be molded into anything useful. Tommy knew, however, that he himself was useful beyond measure.

It was his Uncle Randy who suggested a gap year after high school, a place that didn't appreciate how special he really was. Tommy was convinced he should have been valedictorian, but no, that honor went to a stinking Jew with kinky hair and a nose too big for his face. He wasn't even named salutatorian. They gave that spot to a Paki girl with brown skin who spoke English with an accent! And Mr. Ling, the Chink principal, made a speech about how "diversity was the strength of Members Academy." Screw that! The strength of the Academy was not diversity but rather the money his uncle donated. The money that built the Randall Millguard gym.

Well, Tommy showed them. Shortly before graduation, Uncle Randy withdrew his support from the school after Tommy complained and after Mr. Ling wouldn't budge during a meeting Uncle Randy had with the principal at the Millguard factory.

Uncle Randy was the best. When Tommy was only nine, his father died, and it was Uncle Randy who invited Tommy to spend the summers with him, who took him to the meetings of the Friends of Alabaster, who introduced him to the true nature of mankind and the imperative that whites reign supreme. Once Tommy became a teenager, Uncle Randy gave him more and more responsibilities and let him work in the Millguard factory producing aluminum nitrate, granular urea, and a host of products. Uncle Randy not only financed the Alabaster Brigade, he also invented the explosive the Brigade knew as R-37.

Members Academy and all the kids in it could go to hell for all Tommy cared. The blonde in the ninth grade who wouldn't let him cop a feel. The redhead in the junior class who supported liberals, radicals, and flag-burners, believed in free love, and screwed almost the entire football team but who wouldn't give Tommy the time of day. The English teacher who disdained religion and urged students to adopt a "humanist" viewpoint. Those who couldn't see the absolute truth of every word in the Bible. Thanks to Uncle Randy, Tommy knew it was not only necessary, but also mandatory to conquer and subjugate all nonbelievers, all non-Aryans, and all those whose lives weren't worth saving.

The Alabaster Brigade believed in the Bible. It believed in Jesus, was devoted to elevating Aryans, was determined to extinguish nonbelievers, and was beholden to Uncle Randy. The Supreme Kommander couldn't operate without his infusion of cash.

Phillip was destined for oblivion. The Precept was an uneducated know-nothing who had been promoted as far up was he would ever go. Maggie Mae was a slut. Tommy was more than happy to deceive them all. They looked down on him? Well, let them. He didn't care one iota what they thought. He knew he was destined for worldwide fame despite his young age. The power didn't lie in the Alabaster Brigade. The power belonged to those who controlled the flow of cash that made its operations possible. The power resided with the Friends of Alabaster. Tommy was already a Friend, and soon Uncle Randy would place him on the board.

For Tommy, this Louisiana operation was merely an internship arranged for by Uncle Randy.

Alexander the Great was eighteen when he achieved success on the battlefield.

Tommy was just eighteen, and he would achieve success shortly. With Uncle Randy's backing, Tommy would become Supreme Kommander. It was only a matter of time.

CHAPTER FORTY

"You guys may be hot stuff down in New Orleans, but the marsh is where it's really at." Smokey Saucier, clad only in a pair of cut-off jeans, was sitting on the dock having breakfast, dangling his bare feet in Boueux Bayou, a can of beer in one hand and a link of boudin sausage in the other.

Frankie and Ribeye were lounging in rocking chairs, enjoying the dawning of what they hoped would be their final day in this godforsaken place, with its low-lying grasses, mysterious waterways, poisonous snakes, furtive alligators, and voracious mosquitoes.

"Beautiful, ain't it." Smokey said, more as a statement than a question.

Ribeye harrumphed. "What's beautiful is the fact that Paolo's got cable TV and internet service out here."

"You guys really know Mr. Micelli? I been working for him for almost a year but never seen him."

Stretching out his long legs, Frankie gave Smokey a not-so-gentle kick in the rump. "And you're never going to see him, unless he wants to see you. You better hope you're on his good side if he does."

Smokey was only nineteen but had heard enough stories about Paolo Micelli to believe he never wanted to be on his boss's bad side. He and Duffle Bag had this job thanks to Duffle Bag's cousin, who knew someone who worked for Micelli. A lot better than crewing on a shrimp trawler. Being a deckhand meant long hours, hands all cut up from handling nets and lines, and spotty pay if the catch wasn't good. Here, there was only one run every other week. Twenty-four hours straight work, but then you were free and could relax at this well-stocked camp, fish in the bayou, and pull in three times the pay of a deckhand. There were other perks of the job as well. Your first drink was free at any of Micelli's clubs, including Good Cheeks in St. Bonaventure Parish. The girls there put out for you at a moment's notice if they knew you were one of Micelli's boys. Smokey's favorite was Chastity, the stripper with the green streaks in her hair.

"What I don't get," Smokey said, his mouth stuffed with spicy boudin, "is why you guys prefer bein' in the middle of all that concrete in New Orleans. Duffle Bag's gone back with Captain Clebert to get the bateau, but I'm gonna spend a week here, with clean air, good livin', high flyin' birds and beaucoup wildlife, thanks to the boss making all this into a conservation preserve. Look over there. See that? It's an eagle. More than two dozen nestin' pair are out here. Captain Clebert said that, before the boss took over and did that 'designation' or whatever you call it, to make this an IBA—an Important Bird Area—you'd be lucky to see even one eagle a season."

Ribeye shrugged. "Hell, if I want to see an eagle, I'll go to the Audubon Zoo in New Orleans."

Smokey couldn't understand these two hulking guys always complaining about being outdoors. "How you gonna 'preciate a bird like an eagle all cooped up in a cage, no matter how fancy that cage is? Everythin' out here is all natural-like."

Ribeye wasn't impressed. "I suppose you know all about them birds. Like those things over to the right. Black with some flash of orange, it looks like, near their bills."

"Oh, I don't know those fancy Latin names or nothin'," Smokey replied, "but I sure know lots of birds just by the way they fly or how their silhouette looks against the sky. That thing that you're pointing to is a double-crested cormorant. Lots of folks confuse the anhinga with the cormorant, but if you know what to look for, it's real easy to tell them apart. They flap their wings the same way and both are black, but the anhinga's got a head almost as small as its neck. When it's in the air, it looks like a sharp flying pencil. Man, this marsh is full of neat stuff. Great blue herons, with gray necks and powder-blue bodies. Eagle osprey, with proud, white chests and a black eye stripe down the side of their faces, like an Indian puttin' on war paint in an old western. Northern Parula, lookin' like it dipped its beak in yellow paint and let the liquid drip down its breast. Fact is, that crazy bird likes to hang upside down in the moss droopin' from the cypress and oak trees. Now, ain't that somethin'?"

"You're full of crap," said Ribeye, bounding from his chair and heading back up the wooden stairs to the air-conditioned camp positioned on pilings thirty feet above the water level. "If I want a travelogue, I'll watch National Geographic, and I fucking hate that channel!"

Smokey took another swig from his can of beer. "He got no 'preciation for nature, do he?"

Frankie didn't respond. Smokey was just a stupid kid, a show-off who didn't have a clue what he and Ribeye really did for Micelli. Smokey thought their sole task was to pick up "product" that had been brought in from offshore and deliver it to New Orleans. He had no idea that they were Micelli's enforcers. If Smokey hadn't been Micelli's employee . . . well, Smokey would have been lucky to have only been hospitalized in traction after Ribeye finished with him.

Frankie looked at his watch. He and Ribeye had to make the run to New Orleans in an hour. Easy. Hand over the "product" at a garage Micelli owned near the Achilles Street Projects and then get Friday and the rest of the weekend off.

Frankie swatted at a mosquito that landed on his muscular forearm. He reached down for the can of bug spray under his rocking chair.

The sooner he and Ribeye got the hell out of here and were back in New Orleans, the better.

CHAPTER FORTY-ONE

Kenny left the Precept's farm in the bus and made a slow, wide turn onto the highway leading out of St. Bonaventure Parish. Twenty minutes to the first pickup in Petit Rouge Parish. Eleven stops in Petit Rouge. Drop the kids off at St. Bonaventure Elementary School. Back by 10:30 so that the Precept could finish wiring the explosives to the detonator.

Kenny hoped there'd be enough time to take another spin on the four-wheeler. He dreamed about the fame that would soon be his. I'm more than ready, he thought. I'm primed. I'll be top dog. By tomorrow night, my name will be splashed across the globe. My face will be on every newscast from California to New York, from Canada to all them foreign countries where they don't speak no English. I'll go viral. Be envied and respected. More than that, I'll be remembered. And while I'm staring down from heaven, on a throne of glory, I'll be able to see everyone talking about my grand deed for years and years to come. Immortality on heaven and earth, just as the Precept predicted.

Kenny beamed. Nothing could be better. Absolutely nothing.

His fingers tapped with excitement against the steering wheel. Absorbed by his fantasies, he failed to realize that he had crossed into Petit Rouge Parish driving slightly over its reduced speed limit.

Kenny may not have noticed, but Judson Jorée sure did and caught the infraction on his radar gun.

CHAPTER FORTY-TWO

Kenny's reverie was disturbed by the sound of a siren.

He looked in his rearview mirror. Shit! A cop car. But that siren couldn't be for him. Who would stop a school bus?

Kenny slowed to let the policeman pass.

But the cop didn't speed up and charge ahead. The cruiser with the flashing lights pulled alongside the bus and the uniformed deputy, whom Kenny immediately recognized, signaled him to pull off onto Picox Lane just ahead, an unpaved road that intersected the rural highway.

Kenny turned right as instructed, drove ten yards, and waited patiently in the bus. He knew what to do. The Precept had drilled it into him. If a cop stops you, don't get out. Wait for instructions. Always be polite. Don't ever make a swift move.

Kenny certainly intended to do all these things now that Judson Jorée had a badge. Judson, who was a couple of years ahead of Kenny in high school, parked directly behind the bus, blocking Kenny in. Kenny couldn't see Judson's eyes, which were hidden behind reflective sunglasses, but he couldn't help but notice the self-important sneer Judson always had when he was about to bully someone.

"What the hell are you doing driving a bus, Kenny?"

Kenny almost giggled. Judson would find out tomorrow that Kenny was piloting a vehicle of mass destruction. He calmed himself down enough to respond, "New job, Judson. I'm a substitute."

Judson laughed. "You're a poor substitute for anything, you freaking son-of-a-bitch, and your voice is still up there in the stratosphere. What happened, Mickey Mouse? Your balls never dropped? Or maybe you never had any."

Kenny's face reddened with indignation. Judson was spouting the same old taunts. He hadn't changed, and Kenny was in no position to argue with him, not that Kenny had ever won an argument with Judson when they were in school. Kenny kept reminding himself that, by tomorrow afternoon, Judson would discover just how important Kenny was.

It would do no good to interrupt Judson while he was mouthing off. A ticket? That was nothing but a lousy piece of paper destined for the trash.

Seeing Kenny's flushed face and getting great pleasure from lording it over the little pipsqueak, Judson held up his citation book with a flourish. "You were going six miles over the speed limit, you 'substitute.' So, I'm going to 'substitute' you a big fine. Give me your driver's license and the bus registration."

Kenny pulled the registration papers from the panel below the dashboard, handed them to Judson, reached in his back pocket, and blanched. He didn't have his wallet! He must have left the farm without it!

Judson studied the registration materials. "So, you're driving Boulette's bus? How did you get it?"

Unnerved by having forgotten his wallet, Kenny didn't know how to answer. "I got it . . . well, you know, she got it for me because I had to substitute."

"You're a fucking liar! Boulette's dead. She sure didn't resurrect herself to lend it to you."

Kenny was completely confused. He didn't know anything about Boulette's passing. The Precept told him she was unable to drive, not that she was dead.

"Where's your driver's license, Kenny? Hand it over."

Kenny's face fell. What was he going to do now?

Seeing Kenny's expression, Judson made no attempt to conceal his satisfaction at the situation. "Speeding in a bus that you can't explain how you got and doing it without a driver's license. Do you even have a CDL with a passenger and school bus endorsement?"

Kenny had a Commercial Driver's License with the proper tags. The Precept arranged for that. But it was also in his wallet back at the farm.

"Get out, Kenny. You can't drive that thing without a license. I'm arresting you, confiscating the bus, and running you in. I'll call Cooper at the St. Bonaventure School Board office and tell him to get another driver, a real one, and another bus. Boy, I always knew you were a fuck-up. What are you waiting for? Get out! Now!"

Kenny was in full-fledged panic mode. He couldn't let the bus be taken away. Not when he was so close to glory. How would he explain it to the Precept? What if Judson found the explosives?

"But the kids gotta be picked up . . ." he protested, not daring to move from his seat.

"Right," Judson smirked. "But they ain't gonna be picked up by the likes of you. Last thing they or their parents would want is an unlicensed 'substitute' driving their little black bundles of joy. Now, shut your engine down, toss me your keys, and GET OUT OF THAT BUS!"

Kenny was completely flustered. How would the Precept handle this situation?

"The keys. Now!"

Kenny froze.

Judson pulled out his Beretta. "I'm not fooling with you, Kenny. This isn't some joke. Turn that engine off immediately. Keys! Understand?"

Kenny refused to leave the bus. He would not abandon his one chance at immortality. Summoning up all his courage, his high-pitched voice cracking with the tension, Kenny responded, "I can't do that Judson. Just can't. Let me go on my way, will you? We can sort all this out next week. Okay?"

"Who the fuck do you think you are?" Judson grabbed his pistol with both hands and assumed a firing stance, pointing his gun at Kenny's head. "If you don't open that door and step out this instant, I'm going to book you for resisting arrest. I'll shoot if I have to. Knock will back me up, and ol' Judge Fauchère won't even have to impanel a jury, 'cause there won't be any charges filed."

Kenny grew wide-eyed. His heart pounded so loudly he was sure Judson could hear it.

"I'm not kidding," Judson said, firing a warning shot in the air.

Phillip and Tommy were watching the entire encounter from their truck, which was parked on the side of the road near the entrance to Picox Lane. When the sheriff's deputy fired his gun, Phillip slammed his foot on the accelerator and headed straight for Judson.

CHAPTER FORTY-THREE

Hearing the roar of a big engine and the screeching of wheels behind him, Judson turned and saw a Chevy Silverado fishtailing off the highway and racing at full speed down the dirt lane where he stood by the driver's side of the bus, Beretta in hand.

Realizing that the truck was not going to slow down and would hit him if he didn't move, Judson ran and jumped over the deep drainage ditch on the left side of the road. He was livid. He'd show those fools who was in charge here. He'd issue several costly tickets before seven in the morning. Starner had never done that!

Once the Silverado passed the bus, it couldn't get far. Picox Lane dead-ended a mile ahead. The truck had no way out. Judson knew what he had to do. He would arrest Kenny, handcuff and lock him in the back of his patrol car, move the bus so it blocked the Silverado's exit from Picox Lane back to the highway, and deal with the reckless truck driver. Let's see, Judson thought. Speeding. Endangering a law enforcement officer. Interfering with a lawful arrest. The charges and dollars would add up fast.

But instead of continuing down the road, the driver of the Silverado hit his brakes as he approached the sheriff's deputy. Judson figured it was because the driver had seen the flashing lights on his cruiser and a uniformed deputy brandishing a gun. But the truck was advancing too quickly to stop in time. It clipped the rear of Judson's car, crumpling the side of the cruiser's trunk and slamming its hood into the wide bumper on the rear of the school bus. Though the bus jerked forward, it did not sustain any damage. The collision, however, destroyed the cruiser's grill and knocked out a headlight.

Kenny's hands remained on the bus's steering wheel, his knuckles white. The engine was still running. Even though the Prefect had told him that the explosives could only be set off only by a specific detonation device, Kenny was fearful that the accident might start some sort of chain reaction in the concealed packages.

Luckily, the bump from the police cruiser merely moved the bus a few inches forward. Nothing exploded.

Kenny was relieved, but he didn't dare leave his seat. He was sure the Prefect wouldn't have wanted him to get out. So Kenny waited, sweat pouring down his brow, his armpits moist. He didn't recognize the truck that hit the sheriff's vehicle. He didn't know the truck's driver or the man in the passenger seat.

In the meantime, Judson remained on the opposite side of the drainage ditch and pointed his Beretta at the Silverado. "Get out!" he yelled at the driver, who had a nose that was askew and hair that was razored short.

Judson almost didn't care that his official car, with its sirens, flashers, special souped-up engine, and radar gear, had been damaged. Insurance would cover it. He consoled himself with the thought that, once he arrested both Kenny and the driver of the Silverado, Judge Franklin Fauchère would lock up both of the sons-of-bitches for sure.

The driver of the truck didn't budge, but his passenger, a dark-haired guy, younger than Judson, stepped out, saying to the driver, "Let me handle this. There's an easy way to deal with this dilemma."

Dressed in gray slacks and a white shirt, the kid smiled and held up an envelope. "Officer, I am terribly sorry for any inconvenience that my companion might have caused. I'm sure you can understand his desire to try out the acceleration of his new vehicle on what we assumed was an abandoned route. We did, of course, notice the "dead end" sign at the entrance and we figured . . . well, as I said, I'm sure you can understand. I have the proper insurance papers right here along with—well, isn't that curious—a thousand dollars in one hundred dollar bills. I imagine you'll want to examine all of this."

"Trying to bribe an officer of the . . ." Judson yelled indignantly, not because he was offended or because he was above taking a bribe, but because Kenny was there and he wanted Kenny to think nothing could be done to get him out of the fix he was in, as if Kenny would have any money with which to bribe Judson. Kenny never had a cent to his name throughout high school, and driving a bus as a "substitute" meant that Kenny was hardly rolling in dough now, but if the little wimp, a patsy and a nobody, had a bundle to offer, Judson wouldn't have taken it from him. He wasn't about to be indebted to squeaky-voiced Kenny or give the lunkhead anything to hold over him in the future.

It was just then that Judson caught a glimpse of a beat-up Nissan turning onto Picox Lane.

Judson gripped his pistol in both hands and maintained a shooting stance while trying to absorb the scene. The dark-haired kid was standing in the center of the dirt road, still clasping the envelope. The driver of the truck sat behind the wheel and had a curious expression on his face. Kenny remained motionless in the bus but had not turned off the engine. And suddenly a wreck of a Nissan was pulling up and parking behind the Silverado. A good-looking gal in a tight tank top and ripped jeans got out.

Tommy appeared to be both surprised and disturbed when he saw Imperial Seven. "I've got this under control," he told her. "It'll take just a few minutes to get this sorted out. Then Kenny can be on his way."

She was not happy. "You were supposed to call me first!"

Judson was puzzled. These three people all knew each other, and they also knew Kenny?

If Judson was confused, Kenny was downright flabbergasted. He had never seen any of these folks before, but they knew who he was? By name? How?

Judson kept his Beretta pointed at the kid and said forcefully, "Everyone stay where you are!"

But the kid holding the envelope didn't obey Judson's instructions. Instead, he sauntered over to the side of the road until they were separated by only the four-foot-wide drainage ditch. "Officer, this all can be resolved, I am sure."

Something strange was definitely going on, and Judson was determined to get to the bottom of it. He would show Starner, Ed, and even Knock that he was not someone to be trifled with. The arrests he was about to make would burnish his résumé. He was as good as out of this piddling little parish and on his way up the ladder to a great job in New Orleans. Of course, if the gal in the tank top wanted to show him a little "courtesy," he might accommodate her, but as for the rest, he was going to run them all in, jammed in the back of his now-damaged cruiser.

"Nothing," Judson said firmly, growling in I'm-an-officer-of-the-law-and-you-better-not-mess-with-me tone, "is going to be resolved! Understand? I'm arresting the lot of you."

Judson pointed his semi-automatic directly at the white-shirted kid. "You! Put the envelope down on the ground and go back to your vehicle."

He swung his pistol in the direction of the driver of the Chevy Silverado. "You! Get out and put your hands on the hood where I can see them."

The woman in the tank top started to say something, but Judson interrupted her before she could speak. "You, pretty lady, stay right where you are. I'm a duly deputized officer of the law and I'm in charge!"

No one followed Judson's instructions.

The kid stood his ground and held out the envelope. "You're sure you don't want to examine this? If its contents are not to your complete satisfaction, I'm certain we can find some additional—shall we call them 'items'—to alleviate your concerns."

"DON'T ANY OF YOU UNDERSTAND WHAT I'M SAYING?" Judson screamed. He was astonished. No one had ever disobeyed him. Until now, everyone he stopped had been cowed by his uniform and the reputation of the sheriff's office in Petit Rouge Parish. Judson relished the fear he always saw in the eyes of those he stopped for traffic violations and the docile manner in which they addressed him, whether they were teenagers with new drivers' licenses or the age of his parents, or even of his grandparents. "Yes officer," they'd say with respect. But not this group. These folks were different. Except for Kenny, no one was showing any deference to him, much less fear.

"I MEAN IT!" Judson fired, aiming twenty feet above the kid's head just to scare him and show him who's boss. But the fellow didn't run. Didn't even flinch or duck. He just smiled and continued to wave the envelope.

In the truck, however, Phillip was prepared. The Precept had ordered him to protect Tommy. As much as he disliked Tommy, Phillip was not about to disappoint the Precept.

While the deputy's attention was directed toward Tommy and Maggie Mae, Phillip pulled his hunting rifle down from the rack behind the driver's seat. Once the deputy fired his pistol, it was clear to Phillip that Tommy wasn't safe and dangling the Precept's cash in front of the cop wasn't going to fix anything. He'd have to take out that fucking cop. The Precept's whole plan rested on Kenny driving the bus to New Orleans tomorrow, and it was Phillip's job to make sure Kenny accomplished his task.

Phillip raised his six-and-a-half pound Mossberg Patriot with its lightning bolt action trigger, stuck the barrel out the truck window, adjusted the telescopic scope, calmly took aim at the deputy, and let loose a .308 caliber Winchester cartridge capable of taking down big game animals at three hundred yards.

The powerful bullet tore through Judson's abdomen, knocking him off his feet.

Judson immediately sensed something was terribly wrong, but he couldn't figure out what it was. He wasn't in pain. Not yet. He was in shock. His stomach felt strange, as if a great weight was resting on it. He lifted his head off the ground and looked at his torso, noting with curious dispassion that a red stain was spreading across his shirt as his guts spilled out onto the ground and thinking angrily that no one should be able to do this to him.

The dirt bloody red beneath him, Judson turned and raised his pistol. He had fourteen rounds left in the magazine of his Beretta, and he intended to use them all.

He started firing. At the kid on the road holding the envelope. At the guy in the Silverado with the rifle. Judson squeezed off round after round, wondering why his arm was shaking so much.

Phillip aimed at the deputy. The second shot hit the officer in the forehead. A spurt of gray matter spewed from the back of his skull.

Maggie Mae ran over to the Phillip. "Put that down! What the shit have you done?" Then she looked over at Tommy, who lay face down in the dirt in a pool of blood. He had been killed by a shot from the deputy's handgun.

She'd have to contact Bubba right away. He'd be royally pissed. He'd blame her, not Phillip. Or maybe he'd blame them both. It didn't matter. Bubba would have to tell the Supreme Kommander. And there'd be hell to pay for all of them.

Meanwhile, Kenny, still sitting in the bus, was fascinated by what just transpired. At last, he was party to a real battle. He wasn't disturbed seeing the guy with the envelope, someone even younger than himself, get shot. And Judson getting his comeuppance? That bully deserved to die in pain. For years Kenny had dreamed of doing the deed himself.

Kenny's worry and panic immediately subsided. His fear turned into excitement. He was ecstatic. Today, he witnessed the deaths of two people. Tomorrow, he'd cause the deaths of thousands.

CHAPTER FORTY-FOUR

tarner went right to Florene's café from Graunier's Funeral Home. Watching Gervais work on Debrun's corpse didn't affect his appetite one bit. The only thing bothering him was Gervais's refusal to let him take photographs of Debrun's severed spinal cord.

Blows to the skull. Blows to the neck. Someone wanted to make sure Debrun was dead, but why take his car and run it into the swamp with Gertie in the back seat? If Starner hadn't found the car, Debrun's absence would have been listed as another missing person, along with Boyo. Were those Debrun's blood stains that Starner found at the wrecking yard? If so, why would Boyo kill Debrun? And why kill Gertie?

None of it made sense, and all of it was meant things were happening in the parish that Knock would want to be kept quiet.

Starner's cell phone rang. It was Irénée. She told him Rod had reported an accident that needed investigation. He was already on the scene and wanted Judson to come write a ticket, but she couldn't raise him so she was asking Starner to please go out to where Vizeau Road intersected with Route 2034 right outside of Knock's redline and handle it.

Getting into his truck, Starner sped off, turning on his siren and flashing blue lights. He was rounding the curve that cut through the piney woods just south of town when he saw a school bus creeping ahead. Couldn't have been going more than 20 miles an hour. Starner knew that there were no homes on this stretch where a bus might stop to pick up students. Something wasn't right.

He turned on his siren and pulled even with the bus.

Skinny Kenny Arvenal was driving. That didn't surprise him. Cooper had said that Kenny was Boulette's substitute. But what was strange was the look of panic on Kenny's face.

CHAPTER FORTY-FIVE

Kenny almost fainted when he heard the siren. Stopped by cops twice in one day! He looked down at the speedometer. No question about it. He was driving well below the speed limit. What was going on?

Steering the bus onto the narrow shoulder of the road, Kenny thought that if he had a weapon, he'd shoot this second deputy and then the Precept would have something else to praise him for. It would add to the legend that everyone would soon tell, the story of the glory of a martyr who was brave . . . and fearless . . . and a wiz at offing people, not only in groups but also one at a time. A soldier of the Lord who let nothing stand in his way. Potential Aspirants would pin Kenny's picture above their beds—the one of him standing proud, ammunition belts crisscrossing his chest, AK-47 held firmly in his hand—a screen capture from the video he had made back on Sunday with the Precept. They would look at it every night before they went to sleep, and they would see it when they awoke. He would be their inspiration, although he knew that none of them would ever achieve the heights he had scaled.

Kenny wished that the woman with the great bod—the one who introduced herself as Imperial Seven—had let him have one of the guns from the Silverado driven by the guy with the odd nose and cool swastika tattoo who shot Judson. But no! Imperial Seven told Kenny his mission was to pick up all them pickaninny kids for school and that, as soon as she "took care of the scene"—whatever that meant—she'd catch up with him and make sure everything was all right. Where was she?

Kenny waited for the officer to approach. It was Starner Gautreaux. Everyone in the parish knew the deputy, a middle-aged grump who would never amount to a hill of beans, who would never go down in history like Kenny was about to do tomorrow.

Kenny smiled to himself, for he knew he would never get as old as that deputy. Hell, Kenny thought, he must be near fifty. Kenny knew he would always be young. He would be immortal. The world would remember him just the way he looked in the video, youthful and confident.

Kenny wondered why the deputy did not get out of his vehicle, like Judson did. The cop didn't demand that Kenny throw down his driver's license, nor did he ask to see any insurance papers.

All the deputy did was roll down the passenger window of his truck and call out in that loud, policeman-y tone of voice used to giving commands that would be followed: "You're gonna cause an accident if you keep driving as slowly as that, Kenny. There are kids waiting to be picked up for school. You planning on making them late? Get a move on!"

Kenny saluted. He figured that was what you were supposed to do to any deputy, except to Judson, of course.

Kenny relaxed. He didn't need Imperial Seven. He didn't need anyone. He was invincible.

CHAPTER FORTY-SIX

"That'll do it, don't you think?" Phillip stood back and admired his handiwork. He wiped the rifle clean and put it in Tommy's hands, making sure that Tommy's index finger was on the trigger. "Anyone looking into this will think that the cop shot Tommy and Tommy shot back. Took each other out. No one will be the wiser. Left each of them right where they dropped. I've moved the deputy's cruiser. Drove it into a live oak. It'll look like he lost control and smashed into a tree. From the highway, you can't see it or the bodies. Perfect, wouldn't you say? And look," Phillip said, holding up the bloodstained, cash-filled envelope, "we still got the dough."

"You're so full of shit." Maggie Mae was pacing back and forth in front of her Nissan. "I've talked to the Prefect. You're going to catch hell from the Supreme Kommander. You and Tommy couldn't carry out the easiest tasks around. Get the trucker? You let Saxon Fourteen kill him and then, making matters worse, you blew the truck up and, after it had been towed away, went and stole what was left of it so that no one would find the explosive residue. For 'good measure,' you killed the wrecking yard guy. God, you two are cretins! Couldn't you just follow Kenny as instructed? Couldn't you have just called me when the cop pulled him over? No! You had to get involved in a gun battle. Now you're responsible for Tommy's death. Phillip! It was your responsibility to keep Tommy safe, and you fucked that up, too. Is there anything you touch that doesn't turn to crap?"

Maggie Mae was shocked when Phillip did not show even the slightest hint of remorse. Instead, he was angry. At her!

He snarled, "You little bitch! I don't give a toad's turd if you 'outrank' me in the Brigade. I did exactly the right thing at the right time, every time. Saxon Fourteen shot the trucker. I figured out a way to cover that up. As for the wrecker guy? He pulled a gun on us. I did us all a favor by taking him out. And Kenny? Hell, I protected Kenny. It looked like that cop was about to arrest him, and I was not about to let that happen. Because I acted promptly, the Supreme Kommander's plan is intact. Because of what I did—me, not you—Kenny is on his way to pick up those school kids, and he'll be on time to boot. You want to talk about Tommy's death? That was his own fault, trying to bribe a cop holding a pistol on him. Once the cop fired his gun in Tommy's direction, what did you expect me to do? Stand by and let the pig continue to shoot at him, and maybe at both of us too? No, everything I did was right. There ain't no way you're gonna put the blame on me!"

Maggie Mae withdrew the 9mm Luger pistol that had been tucked into her waistband at the small of her back and pointed it at Phillip. The gun was compact. Though its barrel was less than three and-a-half inches long, it could kill at this distance. "If you ever, and I mean ever, back talk me again, Imperial Ten, I'll shoot your eyes out, cut your balls off, and make you pray for death!"

Phillip stood his ground. "Go ahead. Shoot. What will that get you? The Supreme Kommander needs all hands on deck tomorrow. How are you gonna explain to Bubba that you took out the one person solely responsible for making sure Kenny drives the bus to and from school today and into glory tomorrow? Remember, I knew Bubba before he became the Precept, way before you knew him and fucked whoever you had to fuck to get where you are in the Brigade today. Bubba's sure to side with me."

Maggie Mae was furious. "You're questioning my authority? I outrank you! I give the instructions, not you! How dare you to presume to know what the Precept will or won't do? Get in your truck and continue following Kenny. Call me on one of the burner phones if something happens—call, but don't do anything else.

Destroy that phone immediately after we talk. Do exactly what I tell you to do. Got it?"

Phillip put his hands in mock surrender. "Whatever you say, Maggie Mae . . . or rather," he said with a jeer, "your most esteemed excellency, Imperial Seven."

Phillip turned his back to her and climbed into the truck. What could she do to him? Nothing. He had known Bubba for years. They met at a biker's revival at the NightHawk Church, whose motto was "We pray until the Son rises." A congregation of tattoos and testimony. Of piercings and prayers. Of Jesus and jeans. Of leather chap-clad Christians who met in an old hanger. No benches. No chairs. Worshippers rode their bikes in and sat on them during services. When it was time to make a joyful noise, everybody would rev up their engines.

Phillip was welcomed into the group the first time he drove to a NightHawk Church revival in his customized Harley with its 17-inch high-ride handlebars and chrome street-cannon mufflers. It was Bubba who initially befriended him. It was Bubba who introduced him around. It was Bubba who showed him the way, the true way to salvation.

Bubba was better than anyone. Better at coming up with quotations from the Bible reinforcing what Phillip had always felt, that the white race was superior and meant to control the Earth. Better with his fists. And better on his bike. Bubba's off-roader orange KTM EXC500 Dual-Sport couldn't always outpace the big Harleys, but he was fearless and cunning, cutting off riders and forcing them to give way to avoid crashing.

Bubba was the reason Phillip joined the Alabaster Brigade. Once in the organization, Phillip didn't need the NightHawk Church anymore. The Alabaster Brigade wrapped God into the truth of Aryan superiority. As Bubba liked to say, "History vindicates the supremacy of white Aryans."

"Who created the Renaissance?" he'd ask. Why, white Aryans, of course.

"Who founded our country?" White Aryans.

"Who will lead this degenerate society out of the morass of liberalism, communism, socialism, humanism, and all the other 'isms' that corrupt and debase the supremacy of the superior race?" White Aryans.

Those white Aryans were all men. Not cunts, like Maggie Mae.

Phillip was confident that Bubba would back him up.

CHAPTER FORTY-SEVEN

Abigayle was so excited she was hopping in ever-increasing circles at the bus stop, first clockwise, then counterclockwise. "Watch out," Truvi called to her indulgently, interrupting the conversation she was having with two other mothers who were standing there with their kids. "Don't get too near the road. The bus'll be here any minute."

Abigayle ran back to be by Truvi's side. "You have what I made, don't you, Momma? I want to give it to Mr. Kenny as soon as he gets here."

"It's in my hand, darlin'," Truvi responded, holding Abigayle's art project. "He'll just love it. Why, with that green pipe cleaner stem, the cardboard leaves you designed, the yellow tissue-paper petals, and the little seeds in the center you made out of rice that you dipped in food coloring and then glued down, it looks just like the real thing. Like you could plant it in our front yard and a beautiful sunflower would grow!"

"Oh, Momma," Abigayle giggled. "Hold on to it until the bus comes, okay?" But Abigayle didn't wait for an answer. She ran back to join the other kids who were milling about on the corner.

Truvi's mind was only half on what the other mothers were saying. They were talking about helping to organize a potluck dinner the P.T.A. was putting on for the end of school. Truvi was running through all the things she had to do between this morning and tomorrow morning. Art was so busy that she hadn't seen him again last night. He got home after she went to bed and left before she woke up. The only reason she knew he had been there at all was the note he left on the kitchen table telling her that he slept on the sofa so as not to disturb her because he got in so late.

Her supervisor at Ganderson's had given her tomorrow off so she could be a chaperone, but she had to get the proper form filled out today at work. Friday was usually a busy day at the store, and she wasn't about to risk losing her job by not following Ganderson's rules.

The school was providing snacks and bag lunches, but Truvi wanted to put some extra treats together, not only for all the kids but also for the adults who were going along. That was tonight's task. Homemade chocolate chip cookies and brownies for at least sixty kids. All three classes of second graders would be taking the field trip.

Abigayle's second uniform needed to be ironed at some point today. There wouldn't be time tomorrow, not with Abigayle so hyped up. Truvi would be lucky if her daughter slept past 5 a.m. tomorrow morning. She'd probably come running into the master bedroom, jump into the bed, and urge her momma to get dressed for the big event. No, Truvi couldn't skip the ironing. She wanted her daughter to look her best when the second graders from St. Bonaventure Elementary performed at the Unity Festival. For weeks the kids had been practicing their song, "Love is in Everybody's Heart," and their performance on Unity Festival Stage Five in the heart of the French Quarter was bound to be the high point of their school year.

The St. Bonaventure school bus driven by Kenny slowly rounded the corner and the kids lined up as it drew near. Abigayle ran back and grabbed the paper and cardboard sunflower from her mother. "I just know," Abigayle said, "that Mr. Kenny is going to put this next to him in that little holder he has by his seat. A sunflower reminds me of love. Like in the song we're going to sing. 'Love is in Everybody's Heart.' Won't this put extra special love into Mr. Kenny's heart?"

Truvi kissed her daughter on the forehead. "Of course, sweetheart. It'll make Mr. Kenny the happiest man in the world. If he ever has any worries, he'll forget them the minute you hand him what you made."

CHAPTER FORTY-EIGHT

Starner parked in the center of the street and left his blue strobes flashing. It would take a while to clear out the scene and reopen the intersection of Route 2034 and Vizeau Road.

Rod was already in the deep ditch hooking up a chain to the front axle of a Cadillac Escalade. Its rear bumper was jammed low in the mud against the far side of the ditch while the front tires rose up the steep incline nearest to the road at a thirty-degree angle. The front grill was badly dented, and a dead deer rested against the smashed windshield. On the side of Route 2034, an ancient blue pickup truck listed to one side, its right-front fender crumpled and the tire underneath tilting at an odd angle.

Standing next to the truck were three men Starner recognized immediately. Vernelle, Rod's cousin who worked for the John Deere dealership in St. Bonaventure, and a very unhappy looking Frankie and Ribeye covered in white dust.

"I don't want no trouble, Deputy Starner," said Vernelle, holding a paper sack in his hand. "Rod called you because he thought I would need a report to get insurance coverage, but these nice men have settled up with me just fine. I'm satisfied. No need for you to do anything on my account."

Frankie, a foot-and-a-half taller than Vernelle, walked over and leaned against the damaged truck, dusting off the white powder that caked his clothes. "Looks like we solve all your problems, don't it, Deputy. Didn't need you in St. Bonaventure yesterday, and don't need you here now. We've made an arrangement with this gentleman, and as soon as the wrecker pulls our SUV out of the ditch, we'll be on our way. We'll get the windshield fixed later. Either of you want that two-point buck? Fresh venison. Jumped out of the woods right in front of us. Damn thing got clipped by the bumper, flew up on the hood, and landed smack dab where you see it. Ribeye swerved to try to avoid the deer, but the buck got us, and we got Vernelle's truck. Flipped us around and we slid backward into the ditch. Well, can't be helped." He continued flicking away the powder that clung to his clothes. "Fucking airbags went off too, with white shit that sticks to everything. They ain't cheap to replace, but that's none of your concern."

Starner pulled Vernelle aside. "You sure you don't want me to write up a report? If what they've paid you won't cover the damage, you'll come up short because insurance sure won't cover expenses without an accident report."

Vernelle opened the paper bag so Starner could look inside. It was stuffed with one hundred dollar bills. "I'm not worried 'bout that," he chuckled. "They gave me enough to buy two trucks. New ones! I ain't complaining one bit. Rod told me that once he gets their SUV out of the ditch, he'll load my truck up and drop me off at the new car dealership as soon as he leaves my wreck at the yard. My missus is sure gonna be surprised when I drive up in new wheels today!"

Ribeye was now standing on the edge of the road yelling at Rod. "Get a move on! We don't have all day! Just pull it out of the ditch so we can get going. We'll pay you in cash whatever the cost."

At first, Starner was only surprised to see Ribeye and Frankie at the scene, but now he was deeply suspicious. Why were they paying off Vernelle with such an exorbitant amount? Why were they so anxious to leave in their damaged SUV?

Starner strolled to the shoulder of the road and stood next to Ribeye as they watched Rod climb out of the ditch and attach the chain to the winch. Frankie joined them, standing close to Starner, hoping to intimidate the officer with his size.

"You're about a hundred yards away from the Red Zone, Deputy," Frankie growled. "We got this under control. You can leave now."

Starner took two steps back, out of arm's reach of Frankie and Ribeye. "I'll leave when I'm good and ready. In the meantime, let's see if that thing is drivable once Rod hauls it up on the road."

The winch whined as the chain strained to extricate the Escalade from the ditch. As the hood came into a view, there was a loud popping sound.

"Shit!" Ribeye, said.

The SUV's liftgate had popped open. Dozens of packages the size of hardcover books, each wrapped in red paper surrounded by plastic and sealed with duct tape, were spilling out of the SUV's back storage compartment into the mud.

Seeing this, Starner ran back to his truck and grabbed his rifle.

CHAPTER FORTY-NINE

Frankie and Ribeye clambered down into the ditch. Ignoring the knee-deep mud that coated their fancy shoes and expensive slacks, they started gathering up the packages.

"Don't touch those!" Starner commanded.

Frankie and Ribeye ignored him. They were trying to retrieve and stack as many packages as they could on the far side of the ditch, away from the road, but due to the angle at which the SUV was being raised up by the tow truck, more kept spilling out. One of the wrapped items got caught on the latch of the liftgate. As Ribeye grabbed it to keep it from falling into the mud, the latch snagged on the plastic. Ribeye gave the package a hard yank, and a tear appeared revealing a powdery pinkish beige substance.

Starner fired his rifle into the air. Startled, Rod stopped the winch, leaving the Escalade balanced precariously on the edge of the ditch, held only by the chain.

Frankie paused, looking up with a harsh glare. "Don't fuck with us near the Red Zone. You know Knock's rule. We have a right to reclaim our goods, and you have no right to stop us!"

Starner fired again, this time into the treetops. "Inside or outside the Red Zone doesn't matter to me anymore. I'm not Knock. I recognize what you're hauling, and it's all in plain view. I don't need a warrant. What I do need is for you two to back away. . . . That's right. Up on the other side of the ditch, near the tree line."

Frankie and Ribeye reluctantly obeyed his command.

Starner carefully worked his way down the steep incline to recover the torn package, positioning himself to stay out of the mud while keeping both his eye and his rifle fixed on the two thugs.

Thrusting his finger through the torn wrapping and withdrawing it, the deputy cautiously sniffed the powder and then rubbed a tiny bit under his lips. Just as he suspected. Processed cocaine. There was no mistaking the tell-tale floral scent, the chemical solvent overtone, the numbing of his gums, and the bitter aftertaste the lingered in the back of his throat.

Starner made some quick mental calculations. A brick of cocaine weighed roughly a kilo and, depending on its purity, was worth between twenty-five thousand and forty thousand dollars. There had to be as much as a million dollars of it in the SUV.

Starner tossed the torn package up on the road and put his rifle to his shoulder, pointing its barrel at Frankie. "You're under arrest. Put your hands up where I can see them!"

"No chance," Frankie growled, keeping his arms at his side. "The wrecker is going to pull our Escalade out of the ditch. We'll load everything back up and be on our way. Vernelle here ain't complaining. Rod is going to be very, very pleased with what we'll pay him for his time, and whether he shares that with his boss is his own business. And you, Mr. Deputy, are out of your league. If you know what's good for you, you'll go back to chasing speeders. Everyone ends up happy."

"I said PUT YOUR HANDS UP!" Starner aimed for a spot near Frankie's feet and fired off two rounds.

Recognizing that the deputy had no intention of backing down, Frankie and Ribeye took off running into the woods, the thick underbrush tearing at their muddy slacks.

Starner put down his rifle. He wasn't about to shoot them in the back, and he didn't plan on following them. Besides, where could they go but into to the Red Zone, covered with mud, mosquito bites, and ticks.

Returning to his truck, Starner placed a call to the FBI office in New Orleans to notify the bureau about the drug bust and invited them to immediately send agents. He wanted federal authorities with federal prosecutorial power behind them to supersede the jurisdictional reach of Judge Franklin Fauchère.

Starner had been contemplating burning his bridges with Knock before the old man died. Soon, the FBI would be swooping down into Petit Rouge Parish and the Red Zone. At that point, all his bridges would be enveloped in flames.

CHAPTER FIFTY

"**W**orking here is just like watching something on TV!" Irénée was wide-eyed as Starner locked the holding cell and put the key in his front pocket after he, Rod, and Vernelle brought in the cocaine packages and finished stacking them in the far corner of the tiny, barred room.

Starner flung the file with Rod and Vernelle's statements at her. "If all you're going to do is watch, then go home. You have a job to do here in Ed's absence, and it isn't to sit and gawk. The least you can do is to put these reports into the system."

"Do you have Ms. Ed's login and password? I can do social media if you want, but I've never done anything official-like."

Starner rolled his eyes. "Just pick up the files and put them on my desk. Turn around. Answer the phone, girl! Don't you see that light blinking?"

Without removing the gum from her mouth, she picked up the receiver. "Hello. Sheriff Naquin's office. . . . Yes, I understand. . . . Hold on."

Irénée reached over for the police transmitter. "Judson, come in . . . Judson? Come on, cher, pick up . . . Judson, there's an accident out at Ms. Florene's place . . . Judson? . . . This could be a big-ticket item, cher . . ."

Putting down the transmitter, Irénée handed the phone to Starner. "Here, you talk to Ms. Florene. I can't understand why the Sheriff don't just spring for GPS trackers for Judson's cruiser and your truck. When I'm in New Orleans and use Uber or Lyft, I can see where every car is just by looking at my phone.

With an accident out at the café, guess you'll be getting another big score. This must be your lucky day, but I wonder where the hell Judson is and why he's missing all the action!"

CHAPTER FIFTY-ONE

S tarner wanted to stay at the office and await the arrival of the FBI, but with Judson not responding, it was up to him to handle the entire parish, at least until he could hand his resignation directly to Knock. After he did that, it would be up to Knock to figure out how to deal with problems in the area; however, Starner felt an obligation to Florene, even though he was relieved he would soon have no further obligation to Knock.

Before leaving the station, Starner took the bag of money from Vernelle over the man's objection, explaining that the cash was potentially either the evidence of a crime or the fruits of a crime. Starner assured Vernelle that if it was determined the money was neither, he would get it back. Starner locked the bag in the cell with the cocaine packs and, placing back the key in his pocket, drove over to the café.

When he got to Chez Poêlon, the incident was nothing like the "big score" Irénée imagined. It was a plain vanilla accident. A rich doctor—driving a BMW, of all things, on the way to his fishing camp—backed out of the parking lot right into a guy hauling a brand-new bass boat. Damaged the trunk and back axle of the car, ruined one of the trailer's tires, and messed up the propellers on the big Yamaha outboard engine on the back of the boat.

Starner intervened between the two hopping mad drivers. The owner of the bass boat accused the doctor of not looking where he was going. The doctor complained that the boat and trailer had been parked incorrectly and it wasn't his fault that the rear end of the trailer protruded three feet behind the boat, an obvious hazard.

After issuing tickets to both men—to the doctor for careless driving and to the bass boat owner for having a trailer without a current license tag—Starner went looking for Judson. Starner really wanted to be back at the station to meet the FBI, but Irénée reported she still was unable to raise Judson on the police radio. He wasn't answering the phone at their apartment, and he wasn't at his momma's.

Starner took a quick spin around the parish looking for the young deputy, thinking maybe he parked off the road to take a nap. It would be just like Judson to spend all night carousing with Irénée, write a bunch of bogus tickets to folks passing through, and then hide out to get a bit of shut-eye. Starner planned to ream him out in no uncertain terms when he caught up with him.

Turning on his flashers and speeding up, Starner made a wide loop around Petit Rouge. He did not spot Judson's cruiser on any of the parish's paved roads.

Starner gritted his teeth in fury as he drove. Here he was on a stupid mission searching for that no-good whippersnapper with only bubble-headed Irénée to greet the Feds. He called Irénée and gave her specific instructions. If the FBI showed up before he got back, the only thing she was to do was tell them to call him directly so he could return immediately.

In the meantime, Starner decided to take one more circuitous route, this time pausing to briefly explore each of the many dead-end lanes in the area. These would be just the kind of places where Judson might park, pretending to be watching out for speeders while actually snoring soundly in his cruiser.

Starner drove onto old dirt tracks that led to decaying sharecropper's cabins, inhabited until mechanical harvesters drastically reduced the number of laborers needed to work the sugarcane fields. He steered down overgrown logging trails that wove back behind the tree lines into acre upon acre of clearcuts replanted with pine saplings. He even bumped along rutted paths that led to deer hunting stands.

Starner didn't expect Picox Lane to be any different from the dozens of other dead ends, but as he turned off the highway, he saw what seemed to be a pile of rags in the road. He drove closer.

It was a man. He was motionless, face down in a pool of blood, a rifle in his frozen grip.

Starner parked his truck and rushed over to the corpse. He had been shot.

Starner looked in the direction the rifle's barrel was pointing. He spotted a second body across the ditch.

Judson!

Starner ran and jumped the four-foot span, his knees creaking.

Judson was lying on his back, guts spilling into his lap, and a large bullet hole above his eyebrows. His lifeless eyes were staring upward.

Starner knew better then to touch the body before a forensic team arrived. He was not going to call Acie. Starner was going to tell the FBI, as soon as they contacted him, to get their people over to Picox Lane. This situation might be connected to the cocaine deal, and Starner was not about to let any Petit Rouge "authorities" have a hand in this. What was going on in the parish? Cocaine coming from the Red Zone. Debrun's death a homicide staged to look like a car accident. And now the murder of one of Knock's "boys."

Starner groaned as he leaped back over the ditch to try to determine the identity of the person who had shot Judson. As he approached the center of Picox Lane, he walked gingerly so as not to disturb anything.

Starner noted that the dirt bore signs of multiple tire tracks. Some were seven or eight inches wide, indicating a small car. Others were about ten inches wide. Probably a truck. And a few were over fifteen inches wide. Apparently, a big commercial vehicle had ventured down Picox Lane as well. Yet, the area around the unknown man's body appeared to have been swept clean. It was smooth, just like the bank of the swamp where Starner found Debrun and his car.

CHAPTER FIFTY-TWO

The KTM EXC500 Dual-Sport roared into the yard in front of the rusted metal warehouse in Little Jerusalem, a village of abandoned buildings, shuttered businesses, ramshackle houses, and an aging population trying to survive their last years in a community bereft of youth and hope. No traffic had passed by in the last twenty minutes, except for the orange motorcycle that now approached the parked truck hidden from the road on the far side of the metal framing.

"I came as fast as I could," Bubba said, putting up the kickstand on his cycle.

"Do you know how bad this is?" Art was infuriated. "Why did I fucking make you a Prefect if you can't get your team to follow instructions precisely?"

Bubba knew that the Supreme Kommander was not asking him for a response, and he gave none. He waited patiently, without expression, but ready to react at a moment's notice if necessary. He had seen Art in all kinds of moods. Consumed with intensity as he engaged in the meticulous planning necessary to carry out his elaborate scheme. Cloaked in concentration as he set each of his minions in motion, just as he did in the armed camps in Idaho. Bubba was sure that there were other Saxons and Precepts he had never met. A young vanguard on college campuses to entice potential recruits, students rebelling by rejecting liberal blather and political correctness, convinced that their professors' entreaties to "look at all sides of every issue" were just another excuse to ignore the obvious truth right before their eyes. White-shirt-and-tie-clad men, the type who were seen as reasonable alternatives to sheet-clad, cross-burning fanatics. Calm-sounding speakers who rejected political correctness and spoke of returning America to its roots, to its true Christian origins, while praising the solid, historic Americans who made this country great. Their comments were dog whistles to those who understood the veiled references to white supremacy. Rabble-rousing radio commentators in remote communities broadcasting with incendiary urgency in 20,000-watt circles. Podcasters spewing venom into the ether. Internet and social media trolls tired of lurking in the shadow world of the Dark Web and ready, when Art gave the signal, to emerge into the bright light of publicity that would unhinge nonbelievers while attracting thousands more to the righteous cause of the Alabaster Brigade.

Bubba had seen Art-the-Supreme-Kommander flooded with euphoria when describing the chaos to come that would enlighten the world with the truth the Brigade would reveal.

Never, in all these years, had Art gotten angry at him, but now Art's fury was palpable.

"Do you know what kind of shitstorm Tommy's death will cause?" Art didn't expect an answer, especially since Bubba had no idea of the seriousness of the situation he had created.

"This," Art told Bubba slowly and precisely, "is what you're going to do. Your team has been decimated. It must be reduced even further. There cannot be any more mix-ups, screwups, or fuckups of any kind. It is only a matter of time before someone finds the cop Phillip shot, and when they do all hell will break loose in our quiet little community. First, you're going to eliminate Phillip. After all, I promoted him to Imperial Ten on your recommendation. I want him dead before nightfall. Then, you're going to deal with Imperial Seven, since Maggie Mae is equally to blame for what happened on Picox Lane. From what you've told me, she and Phillip made a bad situation much worse by trying to disguise it. She has to take the fall, and it has to look like suicide. That will keep things nice and neat. Use these cyanide capsules. Make sure she dies at home. Don't leave until you're sure she's dead. I've composed her suicide note. In this envelope is a computer printout free of fingerprints, other than hers. You remember I made each of you sign five blank pieces of paper when you joined the Brigade? This note contains her signature. Use gloves when you open this, press her hands all over it, and then leave it near her body."

Bubba nodded solemnly as he took the envelope and the container of pills from Art.

"Once these tasks are completed, only one thing remains. You and you alone are now responsible for Kenny."

Bubba nodded again. "Understood, Kommander."

"You damn well better understand! I expect a salute at this point, Prefect."

Bubba snapped to attention. "Yes sir! Eighty-eight!"

CHAPTER FIFTY-THREE

When Irénée called Starner to inform him the FBI had arrived at the sheriff's office, he didn't tell her what happened to Judson. He wasn't about to share that news over the phone. Rather, he asked to speak to the FBI agent in charge. Starner told her that, after handing over the receiver, she needed to step outside and wait for instructions from the Feds.

The FBI agreed with Starner's suggestions. Two agents were stationed inside the sheriff's office, guarding the cocaine and money locked in the holding cell and watching Irénée as she sat at Ed's desk.

The FBI's crackerjack criminal forensic team arrived from New Orleans in their portable lab and scoured every inch of Picox Lane. A pathologist examined both bodies, carefully photographing the scene before touching either one. Technicians labeled evidence bags, took measurements, and entered the data they collected into their computers.

Starner sat on the hood of his truck trying to assemble all the puzzle pieces. Never, in all his years as a detective working in the seedier, violent, vicious neighborhoods of New Orleans that tourists never saw, had he ever come across a crime scene so carefully staged. The deceased's driver's license identified him as Thomas Closser from New Orleans. But the driver's license was bogus. The address listed was a street in the Ninth Ward that Starner knew well, a street on which every house had been torn down after Hurricane Katrina devastated the area and which now boasted only vacant, weed-filled lots.

Thomas Closser had been shot in the road. That much was clear from the way blood pooled under his body, even though the surrounding area was swept clean. Why? The scene was arranged to make it appear that Closser had been shot by Judson and vice versa.

But was that really the case? The location of Judson's body was more curious. He wasn't anywhere near his squad car but rather on the opposite side of the ditch. His cruiser was smashed up. Surely, the young deputy didn't back into a tree, crumple his trunk, drive forward another fifty yards down Picox Lane, veer off into the woods, smash into a live oak, run back down the dirt road without leaving footprints, and then leap over the ditch only to get shot.

Who shot first? The man in the road? Why? If Judson fired his Beretta, killing Thomas Closser, how could Closser have then used the rifle to shoot Judson not once but twice?

Starner shared his concerns with the FBI forensic team and pointed out scratches on the trunk of Judson's cruiser, hoping that they might pick up paint samples or other evidence that would explain what Judson's car might have hit or what might have hit it.

There were far too many mysterious deaths in Petit Rouge, starting with Boulette's demise. Then Debrun. Now Judson and Thomas Closser. Beyond that, Boyo was still missing. Was he dead, too?

As much as Starner would have liked the culprits to be Frankie and Ribeye, he knew that couldn't be the case, at least not for these last shootings. The pathologist determined that Closser and Judson both died within the previous three to five hours. That excluded Frankie and Ribeye. When Rod was hooking up the tow truck to their Escalade, he apologized for taking thirty minutes to get there, which meant that Frankie and Ribeye were on the side of the road with a deer plastered against their windshield when the events on Picox Lane transpired.

Ed was out of pocket because of Boulette and Debrun. As soon as Starner broke the news about Judson to Irénée, she'd leave. The FBI would remove the cocaine and cash. Starner would lock the office as soon as they left, go to Knock's, tender his resignation, and leave the entire mess to the old man.

Starner couldn't wait to wash his hands of formerly sleepy, quiet Petit Rouge Parish.

CHAPTER FIFTY-FOUR

Kenny was just finishing a late lunch in the corner of the barn that the Precept had set up just for him, complete with a cozy bed, hotplate, microwave, television, small refrigerator, and computer with internet access. There was plenty of time to savor his meal. He didn't have to head out on the afternoon run for another half hour or so.

Kenny was thankful that the Precept thought of everything. Yesterday he asked what Kenny's favorite foods were and then stocked the refrigerator with them. No beer, though. The Precept warned Kenny that he needed to keep his mind absolutely clear today and tomorrow, though he encouraged him to have as much as he wanted of whatever was there. Two thick muffulettas from Ganderson's, with extra meat and cheese. A six-pack of Barq's root beer. A box of Snickers bars. A huge container of M&Ms. Several large bags of Zapp's potato chips and Cheetos. These were all the delicacies any man could ever want, as far as Kenny was concerned.

Imperial Ten, the guy with the misshapen nose and great Nazi tattoo who shot the cop earlier today, was talking with the Precept. Kenny didn't know what their conversation was about but, from their body language, he could tell it was very important. Imperial Ten arrived in his big Chevy Silverado an hour ago, and he and the Precept had been conferring on the porch ever since.

Of course, Kenny thought, they are discussing me. The fine-looking gal, the one who gave instructions to Imperial Ten, made it clear that it was Ten's job to follow me. Follow me! That was exactly what the entire world would do tomorrow. Follow my example. Follow the blazing light I will ignite to awaken what the

Precept called the "unenlightened hordes of disbelievers" and the "mealy-mouthed liberals" who preached togetherness of unequals without understanding that the Lord really intended things to be separate and unequal. Man was made to rule over woman and the beasts of the field. The saved were ordained to rule over the unsaved. Whites were predetermined to rule over blacks. The Precept was right. Tomorrow all will become clear because of my actions in New Orleans, a city of sin that removed monuments to the great Confederate generals and dumped its memorials honoring brave white citizens who resisted the Darkie-loving carpetbaggers. A city that celebrates mulattos and quadroons and all the other mixed-race monstrosities. I will be the one to bring the illusion of "equality" crashing down. As the Precept proclaimed this morning, I will be the "point of the spear that pierces the balloon of complacency and explodes myths."

Kenny was devouring his third Snickers bar when he heard gunshots. People who don't own weapons, Kenny thought proudly, don't know what real gunshots sound like. They assume pistols and rifles boom like those on TV and in the movies. But Kenny knew the truth, just like he knew the truth of the Lord's love of white supremacy. Real gunshots sound like pops. And what Kenny had just heard were two pops coming from the Precept's house, twenty-five yards away.

He peeked out of the barn door. Kenny wasn't about to interrupt the Precept when he was working. The man with the ugly nose was no longer visible on the porch, and the Precept was just exiting his house, pistol in hand.

Kenny was so happy he almost skipped to the house when the Precept signaled for him. The Precept put his arm around Kenny's shoulder. "This is your day, Kenny. Rejoice in it. Tomorrow, you act, but today you celebrate. You and I will exalt together. We will revel in vanquishing our foes. I have just shown Imperial Ten that I will not tolerate disrespect and disobedience."

The Precept pressed his pistol into Kenny's hand, which quivered with excitement. "Come inside with me and complete the task of instructing Imperial Ten."

As the Precept opened the front door of the house, Kenny could see that the living room was in complete disarray. Furniture was damaged. The curtains were ripped and on the ground. The rods on which they had hung were broken and strewn across the floor.

Imperial Ten lay on his side and was making a strange gurgling noise. Blood poured from two bullet wounds, one in his neck and the other in his groin.

"Finish him off," the Precept instructed, "just like you will finish off all the others tomorrow."

Kenny couldn't believe his good fortune! He would get to kill today and kill again tomorrow. What an honor the Precept had bestowed upon him!

"There are eleven rounds left in the magazine, Kenny. Use them all if you want . . . or don't, it's your choice. Just stand back a bit. You wouldn't want to get blood on your bus driver's uniform."

Kenny could not contain his delight. He pointed the pistol at Imperial Ten and shot. The popping sound of the gun combined with the thud of the bullet as it tore into Imperial Ten's chest. Kenny pressed the trigger once more, aiming at Imperial Ten's cheek. He was sure he heard bones cracking in the man's face as the bullet entered.

Kenny fired three more shots, all into Imperial Ten's stomach.

Imperial Ten stopped his incessant gurgling and was silent.

Nevertheless, Kenny let another two rounds fly, one in each of the dead man's thighs.

Kenny glanced at the Precept for further instructions. "That'll do it, don't you think?"

"Absolutely," the Precept said. He took out his handkerchief, wrapped it around the pistol, and removed the weapon from Kenny's grasp.

In his capacity as Precept, Bubba fulfilled the task the Supreme Kommander had given him. It wasn't easy, but Bubba hadn't expected it to be effortless. Phillip was intransigent. Watchful. Defensive. When Bubba pulled his gun, Phillip lunged, knocking the pistol from his grasp. The two struggled mightily, but Bubba was confident. He knew he was stronger. Better trained. Smarter. Bubba managed to retrieve the weapon and mortally wound Phillip before calmly walking out of the house and summoning Kenny.

"What," Kenny asked, still grinning, "are we going to do with him?"

"Nothing at present. Before you drive off tomorrow, we'll burn everything to the ground. Whatever packages of R-37 explosives we haven't already put in the bus we'll place under the floorboards of the house and near the big posts in the barn. That's sure to incinerate everything."

"But isn't this your family home?"

"The Alabaster Brigade's cause, Kenny, is greater than any one person and greater than any one member's property. You know that. When you join the Brigade, your life, your soul, all your assets belong to the Brigade. This home is nothing. You give the Brigade your undivided loyalty, and the Brigade will provide. That was the problem with Imperial Ten. He failed to follow commands, which meant that his loyalty could not be relied upon. You—on the other hand—you will follow every command to the letter. I have no doubt of that."

Kenny grinned even more. Of course the Precept can rely on me. My loyalty to the Brigade is beyond question! I am the tip of the spear!

Bubba smugly watched Kenny's transparent joy, knowing that the Supreme Kommander would approve of how he arranged things so that only Kenny's fingerprints would be on the pistol laying out in the yard when the firetrucks arrived on the scene. Bubba was sure that, in the unlikely event Imperial Ten's body was recovered, all the evidence would point to Kenny.

Bubba's next task was to rendezvous with Maggie Mae at her place.

The Supreme Kommander's wishes would be satisfied. Kenny would head out tomorrow morning to execute the plan the Supreme Kommander had been working on for over a year.

CHAPTER FIFTY-FIVE

Bea Timms led Starner down the hallway to room in which Knock's hospital bed had been set up. When he came by yesterday, Knock was weak but had enough strength to get to his seat in the garden, even if Bea had to surround him with pillows and lash him to the rocking chair. Today the sheriff lay flat on his back, his breathing slow and shallow. His almost translucent skin had a yellow-green tinge. His cheeks were caved in, and his eyes were closed. He looked cadaverous.

Starner recognized the signs, having seen similar changes in his father-in-law, Fogel.

Before Hurricane Katrina, Starner and his wife moved Fogel, who had early-onset dementia, into a nursing home. After Katrina, it fell to Starner to tell the confused old man that Cheryl Ann and Bucky were dead. It was the hardest message he ever had to deliver. As a New Orleans detective, Starner met with more than his share of grieving mothers to inform them that their preteens had been gunned down in the street. He held collapsing widows in his arms after telling them that their husbands had been caught in the cross fire of gang warfare. And, in his years in Petit Rouge Parish, he once knocked on the door of a family he knew well to inform them that their teenager had perished in a gruesome auto accident.

Starner thought he could handle telling Fogel about their mutual loss. He certainly didn't want anyone else to do it. But, when the time came, he couldn't get the words out. Starner just sobbed and hugged Fogel, who, despite his inability to focus or cogently follow a train of thought, understood what his son-in-law was trying to say. The two of them wept together.

After that, Fogel lost the will to live. He refused to eat. He ripped the IV out of this arm when they tried to feed him intravenously. He developed an infection that attacked his liver and kidneys, and he refused all medication.

Fogel wasted away until he looked just like Knock did now. Skin thin and jaundiced. Kidneys shutting down. The time between inhaling and exhaling taking longer and longer. Slipping away, waiting for death to descend and ready to embrace it.

Starner had come to tender his resignation, expecting Knock to be sentient enough to respond. He wanted to see the old man's expression when he told him about the cocaine from the Red Zone and the FBI's arrival in the parish. Starner wanted to cleanse himself of the shame he felt for having traded his self-respect for a paycheck, for having obediently sucked up to Knock for all these years, and for having turned a blind eye to the corruption that permeated the fiefdom that the sheriff proudly called "his parish."

But seeing the old man on his deathbed, Starner could not summon the energy or the will to carry forward his intentions.

He took Knock's hand. "It's Starner, Knock. Come to visit you. Give me a squeeze if you can hear me."

Knock's skeletal fingers didn't even twitch.

Starner sighed, not out of exasperation or relief but out of resignation. The old man had taken advantage of him, had been amorally venal while projecting personal integrity to the world. The sheriff provided a haven for criminal activity all the while boasting that, because of his tight rein, Petit Rouge was crime-free. Nonetheless, Knock took him in when no one else would.

Starner decided to let the old man die in peace, thinking that the world he had erected was intact and that he would be remembered as a great lawman and the longest-serving sheriff in the entire state. Let Knock coast into oblivion not knowing that everything he built was about to be dismantled. A new sheriff would be elected. He would examine the books the old man kept in his office desk under lock and key and uncover all the discrepancies. Once Knock's will was probated, everyone would find out how much money he managed to sock away, which he couldn't have done on his government salary alone. They would discover how valuable his antiques were and how vast his wealth really was. The sheriff's formerly "unsullied" reputation would be trashed.

Starner kept all these thoughts to himself and simply held the old man's hand as he leaned over and whispered in Knock's ear, repeating what he whispered to Fogel at the end, "You don't have to hang on. You can let go whenever you want."

CHAPTER FIFTY-SIX

Abigayle skipped off the bus and waved goodbye to Mr. Kenny, pausing only to happily touch the paper sunflower she had given him this morning, which he stuck in the cupholder next to his seat. Despite the fact that the other kids made fun of him behind his back for his squeaky voice, his awkward ways, and his yellow bus driver's uniform that was too big for him, Abigayle really liked Mr. Kenny, who today, for the first time this week, had a big grin on his face.

Kenny couldn't stop smiling. His feet were tapping with excitement. He had been training for such a long time, and now all that coaching was about to pay off. He was like all the superheroes he had seen in movies whose true powers were hidden from view, who appeared to be meek and mild, quiet and unassuming. But once they slipped out of their street clothes and into their superhero garb, everyone saw them for what they truly were. Not ordinary at all, but extraordinary.

None of these little pickaninnies I ferry to and from school have any idea what is store for them tomorrow, Kenny thought. They don't know my superpowers. They have no concept of the web of hidden wires running from the storage compartments beneath the bus to the undercarriage above the front axles to the red button that the Precept installed by the driver's seat, next to the cupholder with Abigayle's sunflower. They have no way of knowing that once we arrive in New Orleans and pull into the middle of the French Quarter amidst the vast crowds attending the Unity Festival, a single press of the red button will make them and everyone around them literally disintegrate in an "illustrious cloud of singular power." That's how the Precept described it. They are unaware that their deaths will usher in the splendor and majesty of white supremacy.

The Precept taught that no one can dispute the biblical truth. Blacks? They are despicable in the eyes of the Lord. The Bible is pure. Perfect. Explicit on this issue! As an example, the Precept used the story of what happened to Noah's family, the story of the curse of Ham and the curse on Ham's son, Canaan. Ham and Japheth were brothers. God caused Japheth to be born white and Ham to be born black. Noah himself said that Canaan will be a "servant of servants." It could not be any clearer. The "Hamite race"—which the Precept told him meant all blacks, including those with only a drop of black blood in their veins—were foretold in the Bible to be inferior to all whites. Spiritually inferior. Genetically inferior. Inferior in every way.

The Precept pointed out numerous other biblical examples of black inferiority. There were passages about Zerah the Ethiopian. Black as coal, with an army of a million men. Soundly defeated by God's will. It was all right there in Chronicles. "The Lord defeated the Ethiopians." It wasn't just man who defeated the blacks, it was the Lord himself. God's own hand came down on those uppity enough to dare oppose the superiority of whites.

The Bible is truth! The absolute, literal truth! Every single word.

The Precept taught, and Kenny believed, that God does not countenance whites who advocate mingling with blacks or who pursue the false path of "equality" of the races. Kenny knew that, through his actions, the Lord would unleash his righteous wrath on all nonbelievers. All atheists and humanists. All weak-willed and weak-minded proponents of the "unity" of mankind. All Jews, Buddhists, Islamists, and any others who neither recognize nor acknowledge the white perfection of Jesus Christ. Everyone must accept the judgment of God. It has been foretold.

Kenny was proud to be God's chosen instrument.

Nevertheless, a question crept into Kenny's mind, as much as he tried to deny it. Could an exception ever be made? For just one of the pickaninnies? For a single young Ebonic? Might God make an exception for Abigayle, who was kind to Kenny and brought him gifts, even if she was black and of an inferior race?

Kenny quickly pushed aside such charitable thoughts. There can be no questioning God's will. No! There must be no exceptions!

Death and the grace of God lead the way to a perfect eternity, Kenny thought. He was ready and eager to enter that portal.

CHAPTER FIFTY-SEVEN

Maggie Mae sat naked on the bed drinking a beer.
Bubba returned from the bathroom concealing the three capsules clasped in his left hand. He placed a glass of water on the nightstand, climbed in next to her, and nestled his head in her lap. They had been at it for almost an hour, and the disheveled bedsheets were damp with sweat and bodily fluids.

Maggie Mae lay back against the headboard, beer bottle still in hand, and opened her legs so that he could lick away. It was pleasant enough, but nothing extraordinary. Nonetheless, she forced a little sigh, to give him the illusion that he was turning her on. She would do whatever it took. After all, hadn't she risen from Aspirant to Member to Saxon to Imperial in record time? So many men could be manipulated like Bubba. She'd gladly allowed them do whatever they wanted to do with her—whatever they wanted to do to her—letting them think they were using her, while all the time she was using them to climb the ranks. Tomorrow, after the Supreme Kommander's plan succeeded, he'd need even more troops. He'd require even more leaders, more Precepts. She was ready to be anointed and ascend to a higher echelon once again.

And within a year or less—she could almost taste it—being a Kommander herself would be within her reach. She would be one of the elite, running several cells. Sure, she thought, I won't be the Supreme Kommander, like Art, who not only had his units throughout the Gulf region stretching from Texas to Florida, but who also headed the Alabaster Brigade's National Council. She was sure that when she became a Kommander on the secretive Council, she'd prove herself as clever as Art, if not more so. Art certainly excelled at operating in disguise. Who would ever suspect that the Supreme Kommander of the Alabaster Brigade would be married to a black bitch with a black kid to boot? But once I make Kommander, Maggie Mae thought, my disguise will be even better. No one would ever suspect a leader of the Alabaster Brigade to be a woman, especially not one with my looks and my figure. I will be able to move across the country with impunity. I will attract hordes of female recruits, creating an ever-enlarging pool of Aspirants. I will be in the inner sanctum of the Brigade, joining the other Kommanders at Council meetings.

Bubba paused his slurping for a moment. "You like that, don't you babe?"

Maggie Mae was glad he had stopped. It was getting sore down there. His tongue felt like sandpaper on her at this point, but in response to his question, she merely purred, "You bet," knowing that Bubba would believe her. "Here," she said, shifting around and flipping him over on his back, "let me go down on you."

Bubba grinned. He had maneuvered this just right and congratulated himself on her not suspecting a thing. As she placed her face in his crotch, he wrapped one thigh beneath her neck, one above it, and pressed them together.

She thought he was just being playful, so she grabbed his balls in her hands and squeezed gently.

Bubba was no longer just a boyfriend. He was a Precept assigned a deadly mission. He tightened his thighs, causing Maggie Mae to gasp for air.

She was taken aback. So, she thought, he wants to play rough? She crunched his testicles as hard as she could.

The Precept ignored the pain and forced his thighs together with all his might.

Maggie Mae tried, to no avail, to wriggle out of his grasp. She couldn't catch her breath. She was losing consciousness. What the hell was he up to?

Just before she was about to pass out, he released his grip on her neck.

She lay there gasping for air and coughing, which made it even harder for her to draw oxygen into her lungs.

"Sorry I was so rough, babe." Bubba shoved the three capsules into her open mouth. "Swallow these. They taste terrible, but they'll help."

He lifted her head up, grabbed the glass on the nightstand, and held it to her lips. The water spilled out the sides of her mouth as she got the pills down.

She felt a terrible burning in the back of her throat and began to gag. Something was terribly wrong. She flailed her arms.

Bubba eluded her, slid off the bed, and stood in the corner of the room, calmly pulling on his clothes. He waited until the pills did their job, enjoying every minute of her suffering.

Maggie Mae began to breathe abnormally. She was inhaling rapidly and deeply but not getting enough oxygen.

Her skin began to turn cherry red, just as the Supreme Kommander had told him it would, explaining that cyanide acts as a binder in the bloodstream. Oxygen stays there and does not migrate to the cells, starving them.

The Precept watched impassively as Maggie Mae started to go into convulsions, her body contorted, her eyes wide with fear and disbelief.

She thrashed around the bed, fruitlessly trying to sit up. Her eyes fluttered. Her eyelids closed then opened wide. She stared at the ceiling in panic. After a while, she shut her eyes and stopped moving.

The Precept looked at his watch as Maggie Mae lapsed into a coma. Cardiac arrest would follow in a few minutes.

The training Bubba had received at the Idaho camp emphasized precision. The Kommander's instructions were precise. Bubba acted confidently and unhurriedly. Putting on a pair of gloves, he wrapped Maggie Mae's listless body in the sheets, moved her aside, remade the bed with fresh linens, and placed her back on it. He put the dirty sheets and pillowcases in large garbage bag to dispose of later.

After rearranging the room, Bubba placed the suicide note in her flaccid hands, pressed her fingers over it, just as the Supreme Kommander had instructed, and then positioned it on the bedside table.

As he was cleaning the bathroom, he thought how appropriate it was that the Supreme Kommander wanted Maggie Mae to die like this. After all, the Nazis used Zyklon B in the gas chambers, and Zyklon B was simply a gaseous form of cyanide. It was a shame they were thwarted from fully fulfilling their intention to eliminate all non-Aryans.

The Supreme Kommander's plan would be more effective than the Nazis', for he decreed that the death of every non-Aryan was unnecessary as long as all non-Aryans were subjugated. But examples had to be made, and if many non-Aryans died in bringing God's will to the fore, so be it. Even Brigade members like Phillip and Maggie Mae were disposable if they failed to execute an assignment properly.

Non-Aryans needed to understand they would never be equal to white believers. That was the whole point of tomorrow's great event. The world would be forced to acknowledge the vast power of the Alabaster Brigade and accept the need to bow before the superior race of the Brigade's Aryans. The Brigade represented the only true religion. The world would not condemn the Brigade for its actions but rather grasp the necessity for them, recognizing that destruction was for the greater good. As it says in Ephesians, Jesus gave "himself for us an offering and a sacrifice to God for a sweet-smelling savour." The thousands who would die tomorrow were a necessary offering and sacrifice.

Bubba congratulated himself on another assignment executed to perfection. By the time Maggie Mae's body and her suicide note were discovered, both he and the Supreme Kommander would be long gone, their mission accomplished. Tens of thousands would be dead in New Orleans, hundreds of buildings would be leveled, the French Quarter would be a smoking ruin, and the video he had made of Kenny on Sunday would have gone viral, attracting more and more recruits to the Alabaster Brigade.

CHAPTER FIFTY-EIGHT

Starner sat in a lawn chair in front of his double-wide, a half-drunk beer in hand. Wisps of clouds moved across the night sky, intermittently blotting out stars.

The shackles had not lifted. The burden had not lessened. The wave of exhilaration he expected to feel when he tendered his resignation was never going to arrive. Starner had succumbed to sentiment. He did not have the heart to confront Knock as he slipped into a coma perched on the precipice of death.

What was left, Starner thought? Nothing hopeful. Nothing comforting. He was now the only "officer of the peace" in the parish. The phrase was full of irony. There was no peace to be had. Not for him. Not for Petit Rouge Parish.

He heard his cell phone ring. Wearily, he looked at the number. It was the answering service to which all contacts with the sheriff's office in the evening were being routed. He remained the sole liaison until other arrangements could be made.

"Deputy Gautreaux," said the woman at the answering service, "sorry to buzz you, but we just received a call about something that looks like it requires an immediate response."

Starner took down the details, abandoned the half-filled can of beer, and gloomily climbed into to his truck.

He arrived at the Muscadine Street address fifteen minutes later, siren blaring, and pulled into the driveway behind a car. In the driver's seat sat a teenager texting on his phone. Starner recognized the boy. It was Braydon. His mother was a docent at the Cottoncrest Plantation.

Braydon got out his car, which smelled of cheese and pepperoni. "She's in there. I spotted her from the window on the back porch. Let me show you."

Braydon led Starner around the side of the house, talking nonstop the whole time. "You gotta understand. If I don't make a delivery, or if the pizza is cold when I do and the customer complains, my boss charges me for the pizza, docking my pay. As if it's my fault! Anyway, I knocked on the front door, but there was no answer. Well, I sure ain't gonna be delivering no cold pizza, so I go 'round and knock on the back door as well. Still no answer. Shit! I rapped real hard on the window. That, I figured, would get whoever was inside moving, and if no one answered, then I was within my rights to tell the shift manager that I didn't deserve to be docked for this one. No sir! Since the lights were on, I tried one more time. No answer. So, I climbed up on a rickety chair on the back porch and peeked inside."

They headed over to the back stairs.

"See, here's that chair. Just like I told you. Go ahead. You're probably tall enough that you don't need to stand on it to see through the window. Spot her? Naked and all. Shaved pussy and awesome tits. I thought she was sunburned as hell, which is probably why she took off all her clothes. Figured that this might be my lucky day, so I rapped on the window to get her attention, but she didn't budge. I looked real careful-like, 'cause you know she had a fine bod. That's when I noticed her stomach wasn't moving. Damn, I thought. She ain't breathing. Then I called 911 and just waited. And here you are. So, can I go now?"

Starner, observing that the woman's diaphragm was immobile, turned around to face Braydon and held out his hand. He would deal with the kid first and the dead woman second.

"Let me see your cell phone."

"What for? I know my rights. Learned 'em in civics class."

"You want me to call your momma and tell her you're not co-operating with the sheriff's office?"

Braydon hesitated and then reluctantly handed his mobile to Starner. "Okay, but I need it back before I leave. That's how I get all the delivery calls from the store. This sure ain't my night. I didn't even notice the address problem until I went back to my car to call 911. Cell phone service sucks out here in this part of the parish, and even when you get service, you can't rely on the addresses that show up on the map on your screen. So I pulled in here. No house numbers I could see, but I figured this was the place. 607 Muscadine was where the call came from, but it's clear now that this ain't the spot. And right before you pulled up, I got an angry call from my boss who said that the folks over at 607 Muscadine are hopping mad that they haven't got their pizza yet. Now I'm doubly screwed. I'll have to go back to the shop, pick up four fresh pizzas—one for the delivery I was supposed to make to 607 Muscadine, and three other orders as well. Tonight will put me in the hole for a week. My boss will charge me for all of them, and I doubt I'll be getting any tips from this run."

"Don't worry. I'll call your boss. Phoning 911 was the right thing to do. He shouldn't dock you for this, but . . ." Starner said, having found the pictures the delivery boy took through the window of the naked girl, "I can't let you keep these photos, son."

"Ain't nothing wrong with that, is there? After all, I have to show my friends what I found."

"It's simple, Braydon. Either I confiscate the phone as evidence, where it might sit for weeks or even months, and tell your momma why I took it, or I can erase the photos and return the phone to you right now. If we do that, your momma doesn't need to know anything about the pictures."

Braydon reluctantly agreed.

Starner erased the more than twenty photos the kid had taken, checked to make sure he hadn't already messaged them to anyone else, and handed Braydon his phone back.

"Can I go?"

Starner nodded.

"But you're blocking me in. Okay if I just drive on the lawn to get around your truck?"

"Absolutely not!"

CHAPTER FIFTY-NINE

This is the last thing I need, Starner thought, turning on his blue strobes as Braydon rode away and repositioning his truck so no one could come up the driveway. One more death to handle while I'm still on the force.

He put on the extra pair of gloves Gervais gave him when they were dealing with Debrun. If there were fingerprints on the scene, he was not about to disturb them.

The doors on both the front and back entrances were locked. Starner noted they had key closures, not dead bolts. No way to tell if they had been fastened from the inside or outside.

Starner jimmied the rear door and entered the kitchen, taking note of everything with a practiced eye. There were no dishes in the kitchen sink. Beer and soda were in the refrigerator, along with six small containers of yogurt, a package of sliced cheese, and a quart of milk.

A short hallway led to the bedroom where the deceased was sprawled faceup on the bed, her mouth contorted in agony. Livor mortis had set in. Gravity caused the body's blood to pool to the lowest level. The bluish-purple color of her lividity, where her back touched the bed, was blotchy, which indicated to Starner she had been dead only a few hours. If death had occurred earlier, the blotches would have disappeared, and the color would have been more uniform.

The woman's skin was cherry red, but it was not sunburned, as Braydon thought. This kind of coloration was completely different. Her face, feet, and breasts looked as if they were enflamed.

The dead woman's hand stretched out toward the nightstand on which rested a lamp, a half-filled glass of water, two small capsules, and a letter-sized sheet of paper. Her knuckles rested against a corner of the paper.

Careful not to touch anything, Starner bent down to examine the note, which was typed, except for the signature at the bottom. It read, "I have lived a life of shame. Shot two people today on Picox Lane because I thought it would make me feel better. It didn't. My life has come to nothing. May God forgive me." It was signed, "Maggie Mae Delacourte."

When Starner was a detective in New Orleans, he had been called to the scene of many suicides, but this suicide note was the strangest he had ever come across.

Was she the Picox Lane killer? If so, then why did she want to make it appear that Thomas Closser had shot Judson and vice versa? And why was Judson so far away from his patrol car? If she was so despondent, why would she take the time to type a suicide note rather than dash it off by hand? Why confess to two murders? And why sign it? A suicide note to a spouse, a lover, a parent . . . that was immensely sad but understandable. But a suicide note addressed to no one in particular and signed with a full name? Why?

Starner looked for a computer and printer or even a typewriter on which the suicide note could have been composed. He didn't find any. She wrote the note elsewhere and then came here to kill herself?

Starner went back to look around the bedroom. If she used a weapon on Picox Lane, why did she resort to pills to do herself in? Judson was shot by a high-powered rifle. From the look on her face, she suffered an agonizing death. Why didn't she just stick a gun barrel in her mouth and be done with it? Who takes off all their clothes to commit suicide in bed?

Starner bent over the bed to look at the woman's neck. There were bruises on both sides. Had she tried to strangle herself first? If so, with what? Did she fail in that effort and resort to taking pills?

Nothing in this room made any sense.

Starner performed another quick but thorough check of the house. No gun. No purse or wallet or anything that could help identify her. Who was Maggie Mae Delacourte?

Starner was not about to call Acie. Since the suicide note referred to the Picox Lane killings, Starner phoned the federal agent who had come up from New Orleans. Got him at home. He said he would get a forensics crew back to Petit Rouge as quickly as he could tonight and for Starner to wait on-site until they arrived.

Returning to his truck, Starner grabbed his flashlight and walked around the yard looking for anything that might give a clue to what really happened here. There was a garage at the end of the driveway. Lifting up the overhead door revealed a Nissan. Starner searched the glove compartment. No registration papers. The VIN number that should have been in the corner of the dashboard where it meets the windshield was scraped off, and the information that had been on the driver's side door post was obliterated with what looked like a blowtorch, because the metal was blackened and scarred. The license plate was from Idaho but had no date on it.

Starner went back to his truck and ran a check on the plate. It came back as registered to a 2011 Plymouth Voyager SUV. The database listed the vehicle as "wrecked, sold as scrap, 3/2/2017." Someone had taken great pains to make this car untraceable. He was sure, however, that the Feds would be able to figure out its origins.

Starner stood on the front porch and contemplated what clearly was a crime scene. What happened here had been staged, just like what he saw at Boulette's house, at the swamp behind her house, and on Picox Lane. Corpses were piling up all over Petit Rouge Parish. The burned body of the guy in the missing big rig. Boulette. Debrun. Judson. The young man whose fake driver's license identified him as Thomas Closser from New Orleans. And now this girl, Maggie Mae Delacourte, or whatever her real name was. Moreover, Boyo still hadn't been found. A series of coincidences? Not likely. All these events had to be connected in some way. But how?

What could possibly be the common link? Debrun was a hefty roustabout. He would have put up a fight before letting anyone smash him on the head and break his neck. Judson's assailant tried to make it appear that Judson had been shot by Thomas Closser.

How could Maggie Mae, or anyone else for that matter, have killed Judson on one side of the ditch and Closser in the middle of the road? Why would the killer sweep the dirt to tidy the scene around Closser but not around Judson?

And what about the commercial vehicle tracks on Picox Lane? What kind of truck or bus would have driven that way and to what end?

As soon as that thought entered Starner's mind, however, he sat bolt upright.

Of course, he thought. It wasn't necessarily a truck.

It could have been a bus.

Maybe it was Boulette's bus, with Kenny behind the wheel.

Kenny had been driving unusually slowly when Starner encountered him this morning, just a half mile past Picox Lane.

Had Kenny and his bus been there? It was certainly possible. Judson and Closser were probably already dead by the time Starner pulled alongside Kenny.

Kenny? Skinny, Mickey Mouse-voiced Kenny? Could it be?

Debrun would never have let himself get beaten up and killed by Kenny, would he? How could that wimp have knocked out the roustabout and gotten the huge guy into his car before driving it into the swamp?

Was Kenny a good enough shot to kill both Judson and Closser? And if so, why would he have bothered to wipe the ground around Tommy's body and then drive away so cautiously? Anyone but a cold-blooded, professional killer would have high-tailed it from the scene as soon as possible.

If the tire marks on Picox Lane were caused by the school bus Kenny was driving, wouldn't Kenny have been in a rush to flee the carnage?

Maggie Mae's suicide note said she was responsible for the deaths on Picox Lane. So, were the dead gal and Kenny hooking up? What would she have seen in him? On the other hand, was she using him? Was Kenny easily charmed by an attractive girl, like a moth attracted to a bright flame?

But if that was the case, the flame had been extinguished. By Kenny? And, if so, why would he want to make it look like she committed suicide?

Kenny appeared to be the common thread.

Starner knew what his next move had to be. He would let the FBI run the investigation of the Red Zone and the cocaine, the shootings on Picox Lane, and the "suicide" on Muscadine Street. The walls around Knock's insular parish were starting to crash down, and Starner was happy to open the ramparts and let the outside storm in.

Boulette's bus, however, was a local matter. Even though his job was about to disappear, Starner was determined to make one final effort to achieve the justice he swore to uphold, an oath he had conveniently overlooked in his years of servility to Knock.

He made it his mission to find and interrogate Kenny Arvenal as soon as possible.

PART VI

FRIDAY

CHAPTER SIXTY

Kenny stood in front of the mirror, admiring the snug fit of the suicide vest. Five tubular pockets on the left and five more on the right. Inside of each was a carefully crafted roll of R-37 explosives, which from all outward appearances was a seemingly innocuous cylinder of white plastic.

The Precept checked the wiring, snapped the locks in place, and handed Kenny the yellow St. Bonaventure school bus driver's shirt that hung from the hook on the side of the barn next to Kenny's bed.

"Make sure," the Precept instructed, "that you have enough freedom of movement to drive the bus and manipulate the handle that opens the door."

Kenny waved his arms up and down and side to side. "This fits great! No problem!"

Kenny remembered how, when the Precept first gave him the SBSB uniform, it was too big. Kenny hadn't said anything about it because he figured that was the only size the Precept could get his hands on. But now Kenny marveled at how well the Precept had planned ahead. With his suicide vest in place, the oversize yellow shirt fit perfectly, and, since the bottom of the suicide vest extended below his waist, his uniform pants fit better as well.

"Let's go over everything one more time," the Precept said.

"I got it, Precept, we've talked about this like a thousand times already! I know what I'm doing. Memorized every step! Pick up the kids and the parents who'll be chaperones. Go to the school and pick up the teachers. Drive careful-like to New Orleans. Get on the I-310 ramp at Boutte. Follow it across the Mississippi River 'til it

213

hooks up on the East Bank with I-10, and then turn right on I-10 south into the city. Exit at the sign that says 'Vieux Carré.' Turn on Conti into the French Quarter. Then onto Decatur, to where Stage Five is set up by Jackson Square, a block away from the place that sells beignets. Drive the bus slowly through the crowd so that no one suspects anything. Then, when I pull up to the stage where the crowd is the thickest, push the red button next the driver's seat. Boom! Couldn't be simpler!"

The Precept watched Kenny get more and more animated as he spoke. He needed Kenny to be calm, not hyper. "That's right, Kenny," he said soothingly, "you know exactly what to do. Now remember, I'll be right behind you on my motorcycle the whole time."

The Precept handed Kenny a new cell phone. "Untraceable. Never been used. It fits here, right inside your shirt. There's a pocket on your vest for it. And this is a Bluetooth headset. Latest model. It's like one of those tiny hearing aids that are almost invisible. You put this in your left ear so that the kids, the chaperones, and the teachers can't see it when they get on the bus. You and I will be connected the whole time. This headset has a speaker in it, so that I can hear everything you say. If anything comes up or you have any questions, just talk. I'll hear you and cue you on—not that you'll need any help, of course, since you're so well prepared. You're on your way to being a world-famous hero, admired by all and welcomed by our Lord Jesus to glory."

Kenny took the miniature headset and tried it on in front of the mirror. The Precept was right. It was almost invisible in his ear. He'd wear his SBSB yellow cap low so no one would see it. He turned to the Precept. "You might be speaking in my ear this morning, but before lunch today I'll be speaking directly to God!"

"That's right, Kenny, that's right," the Precept said as he led Kenny to the table where he had set out the food Kenny had ordered for his last breakfast. A bowl of Cap'n Crunch, two Sara Lee cinnamon rolls, and a dozen Krispy Kreme donuts. "Let me put this big napkin around your neck so you don't spill anything on your uniform, and while I'm doing that, look over here, to your left, next to the box of donuts."

Kenny's eyes opened wide with amazement as he picked up the framed certificate. "You don't mean . . .?"

"Yes, Kenny. Last night, the Supreme Kommander authorized your elevation. Yesterday, you were Member Two Thousand Four Hundred Sixty-One. Today, you are no longer just a Member. You are not even a Saxon. You're now Imperial Forty-Three."

Kenny held the frame as if it enclosed the world's most valuable treasure. Little did he know that the Precept had printed it on his computer last night, right after he had returned from murdering Maggie Mae.

"Imperial!" Kenny was ecstatic. "I can't believe it! I'm an Imperial!"

The Precept gave Kenny a congratulatory tap on his shoulder. "Fastest elevation ever. Aspirant to Member, and then directly to Imperial without having to qualify as a Saxon. You, Kenny, are special and unique. I doubt anyone else will ever achieve so speedy a promotion. Now, eat your breakfast, because you've got to get a move on. Can't be late, today of all days."

Kenny carefully put the framed certificate down at the far end of the table, away from the food so it wouldn't get soiled, grabbed a cinnamon roll in one hand and a donut in the other, and alternated taking a bite out of each as he recalled the Precept's predictions on the day he first arrived for training.

Kenny swelled with pride as he once again imagined the Aspirants chanting, "KEN-NY, KEN-NY, KEN-NY," during their daily drills

Life, Kenny thought, was sweet. Death would be even sweeter.

CHAPTER SIXTY-ONE

Starner had been at the office since 5 a.m., fruitlessly trying to make sense of things. The whole situation made him feel like he was staring at a kids' coloring book where pictures became obvious only after all the dots were connected. The problem was that Starner couldn't connect the dots to form a complete image.

What he learned from Cooper made things even more puzzling. When he called Cooper last night while waiting for the FBI team to arrive at Maggie Mae Delacourte's house, the superintendent agreed to go into the School Board office early today to locate Kenny's address.

"After all," Cooper had said, "I got to get in almost at the crack of dawn anyway, what with all three classes of second graders going down to New Orleans to perform at the Unity Festival, thanks to Mrs. Huval's planning. Plus, the sixth graders are having their field day. End of school events tend to pile up and happen all at once. Then there's the double funeral tomorrow for Boulette and Debrun."

Starner looked at the paper on which he had written down the cell phone number and address Cooper gave him. Although he called Kenny several times, no one answered the phone, and its voice mail was yet to be activated. That was puzzling enough, but stranger still were the School Board's records showing Kenny's home address for the past year was at the same Muscadine Street address where Braydon found Maggie Mae Delacourte's body. If Kenny was shacking up with Delacourte, there was no evidence of it. From his search of the Muscadine Street home last night, Starner was certain no man was living there. No men's clothing, shoes, or shaving gear were on the premises.

Further, if Kenny had been coming and going from Muscadine Street, he hadn't done so in the school bus. Both Starner and the FBI examined the grounds carefully. There was no indication a bus ever parked at that address. Muscadine Street was too narrow, and there were no tire tracks of any kind on the dirt driveway or unmown lawn.

Starner crossed the courthouse building hall to check the property files in the clerk of court's office. He had no problem getting in, because Ed kept a set of master keys for the entire building in her desk.

The property sales and tax records for the house on Muscadine not only failed to clarify matters, but also raised additional questions. The homeowner was listed as Thomas Closser of New Orleans, yet the records indicated that taxes had been paid through the end of the year by Bubba Mauvais of St. Bonaventure Parish.

Kenny was still the link, but how and why was Bubba involved? Starner had arrested Bubba twice for speeding in Petit Rouge. Bubba belonged to the NightHawks, a motorcycle club that had its own "church." Services were held Wednesday evenings and Sunday mornings at a hanger in an abandoned airstrip in St. Bonaventure. The NightHawks wore black motorcycle helmets with tinted faceguards that hid their features and leather jackets adorned with the image of a large bird silhouetted against an orange sunrise.

Nothing added up, and Bubba's involvement only increased the confusion. Nevertheless, several things seemed certain. The records concerning the Muscadine Street house linked Kenny, Maggie Mae, Bubba, and Thomas Closser.

Starner wanted the FBI to handle the cocaine, the Red Zone, and the deaths of Judson, Closser, and Maggie Mae, but Starner wanted to be the first person to question Kenny.

According to Cooper, Kenny's initial pickup was at 6:50 a.m., so the bus was undoubtedly already on the road. The last thing Starner wanted to do was stop a school bus full of children on their way to sing at a festival in New Orleans.

On the other hand, Starner didn't want to wait until Kenny returned to Petit Rouge with the kids. Every minute that went by gave the Feds another chance to find a link to Kenny and intercept him before Starner could.

Starner figured the only solution was to wait on the highway that skirted the edge of Petit Rouge Parish and led south to the interstate connection to New Orleans. That was the quickest route, so Kenny was sure to take it. Starner would follow the bus once it passed him and interview Kenny in New Orleans right after he dropped the kids off for their performance.

The fact that he was going to interrogate Kenny in the Crescent City rather than in Petit Rouge did not bother Starner. Nor was he bothered by leaving Petit Rouge without a "peace officer" for the day. If the answering service called him while he was out of the parish, he'd simply tell them to summon the state police instead. He was certain the state police would relish being invited into Knock's reserve.

What did bother Starner, however, was the possibility of not being the first one to confront Kenny and thereby losing the opportunity to prove his worth—to himself.

CHAPTER SIXTY-TWO

Fifty-seven second graders were noisily chatting away when Mrs. Huval clapped her hands to get everyone's attention. "Children, listen up." She pointed a finger at two boys in the back of the bus who were busy whispering to one another. "That means you, Gabe and Caleb."

The two boys turned to face the teacher and, with sly grins, made a motion with their hands as if they were locking their lips shut and throwing away the key.

"Boys and girls, we're off on our big adventure, and I really need y'all to pay attention. I'm sorry that Ronnie, Cassandra, and Krystelle are out sick today. We'll really miss them. Each of you is going to have to sing even louder than we practiced to make up for their absence. I'm also sad that their mothers, who were supposed to be chaperones along with Miss Truvi, Abigayle's mom, won't be with us to help. So, with only four adults—the other second grade teachers, Mrs. Wexler and Mrs. Valentine, along with Miss Truvi and me—y'all are going to have to be on your best behavior. I know you can all do that! Let me see a show of hands of everyone who can cooperate!"

The bus was filled with arms flapping furiously. Gabe and Caleb let out big whoops as well, and Gabe poked Caleb in the ribs, "I can cooperate better than you can!"

Caleb poked him back. "Cannot! I'm the most cooperatingest of all!"

Mrs. Huval smiled. "Hush up, you two. Remember, cooperating means eyes forward, hands to yourself, and brain engaged. It does not mean mouth in motion!"

Abigayle, sitting near the front of the bus with Truvi, straightened her shoulders, folded her hands in her lap, and whispered, "See, Momma? I'm doing exactly as Mrs. Huval says."

Truvi patted her on the head. "Yes darlin', almost exactly. All except for the mouth not in motion part."

Mrs. Huval waited until everyone on the bus was quiet. "We won't get to the outskirts of New Orleans for a while, and then it may be another hour or so to make it through all that big-city traffic. Since our performance is not until eleven this morning, we have plenty of time to get there. Mr. Kenny is driving real careful, and he's going to stop at the state park to give us a bathroom and snack break, because once we get on the interstate highway in all that traffic, he won't be able to stop. Right, Mr. Kenny?"

Not able to stop? Kenny found this too amusing as he struggled to keep a straight face. Nothing could halt the plan now. Before dawn, he had watched the Prefect rig the timer on the explosives they'd placed in the house and barn. The detonators were set to go off this morning. There would be an explosion and blaze so huge that it would keep all the fire units in St. Bonaventure Parish, where the Prefect's property was located, fully occupied for hours. The body of the man with the swastika tattoo that Kenny had shot, Imperial Ten, would be cremated, and all evidence of what Kenny and the Prefect had been working on would be destroyed. The Supreme Kommander's plan was a go. The great day had come. Nothing could stop Kenny now. He didn't take his eyes off the road to respond to Mrs. Huval but simply raised his right hand and waved in agreement.

Mrs. Huval pulled a pitch pipe from the pocket of her slacks and blew a piercing tone. "Hear that note? That's where we start the song, but you know that, because you've been rehearsing for weeks. This is your big day. Huge crowds will be at the Unity Festival, so you've got to sing out as loudly as you can. Let's try it right now! Everyone, belt out the song and use the hand motions I taught you. Ready?"

The entire bus filled with the sounds of children's voices singing:

Love can make the world go 'round.
Love will bring us up, not down.
Love keeps us to-ge-ther, not apart.
Love is in ev-er-y body's heart.
Each of us has things to share.
Each of us has love to spare.
U-ni-ty is big, not small.
All for one and one for all.
Me with you and you with me.
Let's hear it for u-ni-ty.
U-ni-ty! U-ni-ty! U-ni-ty!

When they finished, Mrs. Huval, Mrs. Wexler, Mrs. Valentine, and Truvi enthusiastically applauded as the kids beamed. "That," Mrs. Huval said, "was just beautiful." She blew on her pitch pipe. "But, as you know, practice makes perfect. Let's sing it again!"

The song irritated Kenny. He found the lyrics stupid. Unity! Love! Meaningless babble. The only thing that mattered was the word of the true God. And completing his mission.

Kenny looked in his rearview mirror. He saw a motorcyclist trailing him. It was reassuring to see the Precept following along, just as he had promised.

CHAPTER SIXTY-THREE

A half hour after Starner parked on a side road south of the parish line, his big Ford Raptor hidden from the main road by the tall sugarcane that rose up from fields on either side, the St. Bonaventure school bus driven by Kenny passed by on the two-lane highway in front of him.

The traffic on the main thoroughfare was sparse. An angler towing a boat behind his truck. A shrimper's van heading back to the coast to pick up its next shipment. And a helmeted motorcyclist in a leather jacket sporting a large bird silhouetted against an orange sunrise.

Letting the boat, van, and motorcycle stay between him and the school bus, Starner drove patiently as the road traced the curves of the Mississippi, the levee looming on his left and acres upon acres of cane and soybeans on his right.

The bus slowed as it neared Cane Break Preserve, a poorly maintained state park with ancient picnic tables, overgrown trails through a small, wooded grove, and a concrete building with toilets. The angler and the shrimper scooted around Kenny's bus as it steered into the park, but the motorcyclist stopped on the shoulder of the road, took off his helmet, used his handkerchief to wipe his sweaty brow, and scanned the paved surface behind him.

The deputy recognized Bubba Mauvais immediately. What was he doing here? Following Kenny's bus?

Starner braked and drifted onto the road's shoulder behind the motorcycle. Exiting his truck, he leaned against its hood.

Bubba did not dismount from his cycle. He just glared at the deputy and revved his engine.

"Hey, Bubba. It's a beautiful day. What's the hurry?"

"Cut the shit, old man. You got no jurisdiction down here."

"Just want to chat a minute. Kind of far away from your place in St. Bonaventure, aren't you? Out for an early morning ride? Guess you don't have to work these days. Rolling in money? Heard you paid taxes on a home on Muscadine Street in Petit Rouge. You're a multi-parish property investor now?"

Bubba didn't panic when he heard that. He realized that if Starner was mentioning the Muscadine house, Maggie Mae's body must have been found. However that happened, Starner being here was not a coincidence, not with Kenny's bus in the park just ahead. Today of all days! Kenny's mission had to be completed, and Starner was just one speed bump to overcome. Putting on his helmet, he withdrew a large handgun from his saddlebag.

As Bubba lifted his arm to shoot, Starner ducked behind his truck.

Bubba calmly walked toward the Ford Raptor, arm extended, looking for a better shot.

Starner inched his way to the driver's side door, jumped in, and slammed the truck into reverse.

Bubba fired off three rounds. One of the bullets pierced the windshield just to the right of the rearview mirror and lodged in the back of the cab.

Starner kept his foot on the accelerator, driving backward down the highway as the Raptor's wheels squealed.

Bubba jumped on his motorcycle and sped down the road in pursuit of the deputy.

Starner, still driving in reverse, saw through the bullet-damaged windshield that Bubba was closing the gap between them. Glancing briefly in his rearview mirror and, grateful that he saw no other vehicles behind him, Starner jammed his foot on the brake pedal. His truck fishtailed sideways, its tires squealing, and started spinning. He wrestled the steering wheel to gain control, and the Raptor came to rest ten yards into a soybean field.

Bubba halted in the middle of the road. He shot twice more at the truck.

Starner ducked low in the driver's seat and turned the truck into the field as one bullet blew out the passenger-side window, piercing the roof, and the other perforated the doorframe.

The Raptor bounced across the field as Starner tore through the soybeans. He didn't risk going directly down a row, because the motorcycle could follow if he drove in a straight line, concomitant with the planting, The truck's four-wheel drive enabled the Raptor to easily climb up one steep ridge, down into the narrow furrow, and up the next ridge, jerking along at 20 miles per hour.

Starner drove until he reached a field cut, the dirt pathway where irrigation lines were laid and, turning onto it, paused to make sure Bubba was not following. Putting the truck back in gear, he steered in the direction of the main road. The field cut ended in clumps of lizard grass and alligator weed that grew up in the low-lying area near the highway. The truck easily maneuvered through it.

The front of the hood was just starting to climb back up to the mounded roadbed when another shot rang out.

Grabbing a rifle from the rack behind his head, Starner slid out the door into the mud. He had no intention of killing Bubba. He needed him alive. But the deputy wanted to be prepared for any eventuality.

Bubba was riding straight toward him, firing as he came.

Starner aimed for the motorcycle's front tire and squeezed the trigger three times. None of the bullets hit its mark, but Bubba, realizing that the deputy was firing at him, got off one round after another while simultaneously steering with one hand and swerving sharply.

Too sharply.

Bubba lost control of his chopper. It skidded out from under him as both he and the cycle spun across the macadam at 30 miles per hour. The motorcycle slid onto the shoulder, leaving metallic marks where the handlebars scraped the road. Bubba's body flipped over and over until it came to rest, motionless, on the side of the highway.

Starner approached slowly, rifle in hand. He bent down and touched Bubba's neck. No pulse. He removed the shattered motorcycle helmet. Bubba's lifeless eyes were open and his lips were locked in a sneer.

CHAPTER SIXTY-FOUR

S tarner weighed his options.

Bubba's unprovoked attack confirmed Starner's suspicions. He had uncovered more than just a link between Bubba, Kenny, Maggie Mae, and the Picox Lane shootings. Nothing was as it appeared to be. Not the deaths of Judson and the mysterious Thomas Closser. Not the "suicide" of Maggie Mae Delacourte. Not even Debrun's "accidental" death in the swamp behind Boulette's house—a house, Starner now recalled, where he had discovered motorcycle tracks leading off the driveway. He resolved to get the FBI to send a team to examine them to see if they matched the treads to Bubba's tires and to check Bubba's place to ascertain whether there was anything there connecting him with Thomas or Maggie Mae.

But, once he placed the call, what next, with Bubba dead and Kenny driving a busload of kids to New Orleans? Starner knew if he called the local sheriff's office they'd come out and have a field day asking why he was operating outside of his jurisdiction. He would be required to wait until investigators arrived. The bullet holes in Starner's truck would validate his story about being attacked by Bubba but would lead to even more queries.

While Starner was pondering the possibilities, his phone rang. He recognized the number. It was the St. Bonaventure Sheriff's Department, the parish where Bubba had his farm.

The moment Starner said hello, Sheriff Isiah Brown came on, and he was none too happy.

"I don't know what the hell you're involved in, Deputy, but why the hell is the FBI calling my office about that fucking

225

racist redneck, Bubba Mauvais? Some wise ass with the FBI just phoned and said that, at your suggestion, they were headed my way to cordon off Bubba's property until they got a search warrant and were informing me as a matter of courtesy! Why the hell are you working with the FBI to initiate something in my parish? I'd sooner shoot my best hunting dog for no good reason then let one of Knock's deputies stick his big nose anywhere outside of Petit Rouge, especially after a Petit Rouge deputy—you, I bet!—insulted my sister the other day and gave her a pricey ticket for allegedly going two miles over the speed limit in Knock's fucking little speed trap. Let me tell you something. You want to investigate activity in my parish? Don't call the FBI and assume I'll just roll over. You come to me first so I can tell you 'Hell no' to your face and kick you in the ass when you turn to leave! What do you think the FBI will find when they get here? Fucking nothing! Bubba's house and barn were practically incinerated in a blast a twenty minutes ago. The fire's so huge that we're calling in fire trucks from all over. The fire chief tells me there's a hole where part of the barn used to be, and the entire area's hot as hell. The chief says that shooting water on it's like pissing on a hot stove. The liquid turns right to steam, and the metal beams Bubba installed in that barn of his are melting like they were made of wax."

Starner couldn't believe what Sheriff Brown was saying. Melted metal beams? Like the blast on Sunday morning that engulfed the tractor trailer? What had Bubba been up to?

Kenny was in the middle of something massive and dangerous. Something involving not only shootings, but also explosions so intense they caused infernos that melted metal, like on the tractor trailer missing from Boyo's yard.

Starner was more concerned than ever. A melted truck. The melting metal on Bubba's barn. A web of murders that Bubba and Kenny were either weaving or in which they were enwrapped.

It was dangerously possible that something else could be on that bus in addition to innocent children.

Starner chose his words carefully. "Sheriff, I suggest you tell the fire chief to pull his folks back and ask the FBI to get a bomb squad over there."

Leaving Bubba's body and motorcycle where they were, off on the side of the road, Starner next phoned the FBI, telling them where to find Bubba's body but not disclosing he would not be on-site when they arrived.

There was no way to convince anyone to act quickly enough. It was up to him and him alone to catch up with Kenny before the bus made its way into the French Quarter. Getting into his truck, with its shattered windshield and bullet-pierced passenger door, he turned on his siren.

CHAPTER SIXTY-FIVE

Having gotten to the Crescent City early, Art Brady walked to the levee at the foot of Canal Street. He confirmed with Imperial Two that all five Saxons were in place and none of them were aware of the others' existence or mission. Each Saxon assumed he was the sole person privileged enough to witness, record, and immortalize an event whose details could not be revealed in advance, but which would readily be apparent when it occurred. Imperial Two guaranteed Art that he would live-stream what they were about to behold directly to the Alabaster Brigade's computer servers. And yes, Imperial Two said, they were all positioned appropriately.

Despite the current problems, Art was confident his master plan would still come off without a hitch. Even Imperial Two did not know that he, along with the other Saxons, would become martyrs as the conflagration flared, destroying the buildings they were stationed in and turning blocks and blocks of the French Quarter into an incandescent pyre.

The planes that hit the twin towers in Manhattan, Art consoled himself, merely brought down two buildings and damaged a few others. Only three thousand lives were lost. Even the planes that hit the Pentagon on 9/11 didn't destroy it. Today, however, the world would witness real destruction. Not just the loss of two iconic buildings in the heart of New York, but rather a force so strong that it would tear the heart out of the Crescent City. Blocks upon blocks of hotels, restaurants, businesses, apartments, and houses in the French Quarter will disintegrate. The St. Louis Cathedral in Jackson Square, the oldest continually active church in the country,

will be reduced to rubble, its Rococo altar destroyed, its steel but-
tresses liquid puddles. The Pontalba Apartments, dating back to
the 1840s and surrounding Jackson Square on two sides, will be
in ashes, their red bricks crumbled, their wrought iron balconies
reduced to unrecognizable metallic lumps. The Cabildo on Jackson
Square, a museum in the old Spanish seat of government, and its
companion building, the Presbytère, would be annihilated along
with their historic collections. The records of the past had to be
extinguished to usher in the new order.

The old hotels that filled the French Quarter, with their liver-
ied doormen and French-themed décor? Art smiled, knowing that
when the time arrived, they too would be gone.

The trendy new boutique hotels filled with affluent nonbelievers? Destroyed.

The beignet shops? The antique stores? The jazz clubs? The up-
scale bars and the low dives? The tourist haunts? Gutted and ravaged.

But it will not be just buildings, Art exalted. The Unity Festival's
thirty thousand or more attendees jammed in the Quarter also
would be incinerated in a flash.

In light of that, every other perceived problem was small.
Yesterday, Randall Millguard, Tommy's uncle, accused Art of having "overarching hubris coupled with gross incompetence." He
threatened to cut off all funding because of Tommy's death.

Millguard's threats did not deter Art. At this point, they were
meaningless. Millguard thought he could hide behind his money,
a puppeteer pulling the strings of the Alabaster Brigade. But Art
knew that the future was his and his alone. Once the world saw the
power of the Alabaster Brigade, others would flock to support it.
Money would flow in, first in a stream, then in a river, providing a
Niagara of resources. Even the Friends of Alabaster would not be
able to deny the mastery of Art's plan. They would fall in line, Art
felt certain. If you dream big enough, if you allow nothing to stand
in your way, and if you accomplish what you promise, the world
will follow. They will overlook anything and agree to everything
a true visionary espouses. Look at Hitler, Art thought. He failed

not because his vision was tainted but because his generals let him down. Art was not going to let the imperfections of his underlings undermine his goal.

Bubba's phone not working? Bubba not answering? There was still time. Bubba's failure to keep his line open and respond immediately would be addressed in due course.

The mission was underway, and nothing was going to interfere with it. From his perch on the levee, Art could see the packed streets of the French Quarter, the crowds pouring in packed shoulder-to-shoulder for the Unity Festival. On his cell phone he watched the real-time videos streamed by his Saxons showing street upon street of vendors hawking balloons and T-shirts to the thousands upon thousands filling the Quarter, buskers playing guitars and trumpets straining to be heard above the cacophony, and the massive stage on Jackson Square where the main performances were occurring and where, right now, a high school band was performing.

Art checked his watch. The St. Bonaventure school children were scheduled to perform soon. Art had not the slightest concern that Abigayle would perish with all the others when Kenny detonated the explosives. Neither she nor Truvi meant anything to him. Each was as insignificant as a fly you flick away. They were black. They deserved to be discarded in pursuit of the greater good.

He tried Bubba again. No answer.

No problem.

Art dialed into the line he had set up for Kenny's phone. "Imperial Forty-Three, listen up. This is the Supreme Kommander."

CHAPTER SIXTY-SIX

The first time Kenny heard the Supreme Kommander's voice through his earpiece, he gasped. The Supreme Kommander was actually talking to him! The Supreme Kommander who planned it all! The Supreme Kommander who anointed him an Imperial!

The Supreme Kommander instructed Kenny to report directly to him from now on because the Precept was "otherwise occupied."

Report directly to the Supreme Kommander! Kenny could barely believe it. He was going to change history today, and he would be under the direct supervision of the Supreme Kommander!

Kenny intended to follow the Supreme Kommander's instructions precisely. Continue into the French Quarter and execute the plan.

Following orders, however, proved harder than anticipated. The interstate was backed up. Near the airport it was bumper-to-bumper, and by the time Kenny finally reached the point where the road curved into the Central Business District and skirted the French Quarter, gridlock had set in. The bus could barely move faster than a crawl. Kenny never expected the Unity Festival to be such a draw. The roads were as snarled as they were during Mardi Gras.

When Kenny finally reached the Vieux Carré exit, he was completely stymied. Police had set up barricades across every nearby street leading into the French Quarter. All vehicles were being directed to Esplanade, blocks and blocks away from the main stage.

The second graders didn't seem to mind the delay. They ran from one side of the bus to the other and talked excitedly among themselves as Mrs. Huval pointed out the sights. The wrought iron balconies with their thick baskets of drooping ferns. The crowds of colorfully dressed people streaming on foot into the Unity Festival area, swarming around the bus headed for the entrance gates and waving at the kids as they passed. The huge archway beckoning visitors to enter Louis Armstrong Park.

Mrs. Huval walked up and down the aisle, reminding the children that they had to stay seated until they reached the drop-off point at the foot of the festival stage.

Kenny honked his horn and tried to turn on the street the Precept had told him to take, but as he did so, a cop with a nightstick tapped on the school bus door.

"Get a move on!" The policeman pointed in a completely different direction than the route the Precept made him memorize.

Kenny whispered urgently, "Supreme Kommander! Can you hear me. They're not letting me turn on the street the Precept insisted I use. A cop is telling me I can't drive into the Quarter from here!"

The Supreme Kommander's voice was calm and reassuring. "No problem, Imperial Forty-Three. Do you have the Unity Festival permit sign on your windshield?"

Kenny nodded, forgetting that the Supreme Kommander couldn't see him.

"Can you hear me, Imperial Forty-Three? Is your Unity Festival permit visible?"

Kenny checked again. The large purple and green card with the Unity Festival insignia and the big letters written across it in gold reading "Performer's Vehicle: 11 a.m. Show" was firmly taped to the bottom-right side of the front windshield. "Yes, Supreme Kommander." Kenny started to salute, but he caught himself and used his hand to scratch his forehead, hoping that no one aboard noticed.

"Good," the Supreme Kommander said. "Just follow the instructions the cop gives you until you're on Decatur Street. Then, point out the sign to the officer. He'll let you in. From there, proceed as planned. I have complete confidence in you, Imperial Forty-Three."

Kenny was elated. No way he would let the Supreme Kommander down. "Yes sir! Eighty-eight!"

Mrs. Huval was returning to her seat and only caught the very end of what Kenny had said. "Kenny! Of course you ate! Remember? You scarfed down the Snickers bar you brought with you when we were at Cane Break Preserve, even though you wouldn't get out of the bus to join us at the picnic tables. But don't worry, we'll have lunch after the children's performance. We'll all be hungry by that time."

Kenny bit his lower lip to keep from laughing. Little did Mrs. Huval know that there would be no second grade performance today. No performance at all except for the performance of his final deed when the time came for him to push the red button.

CHAPTER SIXTY-SEVEN

As Starner neared the city, the scrum of cars did not automatically move out of his way, despite the fact that his siren was blaring. Even from his high perch in the Ford Raptor, he could not see any sign of Kenny's school bus through his bullet-shattered windshield.

Steering onto the wide thoroughfare's narrow shoulder next to the concrete barriers and honking his horn constantly, Starner maneuvered through the traffic on the interstate. He impatiently wended his way through the suburbs, passed the Metairie cemeteries with their acres upon acres of above-ground tombs, and crossed over the elevated span that skimmed the campus of Xavier University. At the wide turn by the Superdome, the expressway backed up even further, and when he was finally able to exit on Basin Street, the traffic ahead was at a complete standstill. There was no hope at this point of intercepting Kenny's bus before it entered the French Quarter. Starner was undeterred. He would find Kenny, question him, and inspect the bus.

Ignoring the "no parking" signs, Starner ran his truck over the curb and onto the grassy median lined with crepe myrtles and palm trees. Turning off his siren but leaving on the blue-strobe flashers, he locked his truck and took off on foot.

Starner knew this area well from his years on the Crescent City police force. Once he was in the Quarter, it was a short jog to Jackson Square where Cooper said the St. Bonaventure kids would be singing. It would be standard festival procedure to have a drop-off area for performers' vehicles set aside somewhere near Jackson Square.

It was just a matter of locating it. He was certain Kenny's bus was headed there, and, once he spotted it, he was sure to find Kenny.

All the streets leading from Rampart into the Quarter, however, had been cordoned off by the N.O.P.D., and officers were manning every entry, directing pedestrians to one of the six Unity Festival entrances, and allowing only French Quarter residents who had the appropriate stickers on their cars to go in or out.

Seeing Starner's Petit Rouge Parish uniform, the cop on duty on the corner of Rampart and Conti allowed him to enter.

Starner glanced at his watch as the metal barrier opened. Starner accelerated his pace. The more he thought about what Sheriff Isaiah Brown said about the conflagration at Bubba's farm, the more he became convinced he had to get the kids as far away from Kenny as possible.

This end of the French Quarter was residential, lined with two-story, pastel-painted buildings. Narrow wrought iron galleries protruded over the sidewalks on both sides of the street. Every ground-level window and entrance was concealed by wooden hurricane shutters pulled tight to protect the inhabitants from the prying eyes of passersby.

As Starner neared Bourbon Street, the apartments and condos closeted behind locked doors and high walls gave way to restaurants, bars, and shops selling New Orleans-themed paraphernalia, Mardi Gras beads, decorative masks, and T-shirts. The press of human flesh grew so tight that Starner could no longer trot broken-field around all those enjoying the sights and sounds as music blared from every bar's speakers, musicians performed on temporary stages set up at street corners, and street peddlers tried to entice everyone with trinkets ranging from the gaudy to the risqué.

Starner finally reached Royal Street. He turned and could see the St. Louis Cathedral on Jackson Square ahead of him. Panting heavily, he redoubled his efforts.

CHAPTER SIXTY-EIGHT

Truvi was conferring with Mrs. Huval at the front of the bus. "Are we going to make it to the stage in time?"

"What do you think, Kenny?" Mrs. Huval asked. "We just cleared the security barrier, but we're at a dead stop, still four blocks from Jackson Square." She looked out the windshield and sighed, seeing the long lines of anxious festivalgoers jamming the French Quarter streets in front of them. "Oh, never mind. We can walk faster than you can drive at this point. Just open the door and let us out. We'll meet up with you after they sing. If I don't get the children to Stage Five before eleven, they'll miss their performance slot. We can't let that happen, now can we?"

Kenny seethed. Why was she talking about "we"? What was going to happen at 11 a.m. had nothing to do with what she wanted. The destiny of everyone on the bus, and everyone in the crowd, was preordained. The Supreme Kommander's orders must be obeyed. Death was decreed for everyone in sight and beyond. The performing pickaninnies and their chaperones. The black man ahead of him in the crowd with a white gal on his arm. The brown-skinned families presuming they could ever be the equals of anyone other than those of even darker shades. The young couples pushing strollers with fair-haired children who looked Aryan but whose parents mistakenly believed in "unity" instead of God's truth of the supremacy of the white race.

Mrs. Huval, neither appreciating the angry look of impatience that Kenny gave her nor his failure to respond to her question, grabbed her purse off her seat. "Children! Listen up. That means all of you! We're going to have an adventure. We're going to have to walk, double-quick, through the French Quarter so that we'll make it to Stage Five in time for you to sing our Unity Song. Stand up and follow me. Mrs. Wexler will line you up on the sidewalk. Mrs. Valentine will count heads. And Miss Truvi will bring up the rear to make sure we all keep up. Right, Miss Truvi?"

Truvi nodded. "No one is going astray on my watch."

Abigayle was triply excited. Not only was she going to get to actually walk through the famous French Quarter, and not only was she going to perform the Unity Song with her classmates in front of lots of people, but now her mother also had an official role in all of this.

"Kenny," Mrs. Huval said firmly, "open the door!"

Kenny didn't budge.

Mrs. Huval leaned over and, before Kenny could stop her, yanked on the handle that operated the double folding door and started ushering the children down the stairs and out onto the street. "Everyone! Let's go. Lickety-split."

Mrs. Wexler hopped out and briskly began organizing the second graders as they exited, making them stand in pairs on the sidewalk.

Kenny froze. Should he slam the door shut to keep the rest of the kids in the bus? Should he push the red button right now? What would the Kommander want him to do?

But as soon as these thoughts entered his head, Kenny pushed them aside. He knew the Supreme Kommander's instructions were precise and were to be followed without deviation. The red button should only be pushed after he reached Stage Five at the foot of Jackson Square, where the detonation of the R-37 packed on the bus would kill the multitude of festivalgoers and initiate a fire that would incinerate all the buildings within blocks, including St. Louis Cathedral. If he pushed the red button early, the full scope of the Supreme Kommander's plan would not be achieved.

"Imperial Forty-Three. I have you in my sights. What are you doing? No one should be getting off your bus. No one!"

Kenny looked around frantically. The Supreme Kommander could see what was happening? How?

"Drive on, Imperial. Straight ahead. The pedestrians are about to die anyway. It matters not if they are crushed by the bus or consumed by the flames. Do anything and everything to get to Jackson Square. It is critical that you be in position at eleven."

The Supreme Kommander wanted him to drive forward. Kenny would obey.

The last few children were exiting the bus. Abigayle and her mother brought up the rear. As she passed him, Abigayle paused. "Mr. Kenny, you'll be there for my performance, won't you?"

Kenny brusquely shooed her and her mother out the door. He had a mission to complete.

Slamming the door shut, Kenny put the bus in gear and, honking his horn, lurched down Decatur Street into the crowd.

The Supreme Kommander had said to run people down if necessary.

It was necessary.

The pedestrians headed toward Jackson Square, meandering across the middle of the now-closed-off street, unaware that a bus was coming toward them from the rear.

Kenny sped up and steered directly into the Unity Festival attendees.

Mrs. Huval, seeing Kenny driving wildly, couldn't figure out what he was up to, but knew she didn't want the children to witness it. She shepherded her students onto a side street. "We're going to take a short cut!" she announced as cheerily as she could. "Remember, boys and girls, lickety-split if we're going to make it to the stage on time. Stay in line. Eyes forward and mouths shut."

Meanwhile, Kenny accelerated, cutting a swath through the crowd, indiscriminately mowing them down from behind. As the bus moved relentlessly forward, moans, sobs, and horrified wails arose from the injured and those witnessing the tragedy.

Panic ensued as the bus jolted up and down as it ran over those who, moments before, had been enjoying their day, calmly strolling through the Quarter.

The seething mass tried to make way for the vehicle, but the frenzy enveloping the crowd made escape difficult. Some dashed to the side of the road, overturning the tables of the arts and crafts vendors whose wares crashed down and were trampled underfoot. Others shoved and pushed one another until some fell, causing those behind to stumble. Teenagers leaped heedlessly forward like frightened gazelles, parents clutched wailing children in their arms, and elderly couples clung to each other amidst the constant jostling.

The unarmed private security guards hired by the festival stood by helplessly, unsure of what to do other than to call for help on their two-way radios.

More and more people were crushed beneath the wheels of the approaching yellow behemoth. Broken bloody bodies and shrieks of agony were left in the bus's wake.

Kenny's eyes grew wide with excitement. Adrenaline pumped through his veins. He steered to the right, then to the left, then to the right again as he careened down the street, intentionally hitting as many pedestrians as he could, relishing each thud and rejoicing in each death.

Kenny was high on the power he possessed.

He started yelling as loudly as he could, even though his voice could not be heard over the screams of the panicked people in his path. He was proclaiming his victory.

"Escape is not possible! You have but moments to live! The one true God sees all. His wrath is righteous. His ways are pure! And I am his messenger!"

Kenny began laughing hysterically. He was delirious, filled with euphoric rapture as he hit one human bowling pin after another. Each life was like a stalk of wheat waiting to be harvested, of no more importance than chaff to be discarded after threshing. The time to winnow the souls of the nonbelievers had begun! The bus was a scythe, and he was wielding it as an angel of death clad in yellow rather than black. All of this was a brief prelude to the ultimate destruction to come when he pressed the red button.

Stage Five loomed straight ahead at the foot of Jackson Square.

Kenny would carry out the Supreme Kommander's plan, thus assuring his own ascent into immorality.

CHAPTER SIXTY-NINE

S uddenly, a bullet pierced the windshield of the bus.

Kenny felt as if he had been whacked in the right shoulder with a lead mallet.

His entire right side went numb, and he couldn't move his arm.

He looked up through the cracked windshield and saw a uniformed female N.O.P.D. officer shooting at him.

Two more bullets hit the windshield, causing spider-vein cracks to spread across it until, to Kenny, it was like looking through a fun-house mirror covered with gauze.

He felt no pain. He was not going to let anyone, much less a black cunt cop, halt his ascent to glory or interrupt the Kommander's plan.

Using his left hand, Kenny steered the bus toward the woman, who kept firing. How dare she! Women are inferior to men! Blacks are inferior to whites! Everyone is inferior to the Alabaster Brigade!

The Unity Festival crowd, already fleeing in terror from the deadly path of the bus, went into full panic mode upon hearing multiple gunshots. Not knowing which way to turn, people ran as fast as they could toward whatever shelter they could find.

Distraught parents, separated from their children, shouted their kids' names.

Elderly retirees limped along as fast as they could. A few teenagers tried to assist them while others ran carelessly by, elbowing the senior citizens aside.

A wave of humanity sought refuge from the turmoil, only to encounter more chaos as the side streets became jammed. Shop doors slammed shut as stores filled up. Those already inside tried to prevent more frightened festivalgoers from piling in and crushing them.

Firing off one last shot, the officer tried to leap out of the way, but Kenny had no intention of letting her escape. He tugged hard at the wheel with his one good hand and the bus made a sharp turn. The bumper clipped the officer's knees and she fell under the bus. Kenny felt the thump as its tires crushed her.

But he had steered too hard. Seconds later the bus was climbing up the curb.

There was a terrific jolt as something large crashed down onto the roof right behind Kenny's head, and then an ominous grinding noise mixed with the sound of glass breaking under the bus.

He looked around.

The front end of the vehicle had not only demolished one of several metal pillars holding up a wrought iron balcony, now listing at a low angle, but it had also broken off one of the French Quarter's decorative metal lamp posts. The top of the pole, with heavy scrolled ironwork encasing a metal-halide bulb, had fallen onto the roof of the bus, denting it and breaking a side window. A second later, the wrought iron railing from the balcony toppled over and lodged itself into the cracked windshield.

Kenny tried to put the bus into reverse, but he needed his right hand to do that, and it wouldn't move.

He stared at his shoulder, trying to figure out what was wrong.

His yellow SBSB shirt was turning red. Its sleeve was soaked with blood.

All of a sudden, the numbness of his arm gave way to a burning sensation, then to excruciating agony.

"Kommander! Can you hear me?"

"Of course, Imperial Forty-Three." Art was watching the video feed and had seen the bus run off the road.

"I can't move the bus."

"Of course you can. The balcony above you is not going to fall. Nothing is stopping you. Back up and maneuver that vehicle straight to the stage at Jackson Square. You're already late. Do it now!"

"I've been shot!"

"Pull yourself together, dammit! You're an Imperial. You can do anything!"

Kenny tried again. He reached over with his left hand to shift into reverse, but the pain was too great.

He struggled to his feet.

"I can't drive, but I can hit the red button now. I'm only a block from Jackson Square. The time of destruction is upon us! Eighty-eight, Supreme Kommander!"

"No! Not yet!" But Art's insistence was too late.

Kenny closed his eyes and prepared for death as he forcefully pressed the red button with his left hand.

Nothing happened.

Kenny opened his eyes and hit the button a second time.

Nothing.

He pounded on it again and again.

Still nothing.

"It's not working, Kommander! Something must have torn the wiring under the bus. But immortality is mine!"

Art was glued to the video feed as Kenny stumbled out of the bus, ripping his bloodstained SBSB shirt on the wrought iron protruding from the windshield and tilting down to the street. The slit exposed Kenny's suicide vest.

Art could not wait any longer. The explosives on the bus had to be detonated.

Kenny had failed him.

There was only one thing left to do.

CHAPTER SEVENTY

Starner was nearing Jackson Square, pushing his way forward as the mass of people running in the opposite direction impeded his movements.

Ahead of him lay Stage Five. A high school jazz band was scurrying off the raised platform, overturning chairs and music stands in their rush to evacuate.

Starner couldn't see what was causing the panic, but he kept pressing forward.

He heard gunshots, but he didn't know who was shooting or why. Yet Starner refrained from drawing his Glock. He was not going to run through the crowd with a loaded gun in his hand.

As he neared Stage Five and entered Decatur Street, Starner saw that the St. Bonaventure school bus had crashed into a balcony support. The broken body of a policewoman was crushed beneath the bumper, her torso flattened by the wheels. Behind the bus lay a path of human destruction.

Kenny was on the sidewalk. His yellow uniform was torn and bloody. His right hand hung uselessly at his side under his slumping shoulder. He had a wild look in his eyes.

To his horror, Starner realized that Kenny was wearing a suicide vest. There was no mistaking it. It had pockets upon bulging pockets and wrapped around Kenny's waist were chains secured with padlocks.

Starner did not hesitate this time. He unholstered his gun.

CHAPTER SEVENTY-ONE

Art was astounded that Kenny hadn't blown up the bus. If there was something wrong with the red button, the only way to activate the explosives was to trigger Kenny's suicide vest. But, in order to detonate the dozens of packages of R-37 that Bubba stashed on the bus, it was crucial that Kenny's vest go off inside the vehicle to start the necessary chain reaction.

Art had to get Kenny back on that bus one way or another. He started running down the grass-covered levee into the heart of the French Quarter.

Art never intended to be a suicide bomber. He was a general, not a foot soldier. Until moments ago, martyrs were, to him, just disposable wannabes, failures in life until he inspired them to a greater goal. As Supreme Kommander, he carefully cultivated his recruits, molding and inculcating them into the teachings of the Alabaster Brigade.

Art spent untold hours planning the Brigade's emergence. Its domination depended upon the massive public spectacle he planned for New Orleans today at the Unity Festival.

The scores of people run down, mangled, and murdered by a barreling bus in the French Quarter? No seismic change in worldview would occur because of that. The news of the tragedy would create headlines, sure, but they would quickly be forgotten. After all, a truck had rolled over people on holiday in Nice, France, killing them, but no one remembers the name of the driver or the real motivation behind the attack. Hundreds were injured at a concert in Manchester, England, but life went on as usual shortly after. Small events attributed to terrorists occurred every month or so around the globe, but nobody paid attention to them for very long. Such small tragedies were nothing more than background noise that barely penetrated the public's awareness, only to be quickly forgotten.

Sure, the Twin Towers spectacularly fell in New York City, but even that didn't fundamentally change the world order. Sure, the Proud Boys stormed the Capitol, but the next day, nothing really changed. Art intended to initiate an incident that could not be ignored, something that would roil the status quo, create a cataclysm, and be indelibly etched in history.

The explosion that leveled downtown Beirut was caused by ammonium nitrate. The R-37 that Randall Millguard created was just as powerful and more compact. How Jackson Square looked now would be a memory in a few minutes, utterly obliterated by the Alabaster Brigade, thus guaranteeing its supremacy.

The world was long overdue for a real taste of God's wrath. Only the death of tens of thousands could accomplish that, along with the leveling of the core of New Orleans's world-famed historic district.

Art knew in his heart of hearts that the Lord is vengeful. God's will is to purge the earth of detestable people. It says so right in Leviticus. "The nations I am driving out before you have become unclean, and the land became unclean, so that I punished its iniquity, and the land vomited out its inhabitants."

Leviticus calls for the regurgitation of the foul and debased. The retching of the wretched. Purification by fire ignited in the name of the true God of all Aryans. Those who falsely preach "togetherness" and "unity" fail to obey the Lord's clear directives. As God himself said in Deuteronomy, "it is because of these detestable practices the Lord your God will drive out those nations before you."

Art knew that his destiny awaited him. The success of the Alabaster Brigade rested with him. It was an inexorable movement whose future momentum depended upon today's events.

As Art rushed down Decatur Street, gun drawn, pushing his way through the terrified throngs running in the opposite direction, a joyous calm enveloped him. If I die, he thought, it is because the success of the Bible's predictions depends upon what I do. I've primed the ranks. Hundreds of believers are now members of the Alabaster Brigade. Kommanders of lesser rank, plus scores upon scores of Precepts, Imperials, Saxons, Members, and Aspirants lurking in the shadows waiting to emerge into the sunlight of publicity that will shine upon this deed. A vast battalion of like-minded believers affiliated with us, waiting to be activated, will reinforce the cause. None of them will ever be as effective as me, but when that bus explodes in glory, raining down destruction, as is God's will, the Alabaster Brigade will be written into the history books and celebrated as the movement that heralded the start of a new world order.

As revealed in Samuel, God imposed a pestilence, but it was insufficient.

The deaths of the first-born heathens that occurred before Moses led his people out of Egypt was also insufficient.

To start a revolution will take deaths so vast and destruction so great that the world will be in shock. The tragedy must exceed even the horrifying downing of the twin towers. The false idol of "unity" must be destroyed!

Art knew his plan would assure such a victory, but it necessitated that he get Kenny back on the bus.

No longer concerned about whether he would live to see his Alabaster Brigade emerge victorious, Art was at peace. It was God's will. An eternity of joy awaited him. He knew his reward would come not in this life but in the next.

CHAPTER SEVENTY-TWO

"Two at a time. Don't let go of your partner's hand!" Mrs. Huval struggled to keep the children together on they moved quickly down the side street, trying to put as much distance as she could between them and the bus. The cries and screaming behind them on Decatur Street were unnerving her and, she was sure, terrifying the kids.

Mrs. Valentine and Mrs. Wexler tried to run interference as the uniformed children were jostled by all those scurrying past them. Truvi was doing her best to keep those in the rear from falling behind when she realized that she didn't see her daughter in amongst the group.

"Abigayle!" Although Truvi called out as loudly as she could, her voice was no match for the cacophony of the crowd.

Truvi agitatedly spun around in circles, trying to spot her small daughter as person after person surged by them in the narrow street.

Abigayle was nowhere to be seen.

Truvi ran forward to Carole Valentine, asked her to drop back a bit to protect the rear of the procession, and anxiously whispered that she was going to find Abigayle. Turning abruptly, Truvi rushed into the pulsating press of humanity, swimming upstream against the torrential human current.

In and out of French Quarter shops she flew, glancing inside and repeatedly calling Abigayle's name. Getting no response, Truvi raced on to the next doorway, scouring every opening, looking for her daughter, whom she was certain was petrified, but all she encountered were terrified adults surging forward in a heedless panic.

She had covered a block and a half and had almost given up hope when, on the next corner she spotted Abigayle, who had climbed up on a street vendor's table and was waving her arms as if trying to attract someone's attention. Abigayle showed no sign of fear. If anything, she was happily excited. But she was not looking in the direction of Decatur Street, where Kenny and the bus remained, nor toward where Mrs. Huval was leading her classmates.

Truvi ran up and reached out to grab her daughter and help her off the table, but Abigayle shrugged off her embrace and pointed to the street ahead. "Look, Momma. Over there? It's Mr. Art! I knew he wouldn't let me down. He's here to surprise me, and he's running to save us and catch our performance!"

CHAPTER SEVENTY-THREE

Kenny stumbled to the center of the street. The searing pain from the bullet in his shoulder was punishing. But he was deliriously happy.

He was the center of attention. Whichever direction he took, the panicked crowds scattered to avoid him. He felt like Moses parting the Red Sea.

Kenny extended his uninjured left arm like a conductor, pointing this way and that while watching the fear in everyone's eyes with jubilation.

He pivoted, getting ready to strike terror merely by gesturing in another direction, reveling in his power to instill dread, when he saw a uniformed officer, gun drawn, coming toward him. It was Deputy Starner, the one who had stopped him yesterday.

Good, thought Kenny. He needs to die, like everyone else today.

Kenny cocked the fingers of his left hand, making an imaginary gun, and pointed it at Starner, who by this time was closing in on him.

Kenny was manic. "Boom! You're dead. You just don't know it yet."

He aimed his fingers at the fleeing crowd. "Bang. You're dead, too. You're all dead!"

Starner came within ten yards. "Calm down, Kenny. You know me. We can reason this out."

"You are as ignorant as the rest of them! It's never a matter of reason. It's always a matter of belief. Well, get ready to believe in this!" Unable to move his right arm, Kenny spun in a half-circle attempting to use his left hand to grasp the cord entangled in his suicide vest. Each movement forced blood to spurt from his right shoulder. His vest turned crimson.

"Kenny! Stop!"

"Stop what? Can you stop the sun from rising? Can you stop the stars from shining? Can you stop God's will? I am God's will!"

Kenny finally snagged the switch with his left hand, held it heavenwards, and screamed, "The world will remember me."

Starner raised his gun. He didn't want to fire for fear of hitting anyone other than his target. The crowd was too thick. An errant shot might kill an innocent person. But it was now or never.

Starner was about pull the trigger when he heard the sound of a single gunshot behind him.

Someone else's bullet struck Kenny in the forehead. The deranged man fell backward onto the street, lifeless.

The deputy turned around and saw the shooter.

It was not an N.O.P.D. officer, although a phalanx of uniformed cops were now pushing their way through the crowds, guns drawn.

The man who fired was Art Brady.

Starner was baffled. What was he doing here? Numerous times, on his late-night patrols, Starner encountered Art driving back into Petit Rouge, sometimes at two or three in the morning, always going the speed limit, returning from whatever his job was that kept him on the road.

Art approached. "Thank God Kenny's dead."

Starner was puzzled. Here was yet another person with a connection to Kenny? A Petit Rouge local who miraculously appeared just in time to shoot with unerring accuracy? What was going on?

But before Starner could say anything, the N.O.P.D. officers had reached the street. Some were establishing a perimeter, while others had their guns drawn and were aiming at both Art and Starner.

"I got this covered," Starner called out, signaling them to remain where they were. "I'm from Petit Rouge Parish. I know this guy."

"What in the hell are you talking about? Is that you, Starner? We all thought you were long gone! Put down your weapon and let us handle the situation. This is our jurisdiction."

Starner recognized the voice. He turned around to see a heavy-set officer twenty yards away. Chuck Cifaldi, one of the "Achilles

Three" cops Starner had testified against years ago, had always been beefy, but in the intervening years he had put on three times the weight that Starner had. Cifaldi's jowls poured over his collar, his belt was almost obscured by his stomach's paunch, and his pants creased tightly around his bulbous thighs.

"Art," Starner said, "give me your pistol. I don't want these guys to shoot you and, believe me, they have no hesitancy about shooting first."

"Hell no! I've got a concealed weapon permit!"

Chuck Cifaldi waddled toward them. "Shut up, both of you!"

Art didn't back up as Cifaldi approached and didn't remain silent. "Look at Kenny! You can't leave him in the street like this. Did either of you guys serve in Iran, Iraq, or Afghanistan? Don't you know a suicide vest when you see one? It could explode at any minute. We've got to get him out of here now! It can't wait! Look, I'll help you put him back on the bus and drive away, far from where he can endanger anyone."

Chuck Cifaldi stood in front of Art and held out his hand. "Stand down, shithead. I'm not going to ask you again. Give me your pistol. And if that's a suicide vest, we'll clear the area and let the bomb squad handle this."

"Oh," Art shot back. "Like you handled stopping Kenny? Where were you guys when he started mowing people down? When I saw him come out of the bus, his shirt torn and his suicide vest exposed, I was not going to take any chances while you guys sat back on your asses. If it wasn't for me, Kenny could have already exploded that thing!"

Cifaldi puffed out his chest. "I'm not kidding. I'll fucking shoot you if you don't do as I say."

Starner moved close to Cifaldi and spoke softly. "Are you sure want to do that Chuck, in front of all these witnesses? It's one thing to fire in a dark alley with Dolan and Benoit to back you up. It's another thing in broad daylight. Look. Folks have stopped running away and, with all the police around, are now pushing forward to gawk. Let me handle this, then you can take over." Turning to Art, he said, "Give me the gun. You've shot someone in a suicide vest. You're a hero. Don't turn yourself into a victim."

Art handed his pistol to Starner while speaking in an urgent tone. "Sure, take the gun, but don't stand around here gabbing. You know I travel for a living. My inventory includes explosives for commercial purposes. Kenny worked for me part-time a while back and recently came asking for something to blow up stumps on the godforsaken property where he lives. Maybe he not only has explosives in his vest but also in the bus."

Cifaldi harrumphed. "Enough fucking talking! We'll secure the area and wait for the bomb squad."

"You think there's time to wait? Starner knows Kenny. You think he could have acted alone? There are probably others out there in the crowd ready to remotely detonate the vest! By the time the bomb squad gets here, it could be too late!" Art pushed Cifaldi aside, reached down, and grabbed hold of Kenny's legs. "Are you two blind? Look under the bus! Next to the body of that unfortunate cop. Wires are hanging down everywhere. What do you think they might be connected to? I don't know, but are you prepared to take any chances? We've got to drag Kenny back onboard and take him and his vest and his potential bomb of a vehicle out of here before anyone else is hurt. Both Kenny and the bus have got to be moved!"

"This is not the way we do it," Cifaldi said, his gun now pointing at Art. "Don't move that body or the vehicle until forensics gets here!"

Art started dragging Kenny's body back to the bus. "Are you two going to help or not?"

Starner didn't trust Art, but the circumstances were more than disturbing. Bubba was dead and his house and barn were in flames. The knot of violent death that wrapped around Judson Jorée, Thomas Crosser, and Maggie Mae Delacourte had now ensnared Kenny. Art was right. Kenny couldn't have been acting alone. Where did Kenny get a suicide vest? Why would he agree to wear one?

Starner couldn't afford to trust Art, but with so many injured and dead on Decatur Street already, he couldn't risk the possibility of further mass casualties and destruction.

As he caught hold of Kenny's legs and helped Art pull the dead man toward the bus, Starner asked, "Are you going to assist, Chuck?"

"I'm not going to fucking help disturb a crime scene! On the other hand," Cifaldi said warily, starting to back away, "if there really is a bomb . . ." He turned and jogged slowly back to the police line, his vast stomach bobbing up and down. "We'll clear the way. If you want to go get yourself blown up trying to move both the dead guy and the bus, Starner, well more power to you. Couldn't happen to a nicer guy!"

CHAPTER SEVENTY-FOUR

Starner detested the situation he was in. He did not want to work with Art. He did not want to move a corpse in a suicide vest. He did not want to try to start and steer a bus that might be loaded with explosives.

But the French Quarter was still packed with people, even if they were trying to flee the scene. If there were explosives on the bus, and if they were the same as those that incinerated the 18-wheeler and melted the metal beams on Bubba's barn, there was no time to waste.

Starner had no one left to live for, anyway. Everyone he loved was dead. If he could save even one life in the French Quarter today, it was worth whatever the risk involved.

He and Art managed to wrestle Kenny's lifeless body onto the bus, laying it down in the aisle between the seats, taking care not to disturb the toggle switch. The deputy gingerly placed the switch on Kenny's chest where it would not get jostled when he started the bus.

Starner noticed that Art did not seem the least bit fazed by all the blood that had seeped from Kenny's bullet wounds. Most people would have been unnerved by that. Starner did not have time to speculate further, however. If there were explosives onboard, in addition to those in Kenny's vest, it was imperative to get the bus out of the jam-packed French Quarter immediately.

Sliding behind the wheel, Starner could barely see through the badly cracked windshield.

He shifted the bus into reverse to get it off the curb and out from under the balcony that threatened to collapse on it. The gears groaned, the front axle rumbled as metal ground on metal, but the big, yellow vehicle jerked backward. The brakes still worked, but when Starner shifted into low, it became apparent that not only was the power steering gone, but there also was a problem with the wheels.

"Head straight down Decatur," Art called out from the back of the bus. "Look, that fat cop has his folks clearing a way for you." Art could barely constrain his joy, certain that the cop's actions were another sign of God's will. The path the cops were making for the bus would take them right past Jackson Square and beyond. As the bus drove by it, Art would detonate Kenny's vest, a chain reaction would begin, and the world would experience the power of the Alabaster Brigade.

Hearing the unusual tone of Art's voice, Starner glanced in the rearview mirror. He saw Art standing over Kenny's body, reaching for the toggle switch on the suicide vest.

Shifting the bus into neutral, Starner sprung out of the driver's seat and slammed into Art, pushing him backward down the aisle while using his bulk to jam him between the seats. He was determined not to let Art reach that switch.

The Supreme Kommander would not let anyone stand in his way. The Supreme Kommander was supreme because he was the smartest. The most powerful. Art knew he could not fail. He pummeled the deputy about the head. He was determined to defeat anyone who tried to undermine the success of his plan. He would succeed in creating the hellfire that would guarantee the domination of the Alabaster Brigade.

CHAPTER SEVENTY-FIVE

rt was fifteen years younger than Starner, but the deputy was eighty pounds heavier and had been in more than his share of street fights. He smashed his forehead into Art's nose, breaking it.

While Art was gasping for breath, Starner rammed his elbow into Art's windpipe. Blood poured out of his mouth and broken nose.

Starner dragged the now silent and motionless man down the aisle to the back of the bus and pulled Kenny's body into the front stairwell so he could keep his eye on the vest's toggle switch at all times. He didn't dare try to remove it, fearful that if he tried it might detonate the vest rather than disarm it.

The bus had coasted to a stop. The cops were keeping the crowds at bay. Some of the Unity Festival attendees who had fled minutes ago were now cautiously creeping forward and straining to see what the commotion was about, confident that the police had matters under control. The whine of ambulance sirens could be heard in the distance as they converged on the Quarter.

A confusion of questions cluttered Starner's mind. Why was Art trying to reach the toggle switch on the suicide vest? Did that mean the vest could not be set off remotely? Why would Art want to blow himself and the bus up? Why would Art want to kill himself? Kenny was wearing the suicide vest, not Art.

And then there were all the loose wires trailing from under the bus.

Answers would have to wait.

A small contingent of men sent by Cifaldi were cautiously approaching the bus, apparently to find out why Starner had halted it.

Starner did not want to endanger them, but there was no time to get the bomb squad through the packed Quarter. If something on this bus was going to explode, he had to get it as far away from the crowd as possible. That meant he couldn't wait to explain anything to the officers or follow the path Cifaldi was having cleared, one that led out of the Quarter, onto Canal Street, and from there who knew where.

Jumping back into the driver's seat, Starner put the bus into first gear and honked the horn furiously. The approaching officers backed off.

Starner fought with the steering wheel as the yellow behemoth lurched down Decatur Street past Jackson Square. The axles were making ominous grinding sounds and a light on the dashboard showed that the engine was starting to overheat.

Starner couldn't get the bus out of low gear.

The engine revved as he kept his foot on the accelerator, making a wide curve onto the side road that led to a parking lot at the foot of the levee.

Starner did not slow down. The bus approached the lot's automatic gates, smashed through them and kept on going, crashing through the chain-link fence on the far side of the lot and shuddering as It edged up the steep slope of the massive levee that protected the city from being overrun by the fast-flowing Mississippi River, which carries more water per minute than three Niagara Falls.

The front wheels of the bus bounced over the crest.

The undersides scraped the sidewalk on top of the levee.

The long bus pitched downward, skidding on the slick batture.

Starner did not apply the brakes. He had no intention of doing so.

The front of the bus plunged into the muddy water and shot spray thirty feet in the air. The engine stalled out.

The bus became engulfed in the vast, swirling river as water flooded in.

CHAPTER SEVENTY-SIX

Both the forward doors and the cracked front windshield were torn away by the force of the river. Kenny's body was sucked right out of the vehicle.

The bus was now vertical in the Mississippi, its front bumper pointing to a muddy bottom so deep that it could accommodate ocean-going vessels, but the rear of the bus still bobbed in the water like the long, yellow floats Starner used as a kid when he went fishing.

As the silty current swept through the bus, Starner swam upward inside, pushing off the backs of seats to propel himself though the rapidly rising water.

He gulped for air as he neared the rear door.

Art was floating in the water, his shirt caught on the broken back of a seat. He was face up. He was bleeding but still breathing.

Starner struggled to open the rear door.

The latch was difficult to turn.

He kicked at it again and again until finally it moved.

But the door was too heavy to raise. It was one thing to exit through the rear door when the bus was horizontal on a road, but it was impossible to lift straight up as the bus bobbed, cork-like, in the river.

The vehicle sank lower and lower. In another few seconds, it would go under completely.

Starner took a deep breath, grabbed Art by the belt, and waited until the water came even with the rear door.

As the river pulled the bus down, Starner emerged from the door with one hand across Art's chest using a lifeguard rescue hold. If answers were to be had, they would have to come from Art. The deputy was not about to let him drown.

Treading water, Starner looked around.

They were in the middle of the river.

The nearest shore was a half mile in the distance.

PART VII

LATER

CHAPTER SEVENTY-SEVEN

It was after midnight. Abigayle had awoken again from a nightmare. Truvi had come into the little girl's room and was cuddling with her on her bed.

"Do you want to tell me about your bad dream, honey? You've had a lot of them lately. They're no fun to have."

Abigayle just buried her head in her mother's arms.

"It's okay to talk about it. Sometimes that helps. And anyway, I'm here with you."

"But Mr. Art will never be with us again!"

Truvi tried to speak without tearing up. The day after the incident, the pastor had come to her house to explain that they never recovered his body from the river. He suggested they have a "celebration of life" at the church, which is what Truvi did. But it was not the same as having an open coffin and a chance to say goodbye, as difficult as that would have been. It was not the same as having a grave to visit, or a gravestone with an appropriate inscription to mark Art's existence, or a place to leave flowers every year on his birthday.

"No, he won't darlin', but he'll always be in our hearts. And we can be so, so proud that he was a hero to all of New Orleans. Think of all the stories in the newspapers and on television talking about how he saved the French Quarter from a suicide bomber."

"Mr. Kenny was a bad, bad, man."

Truvi gently stroked Abigayle's hair. "Yes, he was, sweetheart. We don't know what makes people bad, but we know a good man, like Mr. Art, when we see one. Just think, when you grow up and have children of your own, you'll be able to tell the story about being in the French Quarter, about seeing Mr. Art come to surprise you, and about knowing how he saved the city. If he hadn't come to surprise the both of us, think what might have happened!"

Truvi caught herself, concerned she might be scaring Abigayle when her intention was to calm her daughter down.

"But you don't have to worry about that. You'll tell your children about how the FBI came to our house to talk to you and me about Mr. Art, how we showed them all his stuff in the garage, and how they asked permission to borrow it for a bit because it was all so interesting. And, of course, you'll tell them, we agreed. Because that's what you do when someone is a hero like Mr. Art."

"I miss Mr. Art."

Truvi gave Abigayle a big hug. "I do too, honey. But we'll always have our good memories of him. I bet, when you're a mom and I'm a grandmother, you'll still remember the song you and your classmates never got to perform at the Unity Festival but which the principal had all the kids in your grade present to the whole school on the last day of class. Let me just get up, turn out the lights, and tuck you in again. Ready? Let's sing the song together.

Love can make the world go 'round.
Love will bring us up, not down.
Love keeps us to-ge-ther, not apart.
Love is in ev-er-y body's heart.
Each of us has things to share.
Each of us has love to spare.
U-ni-ty is big, not small.
All for one and one for all.
Me with you and you with me.
Let's hear it for u-ni-ty.
U-ni-ty! U-ni-ty! U-ni-ty!"

CHAPTER SEVENTY-EIGHT

Frankie sat on the balcony sipping a beer, his big feet braced against the railing.

"I don't understand why you like this place," Ribeye complained. "Nothing but trees and hills and valleys. Fucking nature. I hate nature!"

"Relax. Paolo sent us here until everything settles down back in the States. Now that his Petit Rouge camp has been abandoned, he's scouting other locations to operate from. All we have to do is make sure that the supply is ready to ship when he's ready to receive it. Why not just enjoy the peace and quiet?"

"What I want is a cold Bud, but the only beer you can get here is Imperial, and when you want it, you've got to order *cerveza* or the shitty locals pretend they don't understand you. They've got to be stupid as shit not to learn English."

"Are you going to bitch about everything?"

Ribeye tipped back the bottle of Imperial, drained its contents, and reached for another one from the ice bucket on the table. "The only reason we're in this goddamned place . . . the only reason the Petit Rouge camp got shut down . . . is that fucking deputy. I've got a good mind to . . ."

Frankie snorted. "When have you ever had a good mind? The one with the brains is Paolo. If you're pissed, think about how he feels. All the deputy did to you was to cause you and me to get an extended vacation. Paolo, on the other hand, has lost millions upon millions. Not that he won't figure out a way to make it all back and more. I have no doubt that he'll find a way to get revenge.

"No matter what Paolo does, it won't be soon enough for me!" Ribeye grabbed the bucket of beer and stalked back inside the apartment. At least Paolo's local contact had supplied them with sufficient firepower. Four pocket-sized .380 pistols. Two M249 light machine guns, gas operated and air cooled. An AR-15 rifle. And enough ammunition to fend off a platoon. He took out his cleaning kit and started disassembling the first machine gun.

CHAPTER SEVENTY-NINE

Florene put a plate of jambalaya in front of Starner and stood over him. "How are you getting on?"

"As I told you when I came in, I'm okay."

"Like I really believe that!" She sat down across him in the booth. "First you were in the hospital in New Orleans. No visitors allowed. You missed Knock's funeral. Now that was a sight. Meanwhile, there are FBI agents crawling all over the Red Zone. I heard there are Coast Guard cutters out in the Gulf patrolling the entrance to the Istrouma River and shutting off Boueux Bayou. Even with all the commotion around here, you didn't come back to work when you got out of the hospital. The Police Jury has called for a special election for sheriff, but until then—as you know—they appointed someone from the state police, Earl Elkins, to fill the post temporarily. I heard you just up and resigned the minute you got out of the hospital and put your place up for sale! So how can you say you're 'okay'? Exactly what are you running from, Starner?"

Starner put a spoonful of jambalaya in his mouth and savored it. "Tell Armond he outdid himself today."

"Don't be evasive with me. You and I go back too far. The television stations ran video over and over again about how you confronted crazy Kenny in the French Quarter. They say if it wasn't for you and Art Brady, there would have been more deaths. Kenny in a suicide vest? The thought of it! Always assumed he was a tad off. As Armond says, he was fifteen ounces short of a pound cake. Damn lucky that this is an open-carry state and that Art had a pistol with him. It's true what they say, isn't it? The only way to stop a bad guy with a gun is a good guy with one. I just can't imagine what was going through your mind as you and Art picked up Kenny in his suicide vest. You two were risking your lives to save others! The newspapers say that when the Coast Guard found you swimming with Art in your grasp, you were unaware that he was dead. As they tried to pull you out of the water, they lost Art's body in the current, never to be found. You're a hero, Starner. Why are you running away rather than running for sheriff? Talk to me."

Starner met her gaze as he sat back in the booth. What could he possibly say that would make a difference? In short shrift, Knock's shenanigans would come to light and Starner's reputation would no doubt be tarnished again. He would be characterized either as a willing participant in Knock's illicit scheme with Paolo Micelli or as someone who was aware of the corruption but did nothing to stop it until it was too late. The Feds were shutting down Paolo's Petit Rouge operation and were searching for him, as well as for Frankie and Ribeye, confident that they'd eventually find all three.

Starner knew he couldn't tell Florene about Art. The Feds instructed him never to reveal the fact that Art had survived. They wanted it to look like he died. They whisked Art to Guantanamo, classified him as a terrorist, and were interrogating him. His grieving widow took consolation in the fact that Art, according to all public accounts, died heroically while helping stop crazy Kenny from killing more people.

After the Coast Guard recovered the mud-encrusted carcass of the bus far downriver, the Feds analyzed the explosives jammed into every water-soaked panel and crevice and linked them to the residue found at Bubba's farm. They scoured the property and located the buried big rig with Boyo's body inside. Traces of the same explosives were identified. The story they announced—for public consumption—was that Bubba and Kenny were two sad, dissatisfied wannabes trying to make a name for themselves. Bubba killed the tractor trailer driver, fought with Boyo when retrieving evidence of the explosives used to destroy the truck, murdered Boyo, and buried the big rig in a futile attempt to disguise his crime. Lydellia could live with that tale and shed no tears.

And Kenny? The FBI's line was that he had been depressed, was infatuated with Maggie Mae, though she didn't reciprocate his affections, and had killed her in a fit of rage. Both the suicide vest and his mowing down random victims in the French Quarter attested to his mental instability.

Judson and Thomas Closser? No one had reason to doubt Judson insulted Closser when giving him a ticket, causing the two to face off and kill each other.

Starner knew these were all lies built on a rickety foundation of partial truths, but he didn't care. The Feds needed the lies to be believed so that they could hide whatever intel they extracted from Art. There was no point in revealing the absolute truth. No one would believe him if he did.

What is the truth anyway? Starner figured that maybe it's a tale that skirts the facts just enough to disguise them.

In any event, Starner did not intend to remain in Petit Rouge any longer. There was no future for him here.

He looked across the booth into Florene's eyes. "I'm not running away from anything. We can't escape our past, but we can chart our future."

He reached into his breast pocket, withdrew a business card printed with a New Orleans address and phone number and slid it across the table to her. It read:

"Starner Gautreaux: Discrete Private Investigations."

CHAPTER EIGHTY

The job was easy and the pay was great. All she had to do was bug an office in a run-down building miles away from the French Quarter and far from the Central Business District.

The side door that opened to the parking lot bore a cheesy plastic plaque that read: "S. Gautreaux: Discrete Private Investigations."

Picking the lock was no problem.

The small warren of offices was freshly painted, although sparsely furnished.

She quickly installed two audio bugs in each room, placed video feed cameras behind each of the ceiling vents, and mounted a hidden camera and microphone on the outside of the building so that they would pick up whatever went on in the parking lot.

She never asked why this place needed to be bugged.

She didn't question why all the bugs had to be tied into an encrypted line.

She didn't give a damn why anyone would want to snoop on a two-bit P.I.

All she cared about was getting paid for this part of the job and lying low until the next set of instructions arrived.

CPSIA information can be obtained
at www.ICGtesting.com
Printed in the USA
BVHW072329260323
661097BV00003B/4

9 781946 160973